Welcome...

To a

Forrest's SHADE OF VAMPIRE.

Introducing:

THE VAMPIRE GIFT SERIES

by E.M. Knight

www.EMKnight.com

www.facebook.com/AuthorEMKnight

EM@EMKnight.com

tVG 02 - Version 2

Books by E.M. Knight

THE VAMPIRE GIFT:

Currently Available:

The Vampire Gift 1: Wards of Night

The Vampire Gift 2: Kingdom of Ash

Coming Soon:

The Vampire Gift 3: Throne of Dust (August 2016)

The Vampire Gift 4

For an updated list of books, and to see the latest dates

for my upcoming releases, check out my website:

www.EMKnight.com

Or Facebook:

www.Facebook.com/AuthorEMKnight

You can also sign up for my **New Releases Newsletter**

(http://eepurl.com/bYCp41) to get a notification the day a new book comes out! That way you don't miss anything new. And don't worry – I never send any spam.

The Vampire Gift 2:

Kingdom of Ash

By E. M. Knight

Cover art by B. Wagner

First Edition: June 2016

Book Description

THE VAMPIRE GIFT 2: KINGDOM OF ASH

A daring rescue has freed Eleira from The Crypts.

But that rescue has come at a great cost, stripping Eleira of her humanity and opening up the battlelines between the world's most powerful covens.

Now, as a creature of the night, Eleira has no choice but to return to The Haven. She must discover the truth of the dark prophecy surrounding her life and learn the extent of her new powers... all the while navigating the treacherous landscape of the heart.

But as the Queen awaits Eleira's arrival, discord grows amongst the The Haven's vampires. The threat of war, of outside attack, has them questioning their monarch's ability to rule... and the necessity of The Succession.

Eleira was supposed to be their savior. Her newfound strength instead makes her a threat. None are eager to welcome Eleira with open arms... and all will fight to bring her down if they think it will help them get ahead.

Chapter One

I do a slow circle of the room at the top of the tower, trying to keep my breathing calm and steady.

It's hard. The only reason I'm managing is because of all the meditation I've done over the last century. Otherwise, I'd be going crazy.

I've never been to this part of Mother's castle before. I've seen the tower's angled spire, but it has always been off-limits.

For the first time, I understand why.

Silver. Hoards and hoards of silver, lining all the walls, piled as jewelry and cutlery on the ground, spilling out as coins and necklaces and rings from intricately-carved chests. Ancient suits of armor stand erect around me, made entirely of the accursed-metal.

The mere sight of the room would fill any vampire with dread. Being *locked* inside…?

It's unimaginable.

I lose track of the safe path along the room and misplace a step. As soon as I do, enormous pain crashes into me, coming from all sides, coming almost as radioactive waves from the silver.

6

I cry out and, with extreme effort, pull myself back. The pain subsides. I'm okay—for now.

When Mother first imprisoned me by latching that silver collar around my neck, I thought she'd put me in a cell underground. I thought she'd keep me where we keep the prisoners awaiting trial—though with her at the helm, the trials had never been more than theatrical shams. If a vampire of The Haven did something to warrant being held prisoner, his fate was all but decided: he would become one of The Convicted. No matter what.

So in a way I was relieved when we emerged above ground. I wish I could say it was a surprise that she would hold me hostage... but Mother never hid her disdain for my choice to stop feeding on human blood. There was a time she was afraid the other vampires would see it as weakness pervading through the Soren family. She believed my decision could start a revolt.

That didn't happen. I can thank James and Raul for that. My two older brothers were her bastions of strength, and with Mother leading, none would dare rise against her.

Except, of course, her cousin Rebecca. Yet Mother put a very effective stop to that by... by...

I can't even think it.

I look around the room, at the gleaming metal reflecting the candlelight... and continue my careful path in that slow, precise circle.

Silver usually does not have this sort of radiating effect. In

7

most cases, it's simple: either the metal touches our skin, and it burns—or it does not.

But I'm sure Mother cast one of her spells on the items surrounding me so that just being in the room is near agony.

If I stood still it would drive me crazy. The reverberations through the air feel as jarring as jackhammers pounding at my temples. But by moving in the path I found, I manage to ease the worst of the silver's effects on me.

Movement. Movement is essential to everything, movement is essential to life. As a vampire, I've watched as our coven has stagnated, because it's been stuck within the protective wards surrounding The Haven.

It all stems from Mother. The other vampires of our royalty look to her for guidance and leadership. It's part of the natural hierarchy. They see her growing restless, and they grow restless, too.

Abruptly the doors slam open. A gust of wind blows inside.

I jerk that way.

Mother stands on the threshold, the wind emanating from her and somehow taking the worst of the silver's effects away.

I try to summon up hatred for her... but I cannot. That she would turn against me and Raul doesn't strike me as a great surprise. She was desperate after having lost Eleira. Desperate people do desperate things.

Besides, it's not so much hatred that swells through me, but...
pity. Pity that she would be so power-hungry as to go to these
extremes.

"Enjoying yourself, are you?" she asks, her voice a sing-song
mockery of its usual self. The wind dies down, but the effects of the
silver remain lessened. "I never understood you, Phillip. How you
could be so calm, so complacent, so..."

"Peaceful?" I suggest.

She narrows her eyes. Both her hands go out to grip the sides
of the doorway.

"Yes," she admits grudgingly. "Peaceful." She steps into the
room, her elegant blue gown flowing around her legs as she walks.
"It's not in our nature to be peaceful, my sweet."

The hairs on the back of my neck go up. She's never addressed
me using that term of endearment before. Raul, yes. James,
sometimes. But never me.

"Come." She holds out her hand. "I think you've spent enough
time here. Don't you?"

"You're letting me go?"

She laughs. "You're jumping the gun. Raul and Eleira have not
returned yet."

A nasty feeling rises in my throat. Enough time has passed for
Raul to find Eleira. It feels like I've been here for days.

"Then where are we going?"

Morgan gives a coy smile. "You'll see."

I follow her down the long, icy hall of her castle. Empty canvases framed in gold hang on the walls.

They're an eerie reminder of what she's capable of.

Nothing—*nothing*—could be worse than severing a soul from its body. It's a crime against nature. If the thought of feeding on human blood makes me ill, what Mother has done to every one of these vampires in the paintings... the *way* she did it... it makes me want to throw up.

We walk to a curling staircase leading down. Mother glances back at me. "You're not stupid enough to try to run, are you?" Out of nowhere, that silver collar she'd flung around my neck appears in her hands. "Please tell me you're not. You don't know how it pains me to use this... *device*... against my own flesh and blood."

"No," I say stiffly. "I won't run."

"Good." The collar disappears up her sleeve. "That makes me so happy."

We descend the narrow stairs. At first I think we're going to the ground floor. But then Mother takes me lower, deeper into the earth.

I begin to grow wary.

At the very bottom is a set of dungeon doors. Morgan shares a conspiratorial look with me. Then she opens them.

My heart sinks when I see what's on the other side.

Patricia and Jacob are hanging limp from the walls. Silver gauntlets bind their wrists and ankles. Their heads droop low, but Patricia manages to look up—weakly—at our entrance.

Mother pulls the doors closed with a bang. The sound echoes through the dark, rocky chamber.

As soon as that happens I sense we're not the only ones here. Sure enough, from behind a jagged column emerges an ensemble of the Queen's personal guard.

There are six of them altogether. I scan the faces. Two of the six I know from before, but the other four are new. Their Commander, identified by the gold stitching on his black coat, is no one I've *ever* seen before inside The Haven.

"You've changed your guards," I say. My mind searches for an explanation. Mother's previous guards had been stable for decades. They had the utmost loyalty to her. "Why?"

"I was hoping you'd be able to tell me that," Mother coos. "After all, it was you and Raul who started the fire in the village—along with these two accomplices."

She casts an arm toward Patricia and Jacob.

"What does the first have to do with anything?" I ask.

"Well..." she taps her lips. "Four of my most trusted guards were found dead in the aftermath." She turns to me. "They didn't burn. They were *murdered*."

A wave of shock passes through me.

Who would kill four vampires?

"These two," Mother continues, walking closer to the husband and wife pair, "have proved surprisingly stubborn in admitting their guilt. But that's not a problem. Because, down here, my word is law... and the law finds them guilty of *murder!*"

I give a strangled choke. "No!"

"Yes." She looks like a puma glorying in the moments before the kill. "Patricia and Jacob have proven their unworthiness to remain part of our coven again and again. This final insult, it was too much."

The hanging woman's eyes roll up and meet mine. The despondent resignation in them breaks my heart.

I look at the guards again. They all have smug smiles on their faces. *They* know what's going on. And I'm starting to suspect that I do, too.

Mother brought me here to witness an execution.

"You think *they* killed your guards?" I say. "Look at them! They barely had the strength to stand after you kept them prisoner and brought them to Eleira's introduction ceremony. How could they have gone against *four* of The Haven's most accomplished fighters?"

Mother gives a little laugh. "Oh, that's the same story they've given me. It's funny how such things align. If I didn't know any better, I'd say that you three are colluding against me." She glances at the ring of guards. "Wouldn't you say, Smithson?"

12

The Commander instantly drops to one knee and holds a fist to his chest. "Yes, my Queen."

Morgan strolls up to him and casually rakes a hand through his hair. "Oh, you're most obedient now, aren't you? Of course, that's just how I like my companions."

The commander glances up and meets her gaze for the briefest moment. There's something more going on between them—I wouldn't be surprised if Mother has already taken him to bed.

I don't know if her promiscuity should repulse me or not.

"Why'd you bring me here?" I ask. I barely stand above Patricia and Jacob in terms of strength, but I try to channel some of Raul's fortitude.

"I brought you here..." Mother turns to me, "to show what befalls vampires who oppose my rule."

Everything happens at once.

She flings an arm toward me. That chained silver collar flies from her sleeve. I raise a hand to protect myself but it does little good. The collar simply binds it to my neck.

The force of the strike throws me back. All the air rushes from my lungs as I slam against the wall. Mother's magic instantly pins me in place.

The guards surround the prisoners. They shove a strange looking sack over each of their heads. Patricia and Jacob start to convulse the instant the sacks are on.

Their bonds are released. They drop to the ground and jerk about with absolutely no control over their limbs.

"Hold them tight!" Mother commands.

Two guards grab either of the pair. Patricia and Jacob don't so much fight the guards, as the guards fight them, doing as much as they can to keep the convulsions in check.

Mother gestures to Smithson. "Bring it now."

The Commander rushes off into the depths of the cave and comes back carrying two empty canvases.

Exactly the same sort that I saw lining the hall.

Realization sinks in. "No!" I exclaim. I fight the silver collar with all my might. "No, Mother, don't—"

"You *dare* call me that?" She turns on me, dressed in all the fury of a Queen. "I am your Monarch, and you will address me as such!"

She slaps me. My head snaps to the side, and my glasses go flying. Everything becomes an indistinct blur.

Jacob and Patricia keep convulsing on the ground. Smithson raises the two canvases onto hooks on the wall, right where the husband and wife pair were previously hanging.

Morgan towers over them. The way the shadows fall across her face make her all the more menacing.

"For the murder of four of your kind," she declares, "I sentence you both to eternal suffering. The lives you stole will never be brought back. I would not do the same to you, but I *will* ensure that

14

all the pleasures of this world are denied to you as you continue to linger, as trapped souls, for all eternity!"

Her voice gets louder and louder as she delivers the two sentences. A wind gusts up from the sides of the chamber and surges around her in a violent tornado. Her dress flaps this way and that. For the first time in my eyes, she looks like a real witch.

She pulls a silver dagger from her waist. The wind howls, ripping away my screams of protest.

Morgan raises the dagger above her head. She plunges it straight down into Jacob's heart. Blood spurts out, but it's caught by that wind and directed straight into one of the empty canvases. Mother chants an incantation, and the flow of blood is surrounded by a glowing blue light. It streams right into the frame, where slowly, the image of a wretched Jacob starts to form.

What little I make out without my glasses is ghastly. The Jacob in the painting is barely a skeleton. The muscles take shape over the bones of his skull. His eyes appear there, too, looking infinitely haunted. The barest layer of translucent skin starts to cover the red muscle fibers...

And then the flow from his body stops. I look at the shell that remains. It's a horrible sight. Inside the painting, he starts to move, but then Mother utters another spell, and he goes still.

She stands and brushes a strand of hair out of her face. "One done," she says. "Never to trouble me again."

Her coterie of guards snickers.

She turns her attention to the woman. "My dear, you're in luck," she says. "You get a few more minutes on this earth while I recover my strength."

I see it as my chance. If I can save Patricia... if I can make a difference...

"Morgan, you mustn't do this!" I stop fighting the collar around my neck—it's not like I can do anything against it. "Think of the consequences! You speak of killing vampires as the greatest crime—surely, this is worse! A soul is not meant to be separated from a body. Not while still remaining on this earth! Please, please, don't mar your rule by doing something while lost in the grips of madness!"

She barely looks at me. "Madness?" She scoffs. "No, Phillip. This isn't madness. Madness would be allowing the seed of rebellion to linger. You think I can turn a blind eye when four of my guards are dead? You think I can sit on my throne and do nothing while *filthy* vampires such as these seek to undermine everything I have? Everything that *we've* built?"

"You're not listening to yourself!" I cry. "You feel their strength. You know Patricia's never been powerful enough to challenge one of your personal guard. How would she or Jacob have killed them? *Why* would they kill them?"

"Because they're filth," she spits. "Because they were humiliated by my guards in front of the entire assembly. Because in the fires that you and my other son began, in the mayhem and confusion, they thought they could have their revenge! *How* they did it, I don't know. I don't care to know. Maybe they took them by surprise. Maybe—"

"Andrey would never have been taken by surprise."

"SILENCE!" she screams. "Silence! Don't you *dare* talk about Andrey. Never again—never again will you speak his name to me. Or else… or else…" she's starting to sound hysterical now, "…or else you'll end up in a painting on the castle wall, too!"

One of the new guards gasps. Mother turns on him in a blind rage.

"You don't think it's within my right to do?" she demands. "You don't think that I have absolute rule in The Haven?"

"No, my Queen. You do, my Queen. Forgive me, my Queen."

The apology seems to appease her. She takes a few deep breaths to compose herself.

Then she addresses me again in a sweet voice. "My son," she says. She walks toward me. "My sweet, precious, youngest son. Don't you know how hard it's been for me to watch you toil away as a result of your… *choice?* Don't you know how hard it's been for me to see Raul and James rise up above you, when you were the one always gifted with such potential?" She touches my cheek.

I stare into her eyes, unflinching.

"You know what I speak of," she tells me softly. "You were always the intelligent one. You sensed the same darkness inside you that I did when you were made. You *knew* it could overtake you, if

17

you only let it, and you *knew* that its power would be unrivalled by any in our coven. You knew that had you embraced it, you would have risen in power, and, eventually, stood above even me."

The silence in the cave is palpable. Each one of the guards is listening to his Queen with bated breath.

"Yes, Mother. I knew," I say. That is my greatest secret—that I can become the strongest of all.

And now it's out in the open.

"But you rejected it," she says. "You rejected it, because of your love for me." She wipes away a fake tear. "You did not want to challenge my rule. Why, then, do you do it now?"

"I made the choice for myself, not for you," I tell her. "And yes, I loved you once, as a child loves either of his parents. But who you've become today is a far cry from the woman who raised me."

She smiles in a cruel way. "You think your words hurt me."

"I don't resort to holding my sons hostage," I challenge, "when things don't go my way."

She gives a flippant little laugh. Then she directs her gaze at Patricia, still being held on the floor.

"You want to save her?" she asks. "You can. I'll tell you how." She leans in, and whispers in my ear, "Feed. *Feed*, and embrace who you are meant to be."

She turns away and clasps her hands. "Bring her," she tells Smithson.

18

The Commander immediately retreats into the far reaches of the cavern. I hear a door open. And right away comes the fresh scent of human blood.

Smithson pushes a girl into our midst. She's bound, gagged, and blindfolded.

It's April.

"I'll leave you alone with her," Mother says. She releases the collar around my neck. I stagger down. "Feed, and I'll spare the vampire's life. We both know that it's much more valuable than that of a *human's.*"

On that note, Mother walks out the door, trailed by her guards. They drag Patricia with them.

April is shaking. She's in very rough shape. I can't imagine the horrors my Mother must have inflicted upon her.

"You wouldn't," she whispers. "Would you?"

Chapter Two

ELEIRA

I sit in the back of the plane, huddled beneath a blanket, holding Raul's hand.

He's turned the autopilot on and come out to see me. I've been trying my best to suppress the vampiric urges roiling inside.

It's been hard. Very, very, hard. With our two prisoners, James and Victoria, sitting bound in silver not more than twenty feet away, the urge to feed on them comes and goes in ravenous spikes.

So far, I've managed to fight it down. I suspect the only reason I'm capable of doing so is that I'm wearing the ring Raul gave me.

"It'll become easier," he promises. "Once we get to The Haven, you'll get to feed from the blood banks. You won't need to kill anyone."

I nod, very stiffly. The vampire inside me wants to kill. It *craves* the hunt.

I'm terrified of letting Raul, or anybody else, know.

I draw into myself even more to help contain the struggle.

My eyes go to the front of the plane. James is reclined in his seat, staring despondently at the ceiling. Victoria is as tight as a compressed spring beside him.

"Why do I want *their* blood?" I whisper. "Vampires aren't supposed to lust that way for each other. Are they?"

Raul coughs and tightens his hand around mine. "You're different," he says. "We knew that from the start." He traces the ring. "This helps. Doesn't it?"

I swallow and nod. I keep my breathing very shallow. I'm afraid of catching either James's or Victoria's scent.

"You're different," Victoria suddenly mocks. "Oh, how naïve the both of you are."

Raul stiffens as soon as he hears her speak.

"You're a *witch*," Victoria continues. "And your transformation has been prompted by the blood of one infused with the strength of The Ancient. No wonder you crave vampiric blood. No wonder you want to kill." She sticks her neck out. "So come on, little vampire. Come here. Do what you were meant to do. Suck me dry. Feed the darkness growing inside you."

"Don't listen to her," Raul growls. He stands up. "I can shut her up if you need me to. Just say the word."

"No," I motion him down. "She can taunt me all she wants.

It won't make a difference."

If anything, resisting will show Raul my resolve.

"It's too bad you're unwilling," Victoria continues. "I would make the most *scrumptious* feast. I'm sure of it."

James's eyes pop open. "You're disturbing my rest," he tells her. "Shut it."

Victoria gasps in indignation. I've only been a vampire for a little while, but even I can tell how the reprimand goes against the hierarchy of power on the plane.

Victoria is stronger than James, who is stronger— slightly—than Raul.

But I am the most powerful vampire here. *That* terrifies me.

I pull the blanket tighter around me and try to become as small as possible.

"If either of you bug her while I'm gone," Raul says as he walks to the cockpit, "the silver sacks are going right back over your heads."

Victoria gives him a nasty glare but doesn't say a word. James simply offers a resigned shrug.

I'm left alone with my own thoughts. Time slows to a standstill. Only the constant hum of the plane's engines keeps me company.

In short order, I find myself drifting off. I didn't know

vampires needed to sleep. In fact, I'm not actually sleepy, but my mind seems to be slowing down. The worries running through it no longer seem so prevalent.

Victoria's voice makes me perk up.

"You're not falling asleep. You're going hypo."

I look at her. "Excuse me?"

"Hypo. Like a diabetic. Low blood sugar? Ever heard of it?"

"Of course I've heard of it—" I start to say—and then stop short.

Victoria hasn't actually opened her mouth.

I stare at the blonde vampire.

She gives a very satisfied grin.

"My blood was the first you tasted." Her voice sounds in my head, but she's not actually speaking! *"You and I have a unique connection now."*

My eyes grow wide.

"Can you read my thoughts?" I wonder.

She gives the most miniscule smile. Then, in contradiction, she shakes her head.

"Not quite," she tells me, again without speaking. *"But you and I can communicate through a telepathic link."* She glances at James beside her. *"Don't tell this one. He won't take it too well."*

I stare at her. *"Do all vampires have this trait?"*

Victoria laughs out loud. "Of course not," she says, this time using her actual voice. "We are special. But... most vampires also *kill* the one they first feed on."

"But I didn't kill you," I whisper.

"No," she say. "You did not."

James looks at us, considering... but doesn't say a word.

"That's why you want to now," she adds.

I struggle against the impulse she's trying to goad out of me.

"Safer to speak this way."

"Who says I want to speak with you?" I counter.

"You have questions only I can answer."

I can't deny that.

"We are not so different, Eleira." She takes a breath. *"I did not want to be a vampire when I was turned, either."*

I can't help my shock.

She continues: *"I was also part of a line of witches. That is why our connection exists. Vampires killed my twin. She was the one they wanted. Not me."*

"You have The Spark?"

She doesn't answer.

24

"Why do you want me to kill you?" I ask. *"Why do you taunt me when you know what I can do?"*

She shakes her head. I feel a *snap,* and suddenly the link between us is no more.

"Hello?" I venture.

There's no reply.

I try to catch the strand in my mind that alerted me to her presence... and find it entirely missing.

Victoria flashes the thinnest grin before closing her eyes.

I make an annoyed sound with my throat and turn away. If she can cut off the connection then so can I.

... I hope. I truly hate the idea of her having unfettered access to my head.

Some hours later, the plane starts to descend. We drop below the cloud cover. I look out my window and see the dense redwoods of the California forest.

Home. I think. *But unlike I've ever known it.*

I keep looking out the window until we land. With an aerial view of the forest, I can't help but wonder where The Haven would be inside it. Can I see it from the Outside, now that I'm a vampire? Or is it just as invisible to me as before?

Raul emerges from the cockpit. "Get up," he barks at James and Victoria. "And behave yourselves. You're on my territories now."

25

James rolls his eyes and gives a lazy smile. He raises his bound wrists to Raul. "You might as well release me and get it over with," he says. "We both know Mother won't stand for seeing her eldest in chains."

"After she finds out all that her *eldest* did," Raul replies with a biting look, "she can decide what to do. Let's go."

"No point dragging this out," Victoria mutters. She stands after Raul eases her chains. James follows suit.

Raul turns his head away from them to address me. "You wait here," he begins. "I'll—"

But the moment he diverts his attention from the prisoners, a look passes between the two of them. Victoria reaches into her jacket and pulls out the thinnest silver stiletto. I have no idea how she smuggled it on board.

"WATCH OUT!" I scream.

My cry gives Raul just enough time to twist back. Victoria's stab, aimed at his heart, instead glazes against the side of his ribs.

Raul roars and catches Victoria's arm. He torques it into an awkward position that makes her drop the weapon. But James is right there. He swoops down to pick it up—

I'm out of my seat and on him in an instant. I don't remember making the conscious choice to do so. It just happened. With Raul in danger, my instincts roar to life.

26

I crash with James into the plane's aluminum wall. He snarls at me, but I pin him there easily. He tries to fight. My hand lashes out and catches him by the throat. I feel the call of blood. *His* blood. I feel it pulsing through the heavy veins in his neck.

I could crush him. The thought is distant, foreign, and strange. It's unlike me. It's laced with such malice and hate and, above all, *desire...*

If I but squeeze, I could break his windpipe and end his life.

Someone grips my shoulder. I hiss and jerk free. The grip tightens, and Raul turns me to him.

"Eleira," he says. He's looking at me with pleading eyes. "Don't."

His voice brings me back to myself. I look down at my arm, see the way my fingers are tightened around James's throat. I see the fear in the other vampire's eyes, the abject horror swimming behind his irises that he's doing his best to hide.

It's the same sort of fear I felt when James first attacked me in the atrium. Back when I was first made a prisoner of the Soren brothers.

With a startled gasp, I let James go. There's a heavy dent in the aluminum wall of the plane where we'd hit.

James falls to his knees. He sucks in air and looks at me

as if I'm some feral beast.

Raul gently brings me into him. His arms wrap around my body. He holds me tight.

Over his shoulder, I see Victoria struggling with that velvet, silver-lined bag over her head. When did Raul manage to get that on? It feels like only seconds have passed...

"You blacked out," Raul whispers, as if sensing my thoughts. "The bloodlust broke through."

"Because you were in danger," I say without thinking.

"Eleira," he holds me by the shoulders and looks into my eyes. "I won't lie and say it'll get easier from here. But you *have* to control it. Do you understand?"

I stare right back at him. Confusion and... anger...? swirl inside me. I just saved his life, and he wants to lecture me?

I try to twist out of his grip. He doesn't let me go.

"Promise me," he says. "Promise me you'll control it in The Haven."

I feel that anger rising. I try to push it down, but it's like a pot of boiling water. The only way to get rid of it is to stop feeding it heat... and my raging emotions are simply adding to the fire.

"I..." I start to say. But the voice that comes from my lips is not my own. It's cruel and savage and threatening.

It's the voice of the vampire borne within me. It's full of

28

anger and hatred. I've never been an angry person, and to feel the emotion so acute inside me, it frightens me.

It takes all the willpower I possess, but I temper it. I speak with my regular inflection.

"I'll... I'll control it."

"Good." Just like that, Raul releases me. He bends down and offers his brother a hand. I stare as Raul helps James up.

What the...?

"I was trying to help." James says to me grudgingly. "To get the weapon away from Victoria."

I can't help the incredulous scoff from coming out.

But Raul only nods. "We might plot and bicker," he says. "But two vampires of The Haven would never kill each other."

Yet even as he says that, a haunted look passes through his eyes.

"Especially not anywhere near our coven's territories," James adds. He looks at the blonde woman twitching on the floor. "She was a fool for trying an attack."

My mouth works, but no words come out. Is Raul just going to stand there and accept *that* for an explanation?

"I *saw* the look that passed between you and her before she drew the knife!" I accuse James.

"You misread it. I was telling her not to do anything

stupid."

"Liar!" I snarl. Tendrils of that ever-present anger rise from my gut. "I know what you're capable of! You'd stop at nothing to get ahead!"

"She's known me for a few weeks and already has such a firm opinion," James notes to his brother.

Raul gives a sour chuckle.

"I can't believe this," I say. "Raul, did you not see what just happened? She—"I point at Victoria, "—tried to kill you. Your brother helped her! If it wasn't for me—"

"Enough." Raul cuts me off. Something in his voice slices right through the hierarchical vampire presence that I naturally exert over him. "That's enough, Eleira. I want you to trust me on this."

Am I going crazy? None of this is making any sense! Why is Raul reacting so… passively? Why am *I* being framed as the bad guy?

Raul gives me a level look. "We're going to deplane now," he says. "I'll take Victoria. James will come next. Eleira, you wait here until I return."

"No!" I say. "Why am I to be left behind?"

"It's for your safety," Raul says. He takes my arm and pulls me aside. He whispers in my ear, "Mother knows I brought you back. But she doesn't know how powerful you are yet.

30

She's waiting for us out there. She'll be able to sense your power from a distance—but she doesn't know it's *yours*. I don't know how she'll react when she discovers it's actually you. Victoria already surpasses her in strength. The Queen won't like that. But bringing *two* vampires, both stronger than her, home with me? Let's just say it makes for an unpredictable situation."

"Fine," I grumble. Part of his explanation makes sense... a bit.

It doesn't mean I like it.

I settle into a seat, cross my arms, and stare daggers at the backs of the other three vampires.

Raul rips the sack off Victoria's head just before he takes her off the plane, leaving James with me.

Chapter Three

SMITHSON

I stand on my Queen's right, shoulders back, chin held high, chest thrust out.

We're gathered at the edge of The Haven for the arrival of her two sons. In my mind, I conduct a quick check of all the guards.

I've posted many around the area. The congregation surrounding the Queen is only a tenth of those under my command.

The rest are spread through the trees, hidden in strategic positions throughout the forest. All are waiting to strike on my command.

When the Queen of The Haven reached out to me and offered me the position of Captain Commander... I was flabbergasted. I could never expect such a boon.

She and I knew each other, many long centuries ago...

I lie flat on the rocky ground, edging my way forward inch by agonizing inch.

A violent fire rages around me. The smoke forms a dense black cloud that covers most of the sky. It hides the summer sun and is the only reason my team and I have any chance of success.

No one would be crazy enough to go into the blasting hell we're approaching without the benefit of such cover.

I look over my shoulder and check on my men. This mission is of the highest priority. We are Knights of the Vorcellian Order. We've dedicated our lives to eliminating the stain of witchcraft and sorcery from the human race.

All of us have taken our vows, forsaking the basal pleasures of this life for the sake of a higher calling.

Our Order has been around since the start of the millennium. We've always operated in the shadows, undermining magic wherever it appears. Witches and sorcerers—they are our targets. They are our prey.

We cannot allow the dark, unnatural forces to spread throughout the world.

Now, my team and I stand on the verge of destroying one of the most powerful family of witches in existence:

The Soren Clan.

The past two decades have been a spectacular success. We've managed to burn, kill, or otherwise eliminate all the weaker families. Only five remain that we know of.

Of course, there is always the possibility that more exist. If they do, my Order will find them, uncover them, and watch them burn.

This has been my whole life's purpose. I was born into the Order and quickly rose through the ranks. As a teen, I was made First Officer. Older men scoffed at my appointment, but I quickly proved their doubts wrong. And the ones who continued to snicker behind my back?

Well, those were the only who found their heads on pikes when I became Lord Commander a short five years later.

Eighteen other Knights are here with me. They are my most trusted men. When I caught wind of the ceremony the Soren witches were planning from an inside source, I knew this was the most opportune time to strike.

Of course, this mission carries a high risk of failure. All our missions do, but taking calculated risks is all part of the game.

Sometimes you have to go by nothing more than the feeling in your gut. And my gut told me to attack.

We continue scaling the rocky hill. Four days ago, we set the fires to trap the witches in the midst of their ceremony.

All supernatural creatures fear fire. It is the one element they cannot control, because it is the one element governed by God.

I mouth a brief prayer and make the symbol of the cross

around my chest. My faith in the Lord is unwavering. It is what allows me to face such monstrosities of nature without fear.

But something went wrong.

The fires we set have not yet been put out. They haven't lessened. If anything, in the past few days they've grown stronger.

Stopping the blaze should have been the Soren clan's first priority. And yet they've allowed it to rage on and on...

We surveyed the land before striking the blaze. There wasn't enough tinder there to fuel the fires for four long days.

That means something else is feeding the flames. Something, I suspect, that comes from the inside.

Something that comes from the witches themselves.

One of my men coughs. Damien. I shoot him a sharp look. The slightest sound could give us away when we're this close. He knows better than to risk our position like that.

He gestures in apology, steels himself, and continues the climb. I tense, waiting for the slightest sound that might hint that we've been compromised.

None comes. I breathe a sigh of relief and continue on.

I see the crest before me. Once we reach that peak, we'll have a perfect vantage of the little makeshift village the witches selected for their ceremony.

I tighten my grip on my sword. I haven't been parted from

the weapon since it was bestowed upon me when I turned ten. The emeralds in the hilt protect me from the worst of the witch's magic.

But the real strength comes from the blade... and the arm that wields it.

Dozens of witches and their vile offspring have met their end on the razor-sharp edge of my sword. Every great weapon has a name, and I named mine Witchbane after my first kill.

We reach the top. I signal for my men to lie low. I brought them here, so I have to take the lead. I raise my head over the edge... and curse at what I see.

Eight little huts stand in a circle in the village below. They are untouched by the flames. A faint blue orb surrounds the entirety of the village like a protective shield.

Along the sides, the fire beats against that shield. But it does not penetrate. Somehow, the flames are repelled.

I sink back out of sight. My mind races. Have the witches found a spell against fire? I would have never—ever—fathomed such a thing possible.

"Smithson," one of my men growls. "What is it? Tell us."

I glance at my most loyal men. All of them knew a time would come when they would give their lives for the Order. I'd been hoping to delay the day as long as possible... but a premonition tells me that the day has finally arrived.

"See for yourselves," I say, granting them permission.

One-by-one they crawl to the top and witness the same sight I did.

Once they all know what we're up against, I stand, not bothering to hide anymore. "Who are we?" I demand.

"Knights of the Vorcellian Order!"

"And what is our mission?"

"To rid the world of all darkness!"

"Then with our Lord as my witness, that is what we will do here, today!" I turn to the village and point my sword straight at it. "Show them no mercy! Strike them down in their homes! Kill them while they're abed, kill them all, because they are creatures of the night, and they have forsaken the light for darkness!"

A monstrous roar goes up among my men. I shift my sword into both hands, angle it in front of me, and scream, "CHARGE!"

We race down the uneven ground. Plumes of smoke rise from the fire around us. The heat is unbelievable. But we're all human, and even if we don't have the element of surprise on our side, we should be able to handle the threat of the fire better than the witches.

A quarter of the way there a dark shape streaks by my side. My attention is diverted for a second. When I look, it's gone.

Suddenly one of my men crashes down. He gives a blood-

curdling scream. A second dark shape flashes, just on the other side of my vision. Damien cries and falls, and when I look I see him pinned to the ground by...

By something not entirely human.

Then, from out of the midst of the fires, come a swarm of black shapes. They move too fast for me to register anything more than the most indistinctive blurs.

They're attacking us. I stop and face the enemy, but wherever I look all I catch is a flash of shadow. It's like fighting ghosts.

The pained screams of my men rain through the air. The dark shapes keep swarming around us, darting in and out so much faster than any witch or human has any right to move.

One by one my small army goes down around me. Blood stains the necks and the breastplates of my men. I spin in a rage, slashing Witchbane through the air.

It finds nothing but empty space.

The black streaks continue darting around me. For a second one of them stops. Our eyes meet.

It's a woman.

My breath catches. Her eyes are tinged with red.

I've seen many things in my life serving the order. But a monster such as this, I've only read about.

Suddenly, she lunges forward. Her arms extend and I see

claws at the tips of her fingers.

Claws stained crimson with the blood of my men.

A rage takes me such as I've never felt before. The creature is fast, but somehow, I manage to get my sword up in time. It slashes up between our bodies. I feel the briefest flash of satisfaction as the monster's body is impaled on the blade.

But the creature looks at me... and simply smiles. Her face is a mask of illustrious, maniacal glee.

She grips the sword running through her with both hands and steps into it, pushing it farther through her body.

All my training, all my experience, all that I know fails me then. I'm stupefied. As the woman moves closer to me, my blade stuck in her side, I cannot break eye contact. Some distant part of my mind is screaming at me that this cannot be real, that this must be an illusion cast by the witches to confuse and befuddle me—

But I know that cannot be true, for I've drunk the elixir of Mirthnettle that immunizes me from spells that affect the sensory faculties of the mind.

The creature speaks.

"Do I frighten you, Lord Commander?" She knows who I am. *"Do I repulse you, as you see me now? Am I not an affront to your God?"*

Her face is inches away from mine and coming closer. I can smell her stench—the stench of a battlefield, of putrid blood, of death.

I try to jerk my blade free. But this woman, this being, this… thing… is so much stronger than I am. It's unfathomable. She should have dropped dead as soon as my blade pierced her flesh. Instead, she's standing here, mocking me, and defying everything I've ever known.

Her hands close over mine on the hilt of the sword. Even through my gauntlets I can feel that hers are ice cold. They steal the heat from my body, sucking it from me like a bat draining blood—

Realization hits. Blood. Blood*! Blood on her mouth, blood over her lips, blood all over her body…*

She hasn't just killed my men. She fed *on them.*

My grip on Witchbane wavers. It hasn't once left my side since I inherited it over thirty years ago. But now I'm on the verge of letting go, if only to get away from this creature—

Where would I go? My eyes flash past her. There are others of her kind all around. They're staring, at me, momentarily distracted from their feast on my dead men.

The most horrible dread crashed into me. My men—all dead. All skewered as if they were no more than children. All ripped apart, devoured, by these despicable creatures.

"What are you?" I whisper.

"Not what," the woman rasps. "But who."

She brings her bloodied lips to my ear. "I am the witch you have come to destroy. I am Morgan Soren. But my powers have grown beyond your imagining. No longer will you pitiful humans be a threat to my kind. For now..." she touched a spot on my neck, making me recoil in disgust, "...it will do me great pleasure to show you what it's like to be as I am."

Her head whips forward and she sinks her fangs into my neck.

All the world goes dark.

***

I wake up with my hands bound to the sides of my body. My head is heavy. Thinking is... difficult.

How am I still alive?

The last thing I remember is that blasted creature lunging for my neck. I was sure I was dead, just like the rest of my men.

But now...

What twist of fate has kept me alive?

I fight through the grogginess and do a check of my body.

It's hard to tell at first, but I don't think anything is broken. Considering the despicable way I saw the mass of creatures rip *my men apart, it astounds me that I'm still in serviceable shape.*

Eighteen dead. One alive. Why me?

It has to be because I'm the Lord Commander. But whatever advantage these witches think keeping me alive will bring them, they are sorely wrong.

There's a stiffness in my neck. That seems to be the only injury I've sustained.

I look around the room. Where am I?

Everything is dark. It's also cold. We're obviously far from the middle of the inferno.

I push against my bonds, testing them for a weakness. But I'm tied tight. The only way I'll be let out is if they decide to release me.

I snort in disbelief at my own thoughts. Release me? They've probably only kept me alive to torture me and get information out of me about The Vorcellian Order.

I'll never give them that. There is a sacredness to who we are and what we do that will ensure I will never give our secrets away.

"Kill me, then, witches," I hiss. "Because I will never give up who I am."

A voice in the darkness shocks me by answering. "Unfortunately, Lord Commander, you already have."

From behind me walks the same creature who I thought

had ended my life.

Immediately, I tense. How had I not sensed her presence?

It's because of the heaviness, *I tell myself.* It's dulling my senses.

But deep down, I know that isn't true. I didn't hear her... because she wasn't breathing.

"What are you?" *I whisper as she steps around me.* "Where are we? What do you want?"

"I want to make you understand what it is to feel fear," *she answers.* "I want you to know what it's like to be hated and reviled. I want you to see the falseness of your Order and everything you stand for. But most of all, my darling..." *she leans into me, tracing a nail along my bare chest.* "...I want to see you burn."

I keep my face strong, and I stare into her malevolent eyes.

"You wouldn't have kept me alive for that," *I say.*

"Oh," *she laughs.* "How wrong you are."

"I know how your mind works, witch," *I snarl. Hatred pulses through me at being so close to her kind.* "You can't deceive me. I know what you are."

"You think you know?" *She laughs again. Then she steps away and considers.*

"Your world is small, Lord Commander. Your beliefs are what limit you. Beliefs in your God, in sins of the flesh, in the

43

rightful order of creatures…"

She trails off. "In the morning, when the sun rises, you will learn what you truly are. And you will discover what your persecution of those different from you has cursed you to become."

She turns and leaves without another word.

*** *

For hours, I remain in the dark, counting down the moments until my death.

I'm now certain that death is imminent. Death by fire. They are preparing my body for it.

I haven't been given food or water. They want to starve me first. They want me to feel the desperation before being given into the flames.

But surprisingly, I do not feel the pervading weakness that indicates a lack of nourishment. There's a distant type of thirst, deep inside my body, and it's both stronger and more subtle than any I've felt before. But I feel it lower than on my parched lips. I feel it down in the whole of me. I feel it in my chest, in my gut, in my torso and loins and legs.

It's not something that mere water can fix.

What is happening to me?

I see a crack of light start to seep in through the darkness. The sun is rising outside. My body tenses—I don't know why. Sunlight should be a relief. It casts away darkness and makes the world whole. The sun gives life and birth and renewal.

But something about that *particular light makes me want to draw away.*

I've never had that reaction before.

I watch, breath caught, as the light advances toward me. The creature, that witch, told me that the morning will teach me who I am.

I strain my ears for sound of an approach. But everything is quiet. Everything is still. The light grows stronger, seeping through the thick fabric curtains of my prison.

Nobody is coming. Why?

The light creeps toward me. A sense of great danger overcomes me. My instincts, honed over years on the battlefield, scream at me that something is terribly, horribly wrong.

And then the light reaches my exposed body. It touches my naked skin.

And the moment it does? A roar of agony is ripped from my lips. The pain is endless, ceaseless. It consumes me entirely.

But in the briefest flash of lucidity, I start to understand:

I've been made into one of them.

Chapter Four

SMITHSON

My eyes widen when I sense her strength.

The vampire being led forward by the Queen's middle son is stunning—a radiant, tanned beauty.

She is also strong. Stronger than any I've ever encountered before.

Suddenly, all the guards I've posted do not seem like enough. She can use our natural hierarchical tendencies to turn them against me. Or, at the very least, to subdue them if a fight breaks out.

My eyes go to the Queen. She and I have history, yes— Morgan was the one who turned me—and my loyalty is unwavering to her for all the things she has opened my eyes to over the centuries.

Or so she's been led to believe.

I am grateful for the gift she's given me. Without her... without her, I'd have long been a corpse in the dirt. The Order I once belonged to would be nothing but a lost speck in the great shadow of time, gone forever to the world.

Instead, The Vorcellian Order is one of the most powerful secret organizations in existence. If Morgan had any idea of its survival…

But of course she doesn't. Few vampires do. Besides, she's been trapped within the boundaries of The Haven for six centuries, boundaries that are entirely of her own making.

She brought me here under guise of needing my help protecting her kingdom. In truth, I suspect her motivations are more sinister than that. She's restless, I can tell, and aching to get out.

But while she rules, she cannot leave The Haven's protective realm. Such is the cost of being a Great Witch.

I glance at her. Morgan is a picture of icy calm. She knows the vampire her son brought is stronger than she is—but she also knows that the magic she wields and the loyalty she commands amongst The Haven's residents makes her untouchable.

It's the second vampire, the one still on the plane, who truly concerns me.

That one is even stronger than the first.

Raul and his captive stop twenty feet before us. It's a respectful distance, but the Queen's son has no qualms showing his disdain for me.

He and I have no love lost over the years.

The Queen steps forward. "Who is this?" she asks, gesturing dismissively at Raul's prisoner.

"Mother, I present to you Victoria Clare," he says forwardly, going to one knee. "She is the one who betrayed Father and tried to draw Eleira's blood."

The short blonde vampire stares impetuously at the Queen. Without any permission being granted, she speaks.

"So, you're Morgan. Much less impressive than I was led to believe." She looks over the ring of trees surrounding us, and the guards I have posted there. "This is all the ceremony I get? Pity. I thought you would have tried harder to impress a member of the Inner Circle of the world's most powerful coven."

The Queen turns toward the prisoner. She walks to her. Victoria Clare stares right back,, defiant and unflinching.

I take a step forward to stay by my Queen's side. She motions me still with a quick flick of her wrist.

Morgan stops half-a-step before Victoria. I feel the static potential for violence crackle through the air.

"You don't impress me," the bold prisoner says.

The Queen smiles through the increasing tension. "And you don't frighten me, my child," she replies sweetly. She brings a hand up to touch Victoria's face.

Raul watches his Mother from his spot.

The tanned vampire doesn't pull back. The clashing power between them makes the air feel thick, like we're on the verge of a storm.

"You think I don't know the secret of your power?" the Queen continues. "Of course I do. What's more," she gives a soft laugh, "I have the ability to take it all away. You did not earn it. You stole it from the one who corrupted my husband's heart. I could take it away and destroy you right now… but I think you would be a much more fascinating subject for us to *study*."

She snaps her fingers to call me to her side.

"This is Captain Commander Smithson," she says. "He will be escorting you to the very generous visitor quarters we've provided. Try not to do anything stupid on the way there. I'd hate for you to suffer an *accident*… and end up in a painting."

Victoria blinks in momentary confusion at the painting reference.

I take her elbow and jerk her away.

"Trust me," I whisper, my voice soft but cruel, "you don't want to know what that last bit means."

I shove the silver sack over her head and push her forward.

Chapter Five

PHILLIP

April stands trembling before me. A thick tension fills the space between us. There are cuts all over her body, freshly given by the guards, obviously as a tactic to tempt me.

"Just do it," she whispers. "Do it. I know you have no choice."

Dear God, how I want to.

"No," I say. I stagger away until my back hits the cave wall.

"They'll kill Patricia if you don't." She takes a small step toward me. "But you don't have to kill me. You can use the Little Drink." Her eyes connect with mine. "You know what will happen if you resist."

I look at her in a mix of awe, shock, and wonder. Has she been brainwashed? Is that why she is offering herself to me like this?

Is that why Mother left me alone with her?

"I know what I'm saying," she says, as if having read my thoughts. Maybe they're so transparent that she can see them on my face. "I'm fully lucid. The Queen's guards did things to me—" A flicker of shame crosses her face, "But they never broke my mind. That was not their intent."

"Then what?" I ask. I'm desperate to steer the conversation away from the choice facing me.

"Do I have to tell you? You're one of them. You know."

It's taking all the self-control I have to not launch myself at her. Having a taste of The Convicted blood has opened my appetite for more. Mother's taunts have not made any of it easier.

My hands grip the rocky wall behind me.

"Why are you delaying?" she asks. "Do it! Don't be a coward. You can *save* Patricia!"

I swallow and shake my head. No matter what choice I make, it'll be the wrong one.

Mother made sure of that.

"Take the Little Drink and save her!" April commands. "That's all the Queen wants."

"You don't know what she wants," I breathe. How can I explain that if I taste her blood, I'll never be able to stop? How do I explain that if I give in now, nearly six hundred years of restraint, of restriction, of self-denial will all have been for naught?

If I take her blood, I'll lose myself. The monster whom I would emerge as on the other side would be a far cry from the

Phillip who stands before her now.

Taking Convicted blood is different. They are creatures without sustenance in their veins. But a fresh, ripe human, full of thick, viscous, *hot* blood...

"She wants to get her son back," April says, defiant and strangely confident. She was so subdued when my Mother was here—was that just an act? "I heard everything from the cell where they held me. And James told me certain things, too. Your Mother wants to strengthen the coven—that's why she needs you."

April takes another step to me. "I heard how you protested against what the Queen has done. Don't you want to save Patricia from that same fate?" She thrusts her arm out. "I do. So don't be a coward. Drink!"

I marvel at her. How can she be so firm and determined? The spark of something I'd long-since considered lost comes to life inside me. I've never felt love for a human before, but April's bravery makes my heartbeat quicken.

It'll only make tasting her blood all the worse.

"You'll die if I do," I say in a faint whisper.

That makes the girl stop and blink. But then she shakes her head.

"No," she says. "You're lying. James has—"

"James has drunk human blood his whole life!" I snap.

"James knows how to stop! James was your lover. I know what he promised you, and I know the sacrifices you made for him! But James is gone, and if you think you can come over to our side by latching your claws into me, you're mistaken."

"So you're going to let your Mother kill Patricia?" April asks. "Because you're too frightened of what you are?"

"Did you not hear me?" I snarl. "If I start now, I'll never be able to control the thirst. It's not just Patricia's life that's at stake. It's yours. How don't you understand that?"

She turns her gaze downward. "Because I saw you in the village," she tells me. "Before you even knew I existed, I saw how you interacted with the villagers. You're not like the other vampires, Phillip. You're *different*."

I scoff a harsh laugh. "You think I don't know that? And the only reason I'm *'different'* is because I've rejected the feeding process that opens the gates of darkness. I've held the creature inside me dormant for so long that it's not a part of who I am any more. But the second I taste your blood, it'll be unleashed. I'll be worse than a newborn vampire. The bloodlust will be unparalleled. I won't be able to stop myself with you. I'll go after others. And because I know these caves, because I know The Haven, no humans will be safe from me."

I ease myself away from the wall. "Is that what you want, April? Because that's the choice you're giving me. It's not, 'Drink and save Patricia's life.' It's 'Drink and kill you, and kill dozens of others.' When the sickness takes over and I black out, there's no going back. *That* is my dilemma. *That* is the choice you're asking me to make."

"I don't believe you," she whispers. "You're stronger than that."

I approach her. She does not move away.

I advance until our bodies are almost touching. Her scent fills my nostrils—that tantalizing mix of mortal innocence and human blood and...

I nearly gasp. *And woman.*

I can see the emotions raging beyond her eyes. Some humans are easy to read. Not her. She keeps everything about her behind those stunning blue irises.

"Why aren't you frightened?" I whisper.

"Because... because I know your heart," she says. She hesitates, then reaches out and takes my hand. She brings it up, between our two bodies. "You're not like the guards or the others. There is good in you."

"It's tainted," I say. "Tainted by evil."

"You've fought it off for this long," she says. "Why would your willpower falter now?" She looks into my eyes. "I know you can do it. You can restrain yourself. Have a drink. Save Patricia's life."

Still I hesitate.

"If you think it'll change you... it won't."

"How can you be so sure?"

"Because all the Soren brothers possess their Father's strength," she says.

I look at her as if seeing her for the first time. "What do you know about my Father?"

"I know that he rules the most powerful coven in the world. I know that his strength on this earth is unrivalled."

"But you're human." The gears spin in my head. "You're human, and you were brought to The Haven from the Outside. No humans know about the other covens!"

"My memory was restored," is all the explanation she offers.

A noise behind us makes me snap around.

"Quick!" she breathes. "This is your last chance! Do it, do it now, or else Patricia dies!"

The conflict inside me rages as strong as a tempest. Do I dare do it? Do I dare fail myself and give in to Mother's demands?

Still the scent of this human girl calls to me. The temptation is unlike any I've felt or known before. It's not just the blood that makes it appealing.

It's the fact that it's *hers*.

She pulls her straight blonde hair back and cranes her neck. Her eyes drift closed as she arches herself into me.

"Drink," she whispers. "But—" she opens one eye. "—But remember who you're doing it to."

With that, the sealed door opens, and my choice is made for me.

I sink my fangs into April's neck and draw deep.

Chapter Six

SMITHSON

I shove my captive out in front of me. The silver sack covering her head does nothing against the natural influence of power she exerts over others.

That influence is the reason I'm taking her beneath ground alone. None of the guards I have command over in The Haven have even a tenth of the discipline my former colleagues in The Vorcellian Order possessed. Since I'm newly arrived here, I have only the most basic surface layer of understanding about the currents of power flowing through this coven.

That is why, for now, the only person I fully trust is myself.

Victoria walks onward without protest. It's almost like she already knows the place. Nothing in the terrain gives her even a second's hesitation despite having her eyes covered. She's as sure-footed as a goat.

So far, she hasn't tried lashing out with the power she possesses. I know it's only a matter of time. A vampire as strong as her does not stay captive for long.

Not unless she wants to be here.

That is the possibility that disturbs me the most.

Suddenly, she stops. I prod her forward with my silver-tipped sword. Witchbane—the same sword from all those centuries ago.

It has only strengthened with time. The moment I understood the sort of creature Morgan had turned me into, I made it my mission to never again be left helpless against vampires. Even if I had been turned into one of their kind, I knew they were still my enemy. I had to arm myself, to protect myself, to learn their strengths and weaknesses so that I could understand mine.

It was I who discovered that silver was their weakness, for example.

"Go on," I grunt. "Don't make this harder on yourself than it needs to be. You heard the Queen's threat."

A mocking sort of high-pitched laughter comes from beneath the cloth. I tense, ready to plunge the blade into her heart at the slightest provocation. If she attempts to escape…

I shift the blade into her. I apply the faintest bit of extra pressure, just to remind her that I'm here.

Or is it to remind myself that I'm in control?

"Your Queen is nothing compared to the ruler I served under for forty years," she replies. "The only reason I allowed myself to be captured is so that I could be led here... to you."

She eases her body forward and starts to turn. She does it smoothly, slowly, with just enough grace to let me know she doesn't mean this as a threat or a precursor to an escape attempt.

She shocks me, though, when she brings her palms to either side of my sword and presses them onto the silver.

"I could snap this blade in two," she drawls, almost lazily. "Such is the power given to me by The Ancient's blood."

I try to hide my surprise but the effort is wasted. A sharp intake of breath is all it takes for me to give myself away.

"Oh, yes," she continues, keeping her head aimed at me, as if the velvet barrier is not even there. "I know how long you sought The Ancient yourself. But you never found him, did you, Smithson?"

"That's enough," I growl. My response to the initial query was all the evidence I needed of Victoria's trickery. Usually, I'd have enough self-control to hold that intake of breath in. But she'd exerted her influence over me in the most subtle way possible, subtle enough that I didn't notice. Had her attempt to control me been more overt, I could have barricaded my mind from it.

But Victoria is slippery. I'm more aware of that now.

"Is it now?" she wonders. "Look at where we are. Alone.

Underground. I could kill you, hide your body, and run free in The Haven if I so wanted."

"There are two hundred guards watching these corridors," I bluff. "You wouldn't get ten feet past the exit."

She laughs again. "Two hundred guards? Is that supposed to impress me?" She lowers her voice. "I know it's just you."

"The silver addles your senses," I tell her. But a bead of sweat trickles down my spine. "Your sense of the other vampires is inaccurate."

"Are you saying that to convince me or to convince yourself?"

"Neither," I tell her firmly. "I am simply stating it as irrefutable fact. Now come on, *princess*. I don't care who you were in your other coven. Here, you're a prisoner of my Queen, and you'd best remember that."

"Or what?" she asks. "You'll skewer me with your little sword?"

"Yes," I grate, pressing it into her belly. "I'll do exactly that."

"I don't think so," she sighs. "You wouldn't kill me."

"And what makes you so confident?"

"Because of the link I have with your Queen's most prized possession."

Is she talking about...

"Eleira," Victoria says. "My blood was the first she drank. It wasn't from the vein, but from a chalice infused with magic. You kill me," she laughs, "...and you write your own death sentence. Because if my link to the girl breaks, so will her mind. And we'll see how well Morgan's succession works then."

I shake my head even though I know she cannot see me.

"You're wrong," I say. "The Queen has taken precautions. Eleira is at no risk. Besides, I don't even know why I'm entertaining this conversation with you. So I won't. Another word, and, link or no link, my sword goes through your pretty little heart."

"You wouldn't dare," she hisses.

I grab the silver layer of her sack and pull it up to see her eyes. Burning pain shoots down my arm, but I force the sensation down completely.

"Just try me," I snarl, so close to her that I can feel her breath on my face.

She looks into my eyes and sees that I am serious. We clash for a strong, silent moment.

Then she nods in final defeat.

As I lead her the rest of the way to her prison cell, I cannot do anything to stop the triumphant smile from spreading across my face.

Without knowing it, Victoria has just given me more information about the Queen's succession plans than I could have hoped to discover by myself in an entire year.

All because she thinks my loyalty lies completely with The Haven's monarch.

What a sweet, naïve little fool she is.

Chapter Seven

JAMES

"Mother," I say grandly, stepping off the plane and placing my foot on the safe, familiar ground of The Haven. "Are these handcuffs really necessary for the triumphant return of your eldest son?"

I roll my shoulder and bring my bound arms forward. Mother's eyes gloss over me, just as they've done so many countless times over the centuries.

Everything I've done and she still hates me, I think. *Some things will never change.*

For a long moment she considers my request. And then:

"Un-cuff him," the Queen orders a member of her guard.

"And when did you find this one, I wonder?" I ask after my arms are free. He's a fresh-faced vampire I've never seen before. I rub my wrists. "A castaway from one of the neighboring covens?"

"Easy," Raul warns from my side.

I look at my younger brother, and then back at Morgan. "So," I say, "Is it true? Did you really send Raul after me and threaten to kill Phillip if he failed to get Eleira back?"

Morgan doesn't answer. Instead, she sweeps up right to me, and slaps me across the face.

My head snaps to the side. I scowl as I straighten and rub my cheek.

"I suppose there could be worse ways of greeting me," I grumble.

"Be thankful I granted your first request," she says. "It was not an act of mercy, nor do you deserve to be free. But you are right. A member of the royal family should not be held prisoner without trial."

"Is *that* what you intend?" I can scarcely keep the incredulity from my voice. "You want to make an example of me? Just like you wanted to do of Patricia and Jacob?" I look at the rest of her guard.

I don't see my friends in their numbers.

"Where's Andrey?" I ask.

"Dead," she says flatly.

The revelation staggers me. From the corner of my eye, I notice Raul stiffen.

"Along with three of those closest to him," Morgan finishes. Her eyes swerve over me, searching for any emotion on my face.

I keep it locked inside. News of his death comes as a

shock, but I cannot show it with the audience around us.

"It seems your rule is crumbling around you, Mother," I say under my breath. "No wonder you went through such extremes to ensure Eleira's arrival. But don't worry," I gesture back to the plane. "The girl is on there, stronger than even you could have envisioned her to become. *All thanks to me.*"

I take a bold step forward. If Morgan calls me on my bluff, I might suffer the consequences for decades... but if I can angle my perspective properly...

"I'd always intended to bring her back," I announce grandly, so that all the vampires around me can hear. "I saw what Father has done in The Crypts. It's quite extraordinary. You sent me there to destroy him—" Gasps sound from the vampires surrounding us. Usually they are not privy to the inner workings of the royal family, "—But I did you one better. I earned his *trust*. And with it, free passage in and out of the coven. He commands power such as you've never seen. It's harnessed from the blood of The Ancient. Had you had just a little more patience, Mother, I could have brought you a vial of that vampire's most powerful blood. I'm sure with your advanced witchcraft you could have made great use of it."

I sigh and tilt my head to Raul. "But instead you send him to bring me back prematurely. I cannot fault my younger brother for listening to your command. I only wish you would have had the foresight to realize that all I did... was done for the good of The Haven."

I stop talking and wait for her reaction. Tension rises in my body, but I do a great job masking it. I've laid it all out on the line: lie after lie after lie after lie.

Now we see if Mother takes the hook.

The silence stretches. I can tell Raul is eager to speak his bit. But I also know that he's nearly as cunning as I am. He understands my gambit. He knows what I'm playing at.

Above all, he understands just how precarious our Mother is.

And because of that knowledge, I can rely on him to keep his mouth shut.

For now.

"Oh James," the Queen says finally. "How I wish it was only *foresight* that I lacked." Her voice takes on a mocking quality. "But the truth is, my son, it was my trust that you were misusing."

She gives a sad smile. "And my trust that you will never have again, after insulting me with that barrage of untruths."

She withdraws a whip from her sleeve and snaps it forward before I can react. The end coils around my neck.

Panic rushes through me. *It's silver!*

I try to grasp for the end but the pain that takes me is staggering. I fall to my knees. I try to fight, but it's not just silver—the damn whip is infused with some sort of magic that makes it stronger. One of Mother's accursed spells is augmenting the silver's effects and making the anguish a thousand times worse.

"I sentence you to become one of The Convicted," she announces. Her voice soars through the clearing as pure horror washes over me. "You will not see the moon or the stars again for as long as you linger. You will not have another taste of blood for the remainder of your existence. From this day on, I disown you as my eldest son. From this day on, I have only two male heirs—and I will treasure them for all they're worth, because neither has ever dreamed of going against me as flamboyantly as you have.

"Your imprisonment will begin the day after the next Hunt. I want you to see what you'll be missing—what you will never again have access to."

"Mother!" Raul exclaims. His voice is filled with urgency. "You can't! Think of the consequences. You mustn't—"

Through the shock of her pronouncement, through the pain lashing through my body, I still find the ability to be astounded that Raul would stand up for me.

"You have *no right* to speak to me!" Morgan shrieks. She's suddenly hysterical. "No right at all! My word is law! The sentence is final!"

Mother tugs on my chain. It drags me to her, making me feel pathetic as a bag of suet. I kick at the dirt and thrash against the onslaught of pain. But there's nothing I can do to lessen it—nothing I can do to ease the horrid sensations raging through my body and mind.

"I'll take him to the prison cells myself," she says to the gathering. "And after... we will welcome our returned runaway, Eleira."

Chapter Eight

ELEIRA

I've been on this plane for what feels like hours. I've been by myself after James left, waiting for Raul to return and bring me out.

I wonder what's taking him so long. He was supposed to be quick. I can feel the presence of The Haven's vampires surrounding the plane.

What will their reception of me be? I wonder. Now that I'm one of them...

But I'm not. Not really. I'm removed from what they are because of how my transformation came about.

Because of how much stronger I am than any of them.

The trouble is that I don't understand what that means for me now. Raul's warning about the vampire hierarchy is something I took to heart. I've been thinking about it ever since.

If the Queen is out there, amongst the mass—as I know she is—then I'm stronger than her. Does that undermine her rule? Does that make me easier to *hate*?

I sit upright as I feel a vampire approaching. The cabin door opens.

Morgan steps inside.

She's dressed in an extravagant red gown. It flows around her body and hugs her shape. The rubies around her neck remind me of the ones used in the chalice during the ritual in the Crypts that transformed me.

For some reason, she's carrying a staff. She grips it hard, putting most of her weight on it as she walks.

It's made of black ivory and comes up just past her shoulder. The top is carved into a menacing, snarling wolf's head. Above it is a fat ruby that looks like a demon's eye. Dark imperfections run across the surface, giving both it and the staff the impression of great age and power. At the opposite end is a speared tip with yet another, smaller, complementary jewel. The edges of that look sharp as a huntsman's axe.

What happened to her? I wonder.

Quietly, she closes the cabin door. The space inside immediately grows colder. She turns around and I gasp.

Her eyes are glowing.

An incandescent blue surrounds them. I have the faintest hint of a memory of that color. It was the same blue that exploded from out the witch's cavern that I discovered as a little girl.

She steps toward me. For the briefest moment, her face looks tired and old. One more step, and the lines around her face disappear. She's fresh and young again, and none of the fatigue shows.

She gives me a smile full of secrets.

"You can see past the vampire mask," she tells me. "It is both a gift and a curse. Only those who belong to the ancient witch bloodline have the ability."

The blue glow fades. But the iciness in the cabin still remains.

I start to push myself up, but she stops me with a wave of her hand. "I should be deferring to you," she acknowledges. "Of course, it would not do to have me admit that in the presence of others. A Queen has to rule, after all. Even in the face of an upstart young vampire such as you."

She sits down across from me. "So," she continues, "just so there's no confusion. You are stronger than I. But your instincts are not honed enough for you to make use of that strength. If you let me, I will teach you to harness your powers. Both those granted to you as a witch—" she holds her hand out, and a small blue glowing orb appears in her palm, wreathed in flame, "and as a vampire."

The orb vanishes. She turns her hand the other way and extends her claws.

"However," her eyes flash, "should you refuse, you will

find me an uncompromising adversary. You best me in pure strength, but I am superior in knowledge and experience. I am going to set out a series of rules for you—"

"Wait," I say. She's been talking to me as if I have a full understanding of what she wants, whereas in truth, I know nothing. "What about The Hunt? What are you going to do with me? Am I still going to be made prey?"

She laughs. "That? That was nothing. A test for my sons, all three of whom failed. You were never in any danger. I'd never let a vampire taste your blood."

My eyes narrow. I don't believe her. But I know better than to voice the doubts out loud.

"When you walk off this plane," she says, "every vampire in The Haven will be in awe of your strength. They will hate you for it. They will whisper amongst themselves and say that your powers were stolen, not earned. They will be envious of the speed of your ascent. They will loathe you for your introduction into the royal family. But most of all—most of all—they will fear who you have the potential to become.

"I'm here to guide you, Eleira. You cannot think of me as your enemy. You and I want exactly the same thing. We want—we need—for you to prosper. We need you to take your proper place and lead The Haven into the 21st century. I'm willing to treat you as an equal, if you give your word you will not go against me or challenge my rule. If I can be guaranteed your loyalty, you and I will be capable of spectacular things.

"But," her voice becomes hard, "if you choose to defy me, I assure you, I will make your life here a living hell."

She stands and gives a little self-congratulatory nod. "I've let it be known to the others that you have complete freedom to roam and explore the entirety of The Haven. There are no restrictions. You will find no doors that are locked to you. Consider it an extension of good faith. I've had your rooms made in the upper reaches of my castle. I'm sure after your escape, you will have no trouble finding your way back, hmm?"

She smiles at me. "Raul is waiting for you outside. Think of what I've said, and what I've offered you. I will beckon you to me in three days. You can tell me your choice then. But truly, Eleira..." she gives a little laugh. "There is only one path forward for you, if you want to keep your life."

Chapter Nine

PHILLIP

April's sweet blood flows down my throat. It sinks into me and is absorbed instantly by my body. Soon it courses through my veins. I close my eyes and lose myself in the ecstasy of the drink.

Never before have I felt anything like it. Never before have I even come close.

I draw upon the carotid artery in her neck. I'm filled with the thick, robust, and precious fluid. It is my nectar. It is the strongest aphrodisiac I have ever known.

The animal inside me struggles to be let free. After centuries of starvation, it is ravenous.

Keeping its instinctual longing at bay is the most difficult thing I have ever done. But I fight it, even as I drink.

I must stay true to myself.

I lose all sense of place and time as I drink and drink and drink. I'm vaguely aware of somebody else having entered the cavern. I give the entrant the same amount of attention that I might to a faraway gnat or a fly. All I know is April. All I feel, all

I taste, all I experience is the precious human girl beneath me.

Her beating heart sends surges of hot blood into my mouth. It's so strong. The blood is better, infinitely better, than the thin animal blood I've sustained myself on. It has kept me alive, yes, but it is putrid and weak compared to this.

How have I ever resisted the call?

I feel April start to weaken. Her body goes slack. Her limbs, which were full of strength only moments ago, fall to her sides. Her heartbeat slows to a dull and ominous *thud-thud-thud.*

Alarm grips me, and I realize I've drawn too much.

It's the hardest thing that I've ever done, but I force my fangs away. I draw back from her and hold her upright.

She looks at me through drooping eyelids. "You stopped," she says, so softly I can barely hear. A weak smile creeps onto her lips. "I knew you had it in you."

And then her eyes close completely, as she falls into me.

"No!" I cry out. "No, April—"

Laughter greets me from behind.

I spin on my heels. That new, despicable Captain Commander of the Queen's guard is there, his sword drawn, laughing at me.

There's a short female vampire at his side. I cannot see her face because she has some sort of cloth sack covering it.

"So," the Captain Commander says. "It looks like your humanity can be overcome by darkness after all. Congratulations, brother. You are now truly one of us."

He holds his hand out for me to clasp. I look at him in disbelief.

He thinks I'd take it?

He shrugs and draws it back after a moment. April's eyes flutter open, for a second. Hope blooms inside me—hope that despite the amount of blood she lost, she might still be able to recover.

"I was a vampire before you were made," I tell him. "Whenever that was. Don't insult me with your congratulations."

The words on my tongue feel false. I have a sense of the Captain Commander's strength. Like nearly every other vampire in The Haven, it is greater than mine.

He laughs in a mocking sort of way. "You truly think so?" he asks. He leans into me. "You don't remember me at all, do you, boy? And why should you? But it was I who introduced your Mother to the idea of this sanctuary." He gestures around the cavern. "All that you know, everything that you've grown up with… it all stems from *me*."

My eyes narrow. "What are you talking about?"

April wavers again. I catch her under the arms. "What are

you talking about?"

"*I* was one of the first vampires your Mother ever made," he gloats. "How do you think she found me so quickly following the death of her former Captain? She and I have a history unrivalled by anybody else. We knew each other before you were even born."

He steps closer. The thirst for more blood is pulsing through me. It's all I can do not to sink my fangs into April again.

But through an enormous effort of self-control, I manage to keep the urge down. April's willingness to offer herself to me, and the value she placed on Patricia's life make me capable of it.

"I know your Mother is using you," he continues. "I can see through the act she puts up. I've known her for longer than you've been *alive*. And because I've known the Queen for so many years, all the things she thinks are clouded in secrecy are to me transparent as glass."

He stops an inch away from me. "I could be on your side. I could help you navigate through all the turmoil that is to come."

"What turmoil?" I ask. My natural suspicions are swinging in with full force.

"You think the succession is going to be smooth?" He laughs. "I considered you more intelligent than that."

"You don't know who you're talking to," I say. "I've been here my whole life. Maybe you were made first, but you're an Outsider. You don't have a tenth of the influence you claim to possess."

He smirks. "Is that so? Then tell me, please, how I managed to subdue this one—" he snatches the bag from the female vampire's head, and all of her strength is suddenly revealed to me. I nearly stagger back from shock.

She is, without a doubt, the most powerful vampire I've ever encountered.

"—with her being so much stronger than I?"

"Oh, hello." She smiles at me. "You must be the youngest of the Soren's. I've heard plenty about you."

I put April behind me to shield her with my body. My venom hasn't yet sealed the wound on her neck. With her blood flowing freely, she's at risk of being made prey by the two vampires here with us.

"Don't worry about her," the blonde prisoner says. She looks at the Captain Commander. "May I speak to him?"

He nods but keeps his sword in hand.

"I come from your Father's coven," the female explains. "Raul brought me here alongside James. I did not think you and I would meet for a long time. But I'm glad we did...even if it comes on such unexpected terms."

"What do you mean, unexpected?"

"You're supposed to be the one to have rejected human blood, aren't you?" she asks. "And yet here I find you, feeding on a timid human girl."

A growl rises from my throat. It's the darkness inside rebelling against the insult.

"Enough," the Captain Commander interrupts. "I'm here for you to swap places." He leads the blonde vampire into a cell and slams the gate shut.

But there's a certain *deference* in the way he treats her that is unlike any I would expect the Captain Commander to show a prisoner.

It's unnerving and intriguing. Something is going on between the two of them. Both are Outsiders with uncertain loyalties.

I'm going to be careful with them both.

The Captain Commander returns to the entrance and holds the door open for me. "Come on, then. Let's get you out of here. Your brother is back, as you've heard. As is the girl. I'm sure you lot have much to discuss."

I start for the exit. The Captain Commander suddenly raises his sword and points it at me.

"Just you," he says. "The human stays."

It's a meaning of how much April's blood has invigorated

me that I make no move to obey, despite our difference in strength. "She's coming up," I say.

I expect a rebuttal. Even my position in the family doesn't protect me from being subject to the hierarchy.

Yet the monster that's slowly waking inside me is making me recklessly bold. It thirsts for blood. Even though I'm under no illusion that I could win, I still see myself attacking the Captain Commander if he decides to stay in my way.

To my surprise, he lowers the sword. "As you command," he says considerably, "my Prince."

Just before we leave the cavern, I notice his eyes flash to the blonde prisoner left behind us. Again, I wonder what that means.

Chapter Ten

RAUL

I walk briskly through the charred remains of the village, my guilt eating away at me for having ruined so many homes.

I try to justify my actions by telling myself this was essential to getting Eleira away. But now that we're both back, all the destruction I've caused seems to be so... meaningless.

I look at her walking at my side. She's kept her arms hugged around herself this whole journey.

But her eyes take in everything. She is as troubled by the state of the village as I am.

"Hey. You all right?" I ask.

She starts in surprise. "What? Yeah. Yeah, I guess I am."

"You don't look it," I note. I hate the growing distance between us. Eleira has withdrawn more than I would have thought possible after the meeting with my Mother. She hasn't told me what they discussed.

"Neither does the village," she tells me. Her eyes sweep over the charred remains of the buildings. "What happened here? Where are all the humans?"

"Most are safe," I say. "They were brought underground for their own protection, once Morgan sensed we were returning. My Mother took precautions…"

"To keep them away from me," she interrupts. There's a sad inflection in her voice.

"No," I say. "Eleira—"

"Don't lie to me!" She stops and looks right into my eyes. Hers are glowing with determination. "I know what I've become. I can feel it. Don't tell me it's not me the humans are hiding from when I know it really is." She blinks, almost in surprise, then says, "I'm sorry. I don't know what came over me."

"I do," I say. "It's the darkness. I'll help you navigate it. But you need to trust me."

"I do trust you," she murmurs. "And Morgan offered me the same thing."

I look at her and ask her for clarification. "What thing?"

"To help me navigate my new… powers." She slumps back in on herself. "But I don't want help. I want to do it on my own."

"You're not on your own," I tell her firmly. I reach across and take her hand. "Don't you forget that. You have me." I touch the large gemstone on her finger. "You have this. It'll help."

"And who will help the villagers?" she asks, her voice a shadow of its former self.

I look into her eyes. "What do you mean?"

"Their homes are destroyed," she says. "*They're* the ones you should be concerned with, not me."

I frown. "Eleira, you're speaking madness. The villagers have always managed. They'll rebuild and resume. Their lives will be back to normal in short order."

She shakes her head. "You don't get it, do you?" She draws her hand away. I feel the loss immediately. "They're not people to you. They're just... pawns. Just sources of blood for you and your kind."

"What? That's not true at all!" I feel a flash of anger go through me. "Why would you accuse me of something like that?"

"Because it's the way *I* feel about them now," she whispers. Even with my enhanced hearing, I can barely make out the words. "I'm fighting it, Raul. I'm fighting it with every bit of strength I possess. But it's... impossible, in the face of the monster lurking within me."

Her eyes take a desperately sad, faraway look. "I thought I would come back and help them. Instead, all I can think about is taking their blood." She shivers. "It scares me."

I step toward her and put an arm around her shoulders.

83

She resists for a moment… and then melts into me.

I let her put her face into my chest as silent sobs start to rock her body.

"Hey," I say softly. I tilt her chin up. "Hey. It'll all be okay. We'll get you to the castle. I'll get you your fill of blood from the banks. Once that's done, you'll feel better.

She clings onto every word like a drowning woman to a life vest. "Do you promise?"

"I swear it." I drop my lips and place a kiss on hers. "Now come on. The sooner we get you nourishment, the easier all of this will be."

Chapter Eleven

ELEIRA

Raul's assurance takes away some of the guilt I feel as we make our way up through the silent trees toward Morgan's castle.

Now that I'm transformed, everything about The Haven feels so much different. My eyes are no longer blind to the beauty of the place.

The evergreens are wonderful. They infuse the night air with so much life and prosperity. It's probably from my enhanced sense of smell, but I don't think I've ever breathed in air this pure before.

When I was here as a human, all I could see was horror, destruction, and death. Now, as a vampire, the night holds new meaning. The very air holds new meaning. This isn't a graveyard or some place to be reviled.

It's a beautiful, verdant sanctuary.

The silence is so pervasive. But at the same time, it's amazing. That a place could house so many people and yet be so quiet astounds me...

Of course it helps when the majority of those people are locked underground.

A pang of guilt takes me. They are there because of me. Their homes were ruined… because of me.

"Raul?" I ask softly. "In the fires you set—how many humans perished?"

He looks around. He takes a long time to reply.

"Those who died in the actual fires? Maybe a dozen."

A dozen. My gut seizes up.

"And… those who didn't?" I ask. A bad feeling of apprehension sweeps through me. "What happened to them?"

Raul clears his throat. "Some of the other vampires took advantage of the mayhem to feed," he says. "I don't know what Mother has done to them yet. I assume they'll be persecuted for their crimes. But…"

He trails off.

"But what?" I ask. "Tell me!"

He shakes his head. "You saw how Mother is." In a softer voice, he adds, "I'm not sure her head is where it was before."

"So they're just going to walk free?" I insist. "Without being punished?"

"Not all of them," Raul says cryptically. "Some have already paid the price."

86

"What do you mean?"

But Raul keeps his lips sealed the rest of the way.

We reach the castle. Just before we walk through the doors, I stop and take Raul's arm.

"Do you think…" I begin. "Do you think your Mother will really make James one of The Convicted?"

Raul sweeps a hand through his fire-red hair. "Truly? I have no way to tell. But I'm going to do all I can to ensure that it doesn't happen."

I hesitate, then make up my mind, and say, "If there's anything I can do to help, you tell me. No matter what James did—nobody deserves a fate like those forsaken creatures." I think back on the way the mindless horde chased after us. I remember the desperate way they fought each other for the bloodied heart that was thrown into their midst.

I remember the look of utter emptiness in their eyes.

Raul nods. "Thank you. That means a lot. I know what he put you through. Despite that, he's still my brother."

"I understand," I say softly. Even though it pains me to admit, James has Raul's loyalty. I wouldn't ever doubt that.

It just proves what type of man Raul is.

Just then a sound interrupts our conversation. One of the side walls in the entrance lobby starts to shift. A hidden door is revealed.

Raul takes a protective step in front of me. But I put a hand on his shoulder to let him know I'll be okay.

I am a vampire, after all.

A grizzled vampire carrying a lethal-looking sword comes out first. His shoulders are wide. His cheeks are lined with salt-and-pepper scruff.

"*Smithson*," Raul says flatly. He shifts to make sure I remain behind him.

The other vampire smiles and sheathes his sword. "Didn't expect to run into you this soon," he replies. "I—"

But he doesn't get to finish the rest. At that moment, Phillip emerges from the darkness beyond him.

"Phillip!" I exclaim. I push by Raul and run to him. Smithson steps aside with a grunt.

Phillip is carrying someone in his arms. A girl. For some reason I don't place her right away. Her face is cradled against Phillip's chest. As I come closer, I see that it's April.

I stop short. There are two vicious red marks on her neck. They're crusted with blood.

Instantly, my hunger flares. I struggle to push it down. I have to; I can't very well attack the girl who became my best friend.

But it's insanely difficult. The beast inside me thrashes, fights to be let free. My vision wavers, flashing from normal to black and back again.

It takes all I have to push the need to feed on her down. The struggle is real, and it feels eternal. My hands ball into tight fists. I feel the gemstone on my finger and try to focus on that instead, knowing it will help me retain my humanity just as Raul promised...

"Easy. Easy now."

I come to with a start, and realize Raul has his arms wrapped around me. We've moved far away from the entrance, closer to one of those horrible framed paintings. Smithson and Phillip are both staring at us with surprised expressions on their faces.

"Easy, easy. There you go." Raul eases his grip. "You okay?"

I swallow and do a quick check of my body... and nod. "I blacked out, didn't I?"

"Yes, but only for a moment. And—" pride fills his voice, "—you didn't attack."

I grumble something about that not being much of an accomplishment.

"No," Raul shakes his head firmly. "You're wrong. It's a huge measure of your growing self-control."

Despite myself, I flush a little at his praise.

Raul lets me go. But before I can take a step forward, he

takes hold of my hand. His fingers intertwine with mine.

"We'll approach them together," he tells me.

"Okay."

Smithson watches us come closer with a wary look in his eye. Raul tenses when we get close. The two have some sort of unspoken history, that much is obvious.

"I don't need to be here for this reunion," the older vampire says. He doesn't acknowledge my presence in any way. For some reason, that makes me feel like I've become even more of a target.

He gives a curt bow to Raul, and strides out of the castle.

Everyone waits until he's gone. Once the doors close, it's like a plug has been pulled to release the tension.

"You've returned!" Phillip says. "You brought Eleira! How is she, she's—" He stops short. He takes a sharp intake of breath.

"She's so strong," he says as he meets my eyes.

"She hasn't yet fed," Raul explains. "We've come here to get her blood."

"Mother has plenty in the upper rooms," Phillip replies. There's something about him that's different from before. I can't quite put my finger on it, but he seems to be more sure of himself. More in his own element, more confident.

It's April I'm most worried about.

90

"What happened to her?" I ask. I see how weakly her chest rises and falls with each breath. "Is she—"

"Just a bit of blood loss," Phillip says defensively. He cradles her in his arms. "I'm taking her to the infirmary. She can recover there."

"She was bitten?" Raul asks. "By whom? Not—" He gasps. "No!"

Phillip nods. "Mother gave me no choice."

"But you—you haven't tasted blood for centuries!"

A bit of sadness creeps into Phillip's eyes. Yet it's almost immediately replaced by determination. "I did it to save Patricia. Mother accused her and Jacob of the murder of her guards."

"That's ridiculous!" Raul exclaims. "They don't have the strength—"

"I know," Phillip responds. "But she hasn't been rational. Her grip on the throne is crumbling. She's scared."

"I suspected as much," Raul murmurs.

"Wait a minute," I say. "You said you saved Patricia. What about Jacob?"

Phillip looks at me and shakes his head. "I'm sorry, Eleira. There was nothing I could do. Morgan held me prisoner."

"She killed him?" I ask. "No. No, she wouldn't do that. She made him a Convicted, didn't she?"

91

Raul and Phillip share a look. "You don't yet know our Mother," Phillip says.

"Then what?"

"She severed his soul and bound it in a painting," Phillip says. "She did it right before my eyes."

A sick feeling washes over me. "No."

Phillip nods. "April was so brave. Mother gave me a choice. Feed, and spare Patricia from the same fate. Or resist, and…" he trails off. "You know what the alternative would have been."

"That's horrible." I breathe.

Raul, meanwhile, seems to have withdrawn into himself. "This is my fault," he whispers softly. "All of this falls on me."

Suddenly, April stirs in Phillip's arms. Her eyelids flutter open. Her head falls to one side, and she looks at me.

There's only a second of recognition in her eyes. "Eleira," she says. "You came back."

And then she drifts back into delirium once more.

"I need to get her somewhere she can heal," Phillip says. "I'll find you two later. You'll need to tell me everything that happened." He looks at me. "Especially how Eleira became so strong."

"We'll do that, brother," Raul promises.

"Then by your leave," Phillip says, and rushes past us out into the ever-present night.

After he's gone, I look at Raul. "What did you mean that this was your fault?" I ask him.

His eyes darken and he shakes his head. "I wish I could tell you. But some burdens are mine to bear alone."

I wish I could disagree, but I've had that exact same feeling for the longest time.

"Come on," Raul calls, taking my hand again. "I'll show you to the blood banks. Once you've had your fill... then we can discuss what happens next."

Chapter Twelve

PHILLIP

As soon as April is secure in the infirmary, and being taken care of by our resident vampire doctor, I set about looking for Mother.

I have a bone to pick with her. The old Phillip, the one who was meek and passive, the one who never stood up for himself, is long gone. With April's blood flowing through my veins, I feel like a new man. One who won't take things as they are handed to him lying down. One who will stand up for what he believes in and let all those around him know.

The first step is to find Patricia and make sure Mother held up her part of the bargain.

I've managed to tame my thirst for now. I thought that tasting April's blood would open up the floodgates and turn me into a veritable monster, no better than one of The Convicted in my lust for blood.

But something about the *connection* I felt with April—imagined or not—tempers that hunger. My body feels invigorated, and strong. Most of all, however, it still feels like my own.

I'm still in control.

Did Mother know this would happen? If so, she deserves more credit than I've given her.

I run through the forested paths of The Haven. On a whim I decide to take the route through the village. I want to see what progress has been made—if any—in repairing it while I was locked away.

When I arrive, I'm left bitterly disappointed. It is in exactly the same state it would have been after the fires died down. No repairs have been made. Nothing's been fixed or salvaged. It just looks like a charred mess.

Where are all the humans?

I run through it quickly, hating the vile smell of ash still lingering in the air. All of this for Eleira... only to have her boomerang right back into our midst.

Well, now that she's transformed, I won't have to worry about the antidote Raul had me searching for.

I come to the vampire compounds high up on the trees. There's movement up there—I feel the presence of others like me mingling about.

I take a deep breath and start to climb. I've never been close to many of the other residents—but even so, they'll all notice a difference when they see me. They'll know immediately that I've fed.

I can't imagine the sort of scandal it will start. Phillip Soren, who has held out fueling his vampiric side ever since his creation, is now a *true* vampire?

Some of the Royal Court will even see it as a threat, I imagine. Well. Time enough to deal with that later.

But when I make my entrance into the common room or the compound, it's not my name that's on everyone's lips.

It's my brother, James's.

"Have you heard what the Queen has done?"

"His sentence is horrible!"

"She's banished her own son!"

"If he's not safe, what does that say for the rest of us?"

"James was a fool." I stop short when I hear a gruff voice make that proclamation. "He went against the Queen, and now he has to pay the price. It's justice."

I look at the vampire who said that. He's an old-timer, one of those who has been in The Haven almost as long as I. He doesn't rank very highly in power—none of them here do— and usually it would be blasphemy to speak against a member of the royal family like that.

It seems things have drastically changed while I was locked away.

I approach him. He notices me and stands taller.

96

"Well, well, well," he says, puffing out his chest. "If it isn't Phillip Soren. What brings you to spend time with the peasantry around these parts?" The vampires around him chuckle. "I wouldn't have thought you'd ever demean yourself by being seen with us."

There's pure venom in his voice, in his stance, in the way he regards me. He's still stronger than I am—April's blood hasn't given me an immediate boost in hierarchical strength—but I *feel* stronger than any of the vampires here.

I don't answer until we stand nose-to-nose. "I heard what you said about my brother."

"Oh? Good thing, that. I meant every word."

"It's dangerous," I warn, not backing away. "To make proclamations like that where others can hear."

He laughs. Right in my face, he laughs. "Is that so? Well then next time, maybe I'll speak a little louder, so there's no confusion. I *want* everybody to hear. I am my Queen's man through and through. My loyalty is to her. Not to James. And certainly not to you, *weakest*.

He stabs a finger in my chest on the last word.

I just lose it. Before I can consciously reconcile what's happening, I have his palm pinned behind him in an arm lock. I press down and apply pressure. He cries out in pain.

"Don't," I warn him softly, bringing my lips right to his ear, "*ever* make the mistake of calling me that—" I press down. He squirms against the table, "—again."

Then I let him go. A space has cleared around us after the brief scuffle.

The other vampire picks himself up. He looks at me, then spits to the side.

"That's what I think of you," he says. "Don't assume mommy will keep you safe forever. One of these days, you'll get what's coming. Just like your eldest brother did."

With that, he storms out the room, cutting a sharp path through the crowd.

I straighten and pull my sleeves up as I watch him go. I make a slow survey of the room.

"Does anybody else here have a problem with me?" I ask. I scarcely recognize the voice coming from my throat. I *definitely* don't recognize the aggression pulsing through me. "Anybody? Anybody at all?"

The vampires closest to me take a step back. Those in the far reaches of the room crane their necks up, curious about what will happen next.

"Thought not," I say. "Now that that's over..." I bend down and pick up the table that had fallen in the fight, "—will somebody tell me why James is the object of everyone's conversation?"

Silence greets me. But then, from the back:

"The Queen has ruled that he's to become one of The Convicted."

"What!" My head snaps to the vampire who'd spoken. It's Bella, a bland woman of medium build, unremarkable in every way except perhaps for the spark of passion in her eyes. "When did this happen?"

"Not more than an hour ago, my Prince," she replies. "Surely, we all thought you would know..."

"Well, I didn't," I snarl. Anger washes through me. It nearly takes me over completely. Anger at my Mother, anger at the vampire who'd challenged me, anger at April's frailty...

These are exactly the emotions I've managed to suppress for centuries. Now they're out in full force.

It frightens me, the things I might be capable of, should I let that anger take over.

I make my voice extra loud. "Where was the Queen seen last? I was just in her castle, she wasn't there."

Murmurs of uncertainty greet my question.

"Well?" I demand, louder this time

Bella shakes her head. "We don't know. Some of us were there when the plane landed and she made the pronouncement. But we all split after she dismissed us."

"What about the humans?" I ask. "What has she done

with them?"

"They're still clustered in the caves underground," a voice answers. "They were taken there in advance of Raul's arrival."

I nod. That makes sense. Mother must have taken precautions...

"I apologize if I scared anyone," I say. "I'm not... quite myself at the moment."

Before they can ask me why, I stream straight out the room and into the hallways of the compound.

I walk briskly toward Mother's room. I fling the door open with force.

She isn't there.

I grunt in frustration. I still can't believe what I was told about James. Could she have really have sentenced one of her sons to such a fate?

Then again, should it really surprise me? Knowing what she did—or tried to do—to me?

Without thinking, I start going through her things. I don't know what it is I'm looking for. Some piece of evidence I can use against her, something that will give me some sort of advantage in the looming confrontation...

"Enjoying yourself, are you?"

I spin around. The Captain Commander is standing at the doors, his arms crossed, glaring at me with no attempt to hide his disdain.

I shift away from Mother's desk. There is nothing there except make-up, perfume, and other such frivolities.

"You know..." he strolls casually into the room and closes the door behind him. "This is probably the last place I'd expect to meet you."

"Oh?" I say. In my mind, I size him up. He's a complete unknown, brought in from the Outside at a time when my Mother needed help.

"I thought you'd be lost in the underground caverns, feeding on humans to satiate your bloodlust."

"You thought wrong," I say.

"So I see. Still, that doesn't explain what you're doing here." He takes hold of the hilt of his sword and withdraws it a quarter of an inch. The metal gleams in the artificial light. "Or if I should let you go."

That anger tries to bubble up again. I know better than to give in to it. I need all my mental faculties intact if I am to negotiate my way out of this.

"So why don't you tell me what you were doing," the Captain Commander continues. "And help me make my choice?"

"I could ask you the very same thing," I deflect. "Why did you come here, by yourself? Aren't you supposed to be at the

Queen's side?"

He shrugs. "I have others posted. Besides, your Mother is quite the spectacular woman. She'll have no trouble taking care of herself." He flashes a wicked grin. "As she's so aptly demonstrated in her treatment of you."

I walk around the table. The Captain Commander pulls out his blade another inch.

"You think you can threaten me with that?" I ask. "All you do is show your own fear."

"Oh, you mistake me," he offers. "That's not me threatening you."

In one smooth motion he withdraws the entirety of the weapon.

"*This*," he says, pointing it right at me, "is me threatening you."

I go still. His blade is coated with silver. I've had enough experience with that horrific metal to last a lifetime.

"They way I see it," he continues, "we can go about this in two ways. One, I do the task that was assigned to me, and arrest you for trespassing—which is entirely in my right as Captain Commander. Or, two—" to my surprise, he sheathes his sword, "—I simply let you go. You walk out the door. We forget this ever happened."

I eye him suspiciously. "Just like that?"

He nods. "Aye. Just like that."

I start to move—but—then a question comes to mind. "What are you doing here?"

"I heard a noise and came to investigate."

"Sounds convenient," I note.

"Are you questioning me? Remember who has authority here, Phillip."

"I'm sure Mother gave you all the assurance you need, *Smithson*," I say. "But I still *am* her son. So whatever happens to me reflects directly onto her."

He scoffs a laugh. "You want to pull that card on me? After everything she's put you through? Please. I know just how much the bloodline means to her."

I think of calling his bluff—then decide against it. I raise my arms.

"Fine," I say. "You see me walk, and I'll pretend I never saw you." My eyes flash to him. "Because I *know* you were not expecting to find this room occupied when you came here."

By the momentary look of surprise that crossed his face, I know I'm right.

Chapter Thirteen

JAMES

I pace back and forth in the small enclosure of the underground cell. There's dirt all around me. The roof of the place is low enough that if I stand absolutely upright, my head would brush the ceiling.

My thoughts are stormy and chaotic. I'd gambled everything when I told Mother that story. She called me out on it right away.

I'd gambled, and I lost.

How had I been such a fool? How have I allowed myself to be so transparent?

But never did I think she would sentence me to such a fate. Even now, hours after her proclamation, it doesn't seem quite right.

I am to become one of The Convicted. I am to become one of those wretched, despised creatures doomed to dwell forever underground.

It doesn't seem real... and yet, the chained silver collar hooked to the wall beside me reminds me that it is.

After Morgan brought me here, she took one end off her arm and hooked it into the wall. The other, she kept around my neck. She did me one small mercy before leaving, by uttering a spell that lessened some of the silver's effects on me.

For that I should be grateful. She could have easily let me endure here in misery. But the sense of betrayal, the horrific sense of injustice at what she sentenced me to?

Well, it makes gratitude just a *little bit* difficult to muster up.

There must be a way out of this. There must, there must, there must. The Hunt is not for another few weeks. Maybe— just maybe—that gives enough time for Mother to change her mind.

But such thoughts are ludicrous. Mother may be precarious, yes, but she has not once reneged on a decision after announcing it publically. Those made in private, yes, or those that she only consulted with me, Raul, Phillip, and the other members of the Royal Court about. But those that all vampires of The Haven heard?

Never. Not even once.

By now, news of my fate will have spread. Hell, I'd bet even the humans know about it. Anger, fury, hatred—all those words are too soft for the emotions raging through me right now.

Countless hours pass. Nobody comes. The silver collar made it impossible for me to keep up with how far Mother led me down through the earth to reach this cell. So I don't even know where I am.

Can anybody ever find me here?

Suddenly, a light appears in the distance. I jerk forward and nearly wrap my hands around the bars. I stop short at the last moment, after remembering that, yes, they are made of silver, too.

I have to squint against the lantern being carried toward me. But once I see past it, I realize that it's none other than Raul who's approaching me.

"Brother!" I exclaim, my voice threaded with all sorts of relief. "I didn't think you'd come."

He stops just short of the bars and puts the lantern out. In the darkness, everything is easier to see.

"I wouldn't abandon you," he says. "But I had one hell of a time finding this place."

"Where are we?" I ask.

"Miles beneath the castle," he replies. "I had to go through passageways that haven't been used in decades just to get to the proper level. I've been searching for hours."

"Tell me you brought good news."

He frowns. "Mother's been unwilling to speak to anyone.

She won't entertain visitors. The only person she'll talk to is Eleira."

"The blasted girl." I cannot stop the venom from reaching my voice. "It's all about her, isn't it? Dammit! I should have drained her dry when I had the chance. Then all of this would have been avoided."

"No," Raul says. The word comes out soft and dangerous. "That, you should have never done."

"Oh that's right. I forget. You're in *love* with her. Ha!" I bark a laugh and then sneer. "Love is the domain of fools and idiots. It weakens you, it makes you vulnerable. Or haven't you figured that out yet?"

"I'd watch your tongue, James," Raul warns. "Remember which of us is standing on the wrong side of the bars."

"You're right. I'm sorry." I grunt in annoyance. I'm not used to issuing apologies. "Being locked away in here has given me a short temper."

"Not much shorter than usual," he quips. "But I accept your apology."

"Thank you," I grumble. "Now, back to the topic of Mother?"

"I think she's grieving," Raul admits. "For having lost you."

"But she hasn't lost me!" I snarl. I slam a fist into the dirt wall in frustration. "I'm right here, beneath her castle, forsaken *because* of her."

"She issued the order as our Monarch." Raul explains. "Yet she grieves as your Mother."

I scoff. "Do you truly believe that?"

"Yes," he says. "I do."

"She hasn't seen herself as our 'Mother' for generations," I tell him. "Do you know she hasn't looked me in the eyes, not more than twice, in the last hundred years?"

"She trusted you enough to send you to our Father," Raul says. "Whatever issues you had in private were not known to me."

"*Issues*." I laugh. "She was always jealous of me, Raul. That's the real reason I'm stuck down here. I was the one with flair, the one with style. I was the one other vampires looked up to in our coven. Not her."

"You think that's enough to arouse her jealousy?" Raul shakes his head. "James, you are so much more self-centered than I thought."

"What else then?" I demand. "Think of all she's done. Think of the way she's ruled us! She's as vain as any other. More so, in fact! Think of how many jewels, how many precious stones are in her possessions. Think of all the riches she affords herself while denying even the slightest luxuries to the humans!"

"I didn't know you cared so much about the villagers."

"I don't," I tell him curtly. "I'm just making a point."

"And yet there's one you do care about." Raul steps closer to the bars. "Isn't there?"

"I don't know what you're talking about."

"April."

I stagger back. Not exactly from shock, but from all the memories that name brings. April in my bed, the night Eleira was taken. April swooning at my side, the very first time I tasted her blood. April, with her little head full of hopes and dreams, which could never come true...

"What about her?" I demand, regaining my composure. "She means nothing to me."

"Then I guess I shouldn't tell you that she and Eleira have become the closest of friends. Or that Phillip has taken a liking to her."

"Phillip? I don't believe it. He doesn't care about anything except his computers and books and plants."

"That's changed," Raul tells me, "after Mother made him feed."

That revelation staggers me. Mother may not approve of Phillip's choice, but she always looked upon him with respect—respect that was severely lacking in her interactions with me. I never knew why she regarded him so. But as long

109

as it did not affect me, I did not mind. Phillip was always too meek to take advantage of that undue veneration.

"Mother made him feed?" I breathe.

"She made him feed on *April's* blood," Raul emphasizes. "You know what that means."

"That the girl is dead," I say stiffly. I shoot down any emotions that try to rise from that acknowledgement. "Did you tell me that to add to my misery? Because as you can see—" I flash my teeth in a malicious smile, "—it didn't work."

"April still lives," Raul says. "Phillip drew on her, and stopped himself before taking the final lethal sip."

"What?" *That* truly astounds me. "But he hasn't tasted human blood in... in centuries!"

"Almost six hundred years," Raul agrees.

"And April was his first?"

"She was."

"That's... astounding." I can think of no other word. Maybe Mother's respect for my youngest brother has a basis in reality after all.

"I didn't come here to mock or ridicule you," Raul continues. "I just wanted to inform you of what's going on above. And to reiterate that I will *not* let Mother turn you into one of The Convicted. Not if there's anything I can do to stop it."

Raul shoves his arm through the cell bars and offers his hand to me. "You are my brother, after all. No matter what's been done in the past, brothers stick together. *Always.*"

I search his eyes for any sign of disingenuousness... but find none. There is only earnest appeal.

I clasp his hand. "Thank you," I say, and I genuinely mean it. "Even if you are not successful, your attempt means the world."

Raul grips my hand tightly. "I don't mean to fail you, James," he swears.

Chapter Fourteen

ELEIRA

After having fed in the blood banks, I find myself alone in the new rooms assigned to me, in the highest level of Queen Morgan's castle.

Raul left me after ensuring I was comfortable. I told him I was.

In truth, however, nothing can make me more uncomfortable than facing the reality of what I've just done.

I drank *blood*. Human blood. I drank it and it fueled me and it made me feel alive and invigorated and raw and whole. It satiated that deep thirst that was ebbing through my bones, that thirst that was unlike any I've felt before.

I sit on the edge of the bed and finger the gemstone on the ring. Raul's gift. I can't believe he's been watching me for so long. How many years have I been known by the Sorens? He said something about the celestial charts, and how my birth was written in the stars…

Even a month ago, I would have found that difficult to believe. But now? Now, it seems like the most plausible explanation in the world.

I look at my hands. I open and close my fingers slowly. I curl them in and look at my nails. I *feel* the claws hiding just underneath the skin, claws that I can push out at any time...

These are the hands of a killer.

Everything about my body is now focused on one thing: Death.

Death, killing, and murder. My enhanced hearing, my acute sense of smell, the strength within my muscles... all of it makes me a perfect killing machine.

Is that what it means to be a vampire?

I want to feel sad and repulsed at what I've become—at what I've had no choice but to become—and yet I do not. I cannot muster up the requisite feelings for those emotions.

Instead, I feel a growing sort of... excitement. The world has opened up to me in a spectacular new way. I won't age. I can't catch disease. If everything I've learned about vampires is accurate, I'm bound to live forever, to remain in this body for all of eternity...

That is a fascinating thought. Yet I don't feel excited *enough*. I don't feel enthused *enough*.

Could the ring be tempering my excitement?

For a few minutes I debate taking it off. I don't know what will happen if I do. Will I be overwhelmed by the

113

bloodlust? Or will I be able to control it, since I've recently fed?

In the end, I decide to leave it on. Better to not take any unnecessary risks.

Not this soon.

A knock on the door makes me leap up. "Come in," I say, quickly composing myself to try to look less like a startled sheep.

The door slowly creaks open… and Patricia steps to the threshold.

She looks horrid. Her face is gaunt and her eyes are rimmed with red. There are tear trails on her cheeks that she hasn't bothered to wipe away. She's wearing a tattered white shirt, translucent enough that all the hard angles and jutting bones of her body clearly show.

Her arms and legs are thin, frail, and borderline wasted away. She keeps her eyes glued squarely to the floor.

"I'm sorry if I'm disturbing you," she says. Her voice quavers. "But I had nowhere else to go."

"You're not disturbing me," I say quickly. I hurry to her. "Come in, please, close the door. It's wonderful to see you!"

She shies away with every step I take. I don't understand why—but then it hits me.

The vampire hierarchy of power.

Patricia is so weak that I can barely feel she's a vampire. And me? Well, my powers are so far above her that she might as well be a candle flame held up against the sun.

I stop halfway to the door. "Patricia, you don't have to worry about my strength," I say. "We're friends. I know how you helped me escape. I owe my life to you."

She glances at me. I see true terror in her eyes. I wonder if a stronger vampire has ever given her permission to be treated as a friend.

"Truly?" she whispers.

"Yes." I say. "Now come in, and tell me what's wrong. You've been crying—where's Jacob? Is he with you?"

"No... no. Jacob's dead!" She emits a sordid sob and rushes to me.

I catch her and let her cry against my body, doing my best to lend her comfort as she relates the horrible tale of her husband's fate.

"And after Phillip fed," she finishes, "that awful new guard, Captain Commander Smithson, he released me and told me that I was free to go. I didn't know where else to turn. Jacob was my life—he was everything to me! And now he's gone, and I have nothing, nothing to live for, nothing left, nothing at all...!"

She collapses into another round of helpless sobs.

"I can't get Jacob back," I tell her, after giving her appropriate time to grieve. "But I can offer you my friendship. And—" I hesitate, "— my protection."

She looks up at me. "Really?"

"As much as I can give," I say. "But I have to be honest. I don't know the extent of my influence or even my powers. But if you stay close to me, I will do everything I can to help." I take her hands in mine. "I just need *you* to promise me one thing."

She wipes her eyes and gives a tiny nod. "Yes. Anything."

"That you won't be frightened of me," I say. "And that you won't defer to me because of my strength. I can be your friend, Patricia, but our friendship has to transcend all that."

She nods again, more resolutely this time. "I... I think I can do that."

"Now." I stand up and feel a new determination growing. "Since I'm back, I need to get a feel for this place. For The Haven. Can you help, will you be my guide?"

She bobs her head up and down once more.

"You need to feed first. Even I can see that. We'll go up to the blood banks—"

"But those are forbidden for all vampires but those of the Royal Court!" she exclaims in alarm. She takes a step back. "The only time I can feed will be at the next Hunt."

"The blood banks are *only* for the Royal Court?" I question.

"Yes," she says. "They are barred to us."

"No, no." I shake my head. "That's ridiculous."

"If all The Haven's vampires were given access to it, it would quickly run out of blood."

"That's what you think?" I ask. "I was just there—there's enough blood to last everybody here for decades."

Her eyes widen. "*You* have access to the banks?"

"Of course," I say. "And as my friend, so do you. Now come on. If you won't go, I'll bring you some blood. But it's obvious we need to get your strength back before doing anything else."

And what comes next, I tell myself firmly, *is finding out where Morgan placed all the humans... and returning them to their regular lives.*

At least, until I can do something to improve their standards of living.

Chapter Fifteen

PHILLIP

I race around The Haven, trying to find some glimpse of my Mother. But every time I get a hint of her whereabouts, she's gone by the time I arrive.

The beast inside me is growing stronger, continuously. I thought April's blood would unleash it, but it only served to nudge it awake. Now, it's using the influx of human blood to stretch out its long-dormant muscles and ready itself for the next time I feed.

Next time... can I even envision such a thing? But what choice do I have? My body will demand more blood for as long as I live. The fast has been broken, and there's no going back.

Not unless I want to end up like one of The Convicted. I'd only managed to survive on animal blood without devolving into their state because I hadn't *ever* tasted human blood before.

But now?

Now, animal blood will never sustain me. All it would do is slow the descent into the horrific existence The Convicted live.

I end up back at the castle. This is where all this began, and this is where everything can come to its end.

As I enter, I look upon the paintings on the walls. I shiver. I witnessed the profane ritual Mother used to cast a vampire into that eternal hell.

She needs to be stopped. Before she can inflict more damage upon The Haven, and have us crumble from the inside, she needs to be stopped.

I start up the stairs when I hear a door open. I sense who it is immediately. Without looking down, I say, "Raul."

He joins me on the stairs. "I just spoke to James," he says.

"You found him?" My eyebrows go up.

"It wasn't easy. Mother put him in one of the deepest cells."

"She's really serious about the sentence, isn't she?"

"Have you known her to backtrack after making a public announcement?" Raul shakes his head in disgust. "I think there's only one way we can save our brother. And it's *not* through diplomacy."

"You mean…" my eyes narrow and I lower my voice. "You mean we need to help him escape?"

"I see no other choice," Raul says grimly. He grunts in frustration. "It seems all we're doing recently is sneaking someone out or bringing them back in."

"Mother won't take kindly to another escapee," I say. "She has Eleira here, too. Aren't you afraid she'll take her frustrations out on her?"

"I'm terrified of that," Raul says. "That's why, if we do it, we need to have Eleira's full support."

"Will she give it?" I ask. "You haven't told me about her rescue. How did you— "

"I love her, Phillip," Raul says.

My head snaps to him. "What?"

"She's it, she is the one, she's the girl for me." His breath hitches. "And I won't do anything, *ever*, to compromise her safety."

"And... does she know?"

"She suspects it, I believe. But we haven't had enough time together since getting back for me to be sure."

"Now that she's a vampire, you have forever," I say. I feel an unexpected twang in my heart when I say the words.

April doesn't have forever.

"It's not that simple," Raul says. "Not with Mother leading the coven. There's also the threat of war."

"War? What war? What are you talking about?"

"When James went to Father's coven he got involved with

120

a woman. She came back here with us."

"I met her," I say. "The Captain Commander brought her down when he freed me."

"Call him Smithson. Don't grant him courtesy of his title."

I nod. "Okay. I didn't get the woman's name, though."

"It's Victoria. She's our prisoner—for now. But something about it doesn't feel right. If we spring James loose, I don't know whether he'll try to free her or not. The woman was part of Father's Inner Circle. She knows all their secrets. Once Father discovers she's gone, he'll send his entire force for her—and it won't be pretty."

"Christ," I mutter. I rub my eyes.

"I warned Mother about it when she sent James on his mission." Raul looks up the stairs. "She didn't listen. Let's hope she does now."

Chapter Sixteen

RAUL

I bang on the doors of Mother's uppermost chamber. Phillip is at my side, shoulders pulled back, staring at the imposing doors with stark determination.

There's not a trace of fear in him. Nor any fragility. Either the things he suffered during his imprisonment changed him...

Or drinking April's blood did.

Whatever the cause, I'm glad for the transformation. Even though it saddens me that he wasn't given a choice, it feels good to have my brother beside me. It feels good to know he's more confident, more assured, more *forceful* than before.

With James underground and Eleira in the midst of the most tumultuous change of her life, I'll need him more than ever now.

"I can't sense her," Phillip says under his breath. "I don't think she's there."

"Neither can I," I say. "But she could have easily put up a protective spell."

Phillip nods. "Good point."

I raise my fist to knock again. At that precise moment, the doors open.

Mother sweeps into view.

"Raul. Phillip!" She smiles. "How wonderful to have my two sons join me."

I scowl without meaning to. Her upbeat air is absolutely at odds with the gravity of the situation.

"We're here to talk about James," I say. Phillip grunts in agreement.

Mother puts on an expression of absolute wonder. "I'm sorry, who?" she asks. "No, no... I don't know any James. I'm sorry."

She starts to close the door.

I kick my foot out and stop her. "This isn't a game anymore, Mother." My voice is low and threatening. "If you think the other vampires will just step aside while you sentence your oldest son to become one of The Convicted, you're gravely mistaken. If you think Phillip or I will just stand by and do *nothing*—"

She laughs. Her eyes take on a cruel glint again. "Is that so? Tell me, son dearest, just what is it you intend to do? The three of us know—" she looks at me, and then at Phillip, "—exactly who is in control here."

A thick band of tension stretches between us.

"But I suppose I might let you in," Mother sighs. "As it so happens, I'm already entertaining company. You're more than welcome to join us."

She holds the door open wider. Inside, I'm shocked to find Victoria—unbound, uncuffed, and completely free.

Opposite her stands Mother's newest recruit, Captain Commander Smithson.

"Raul, Phillip," the Captain Commander of the guard greets us. "It's good to see you."

"Save it," I grunt. I could never trust the vampire. I've known him as a wanderer for many years, living amongst humans, rejecting all claims to a single coven or clan. That Mother would bring him into The Haven now speaks either of her desperation or her madness.

The Captain Commander chuckles. "Always so cordial." He addresses my brother. "And you, Phillip. How does it feel to be a *proper* vampire?"

Phillip glares at him without answering.

"Oh!" Mother says as she joins the tense assembly. "You should know how proud I am of you, my son." She puts her hands on Phillip's shoulders and kisses his cheek. "I heard how you managed to stop before killing that filthy human girl. I didn't think you'd have it in you. But it fills my heart with much joy that you did. Eleira would be crushed if her little friend died."

Phillip goes absolutely still. "You meant for me to kill her," he says stiffly. "So that Eleira would be turned against me. Isn't that true?"

"Oh, pah, pah," Mother says dismissively. She glides to an unoccupied white leather chair and drops down into it. "How you and your brother enjoy making baseless accusations against me. If I were a tad bit stricter—" her eyes flash at us, "—you would not be so free with your tongues. Especially not around such esteemed company as we have now."

"What is *she* doing here?" I demand, looking at Victoria. "You know who she is. You know how *dangerous* she is."

"And that's why I've invited Captain Commander Smithson to provide protection for this meeting," Mother flutters on. "Victoria wouldn't be fool enough to try anything while he's here. Would you, darling?"

To my surprise, the blonde vampire bows her head with the utmost respect. "Certainly not," she tells Mother.

"See?" Morgan asks me. "There's absolutely nothing to worry about. Now, why don't we resume our previous discussion? Before we were interrupted."

"James," I start to say.

"—*WILL NOT BE SPOKEN OF HERE*!" Mother screams.

Her voice rocks the room. In the ensuing silence, not a single breath can be heard.

"I'm sorry," Mother says after a moment, having regained control of herself. "That was… unladylike of me."

"You were provoked, my Queen," Smithson says. He shoots an evil glare at me as he comes to her side. He kneels down and takes her hand. "Just say the word, and I'll escort the two of them out."

"No, no," Mother sighs. "They should both hear what Victoria has to say. After all, if I cannot trust my only two sons with such information… who do I have left?"

It rankles me how easily she dismisses James—and makes light of how easy it was for her to treat Phillip and me as nothing more than vermin when Eleira got away.

"Shall I continue, then?" Victoria asks.

Mother nods. "Please."

I listen on as Victoria starts to describe the inner workings of The Crypts. She talks about their defenses, their strengths, their weaknesses. She goes on and on about the ruling class, and how Father has fortified his coven to be a near-impenetrable fortress.

But her information is only surface-deep. There are no great insights she provides.

I grow tired of it. "Enough," I say. "Mother, James or I

could have told you as much from having visited. She is not telling you anything useful."

Victoria sneaks a malicious glare at me when she thinks I'm not looking. I catch it.

"She should remain in chains underground," I say. "I came here with Phillip to discuss things of *actual* importance to The Haven. Not to listen to her prattle on and on about frivolities in The Crypts."

Mother ignores me. "You must excuse my son," she says. "He's had a difficult few days. He thinks only of himself—"

"That's not true," I growl.

"Perhaps of Eleira, too," she concedes. "But little more."

Mother stands and walks to the open window. She looks out into the night. "Victoria, why don't you tell all of us of the link you have with my eldest son's beloved?"

That request makes Victoria stop short. Her confidence wavers. "Excuse me?" she asks, thrown off-balance.

Phillip and I make eye contact. Ever so subtly, he shakes his head, indicating he doesn't know what Mother's talking about either.

Neither of us missed her referring to me as "eldest," either.

It means she is truly set in her verdict against James.

"The link, sweetest," Mother repeats, still looking out into

127

the night. "Oh, poor thing, you didn't think you'd be able to hide it from me, did you?"

Victoria looks like she's swallowed a plum. "It's only a trifling thing— " she begins.

Mother turns on her in a fury. "Do NOT lie to me!" she screams. Power crackles out from her like a storm. A sudden wind blows through the window, making her dress and hair flare. She looks more menacing than ever. "I *know* it was your blood Eleira tasted first! I *know* the ritual you attempted to perform! How else, why else, would my precious human witch come back here bearing the full powers of *The Ancient*? It is only through you!"

The wind dies. The storm of electricity ebbs away. Everything goes still again, but the reverberations of Mother's words echo around us and through the room like ghouls haunting the place.

Victoria blinks, maybe frightened—maybe acting? She gives a series of small nods. "You're right, of course. You're right. I'm sorry. It's only that, I'm just beginning to understand the link myself—"

"Another lie," Mother cuts her off. "Very well, child. If you insist on playing games, perhaps some time in the Silver Cell would be good for you." She glances at Phillip, who supressed a quick shudder. "Smithson, why don't you escort our guest to her quarters at the top of the castle? She can emerge after I decide enough time has passed for her to reconsider some of her... attitudes."

"With pleasure, my Queen," Smithson bows. He goes to Victoria and twists both her arms behind her back. The petite vampire doesn't struggle against him, even though I know she easily rivals him in pure strength.

"Try anything I wouldn't like," Mother warns, "and you'll find out just how well your borrowed power stands up against my *true* witchcraft." She gives Victoria a nasty smile. "Fair warning. Ta-ta."

With that, Smithson leads her out the room.

The doors close. Mother, Phillip and I are finally alone.

"Well!" Mother says. "That was certainly something. Wouldn't you say?"

"You're toying with her," Phillip says. "She might take it quietly for now, but it only fuels her anger. Did you not see how she looked at you once you made the accusation?"

"You're just the one to speak about meekness," Mother mocks. "Aren't you, Phillip?"

He starts to respond, but I cut in before he can speak. "Enough distractions. We came here to talk about James."

"There's nothing to talk about," Mother snaps. "His fate is sealed. My decision has been made."

"You have the power to reverse it," I say. "Yes, we know he

129

went against you. Yes, we understand that you're angry. But surely nothing he did deserves the harshest punishment!"

"The harshest?" Mother laughs. "Raul, if you think being allowed to *live* beneath The Haven is the harshest punishment, you are mistaken. Your brother here—" she motions at Phillip, "—knows all about the *harshest* punishment. He saw me inflict it upon Jacob."

Phillip takes a step toward her. "You would *never* do that to James," he says.

It sounds more like an order than an admonition. I look at him in surprise.

That is definitely *not* the Phillip I know to use such a tone with our Mother.

The Queen blinks, also taken back by the force behind Phillip's words. But then she sighs and admits, "No, I suppose not. Such a fate is reserved for the usurpers… or those planning to challenge my rule."

"Of which Jacob did neither," Phillip snarls. Something about him is *very* off. The aggression he's showing seems to be almost uncontained.

Mother waves the accusation away. "Jacob and Patricia have caused me more trouble than you know over the years. If it helps your conscience, know that it was not only the murder of my guards that sealed his fate.

My stomach drops. "You charged *Jacob* with murder?" I ask, my voice shallow.

Mother turns to me. "Why yes, Raul," she says curiously. "I did. Funny that you would take such an interest in the matter. Don't you think?"

I clear my throat. "Jacob was a friend."

"And the guards he killed were my loyal servants," Mother replies. "Surely four lives lost is worthy of the punishment he received."

"I'm telling you, it couldn't have been him," Phillip insists. "He wasn't strong enough to take on four of your best."

"Well, he obviously had help," Mother says. "His wife was one, for example. You know, I was hoping you would be more resolute in your stance against taking human blood, Phillip. I would have *loved* the opportunity to be rid of her. But..." she spreads her hands. "A just ruler never reneges on her word."

Even more guilt eats me up inside that Jacob has to suffer because of what *I* did. *I* killed the guards. Somebody else took the fall.

The only solace I have is the feeling that Mother would have taken the slightest excuse to get rid of him, no matter how small or meaningless. The human lives I saved should help balance the scales of my conscience... but for some reason, they do not.

Since when have I become so sentimental?

I clear my throat, "Back to the subject of James—"

"There is *NOTHING* for us to talk about!" Mother screams. "Bring him up again and you'll see how far my good will goes." Her eyes blaze at me. "Don't test me. Especially not now. Don't test me, son."

A terse silence descends on the room. Phillip moves to speak—but is interrupted when the door swings open.

A breathless vampire guard stands in their midst.

Mother turns on him in a rage. "You better have good reason to interrupt."

"The humans," he gulps. "They've begun to riot."

The Queen curses.

"That's not all," he adds. "Your eldest son, James? He's missing."

Chapter Seventeen

JAMES

Seeing Raul was an unexpected ray of hope in the dark. However, it was extinguished the moment I understood that no matter his intentions, there was nothing he could do.

Mother made her decision, and I don't expect him to change that. No matter how persuasive Raul manages to be.

And yet... only minutes after he left, a strange sort of resonance descends in the air. At first I think it's my imagination. After all, the silver bars and the silver collar could be making me delirious.

But as I try to ignore the sensation, it only grows stronger.

It grows and grows and grows until the tautness is palpable.

Then, without warning, the entire cell starts to shake. There's a breaking roar, and the ground beneath me gives way.

I leap aside to avoid falling. Everything goes still. The resonance is gone. Only the sound of crumbling soil reaches my ears.

I edge closer and peer into the crater. Far, far below me, I can see the faint outline of an underground river.

"Jump," a voice whispers in my mind.

I am so shocked by it that I lose my footing. Before I know it, I'm throttling through the air toward the water below.

I hit the surface with a gasp. An icy cold takes me. The water is freezing. I have never been the best swimmer...

Still, I fight the current until I emerge at the surface. The river thrashes me this way and that until I cling to a jutting rock in its middle.

I look up, trying to make out how far I've fallen. But the rapids sweep me far from where I hit the water. All I see is the enormous, cavernous ceiling above.

The collar around my neck distresses me. I try tugging on it to help me breathe easier, but the silver burns my fingers.

At least I'm free.

Was Raul behind this? The timing was impeccable. It couldn't have been just blind luck that let me free, could it?

No. If there's one thing I've learned over my long centuries of life, it's that luck does not exist. Luck is what those fools jealous of others' ascent to the top claim was behind their success.

And yet... I can't help but feel that my escape was engineered by... *somebody.*

134

I don't know who. And I'm not out of the woods yet. The voice I heard—was that real, or just imagined?

I've dawdled for too long. As soon as my cell is discovered empty, Mother is going to send all her guard after me. And I don't know yet where this river leads.

"So long, Haven," I mutter under my breath. "You hold no meaning for me anymore."

And so I dive back into the river and go wherever the current takes me.

Chapter Eighteen

ELEIRA

No matter my insistence, Patricia absolutely refuses to come with me to the blood banks. In the end, I resort to bringing her bottles after bottles of fresh blood.

She devours them with a speed I never thought possible.

How long has it been since her last drink?

Her appearance improves by the minute. After she's had her first sip, the changes sweep over her like tides retreating from a beautiful beach.

Her skin, which was borderline translucent before, becomes plump and shining. Her hair, so brittle when she came into my room, turns full and thick. Even the muscles on her body look stronger, fuller, more toned.

By the time her thirst is satiated, she even has her womanly figure back.

"How do you feel?" I ask when she's done. I have a burning curiosity about the whole process—about how rapidly the change came about and how quickly she was restored and what it must be like to go through it.

"B-better," she mumbles. Despite the outward difference, she's still meek as a babe.

"Patricia, we're alone," I remind her softly. I look around my room. "There's absolutely no need for you to feel inferior to me."

Her eyes widen, then take on a haunted look. "It's not that," she utters under her breath. "It's just… now that my senses are back, I can better tell how *strong* you really are." She meets my eyes for a second, and then quickly looks away. "It's astounding."

I click my tongue in annoyance. This blasted vampire hierarchy is going to be the end of me. What use is being so strong if it means everyone around is either terrified, envious, or hateful toward you?

"Can we not talk about that?" I say. "I'd much rather discuss—"

I'm cut off by the sound of stamping feet outside my door. I feel a bunch of vampires rush by in the hall.

One of them stops on the other side. He's about to raise his fist to knock, but in my excitement to see him I preempt the attempt by arriving there first. I fling the door open.

"Raul!" I exclaim. I want to embrace him—but stop short when I see the Queen watching us from behind.

His expression is ghastly. "James has escaped," he tells me

without preamble. "And the humans are rioting. We think this is an attempt against The Haven, but—" he glances back at his entourage, "—we're not sure."

"Why? An attempt? By whom?"

"Who else?" the Queen laughs. "By my husband's coven."

Raul turns back to me. "If it's true, we have a fight on our hands. I need you to stay here, where you're safe—"

"No!" I prompt. "I'm not going to be cooped up while you face the danger."

"Eleira, you're newly made," he tells me in the same tone one would use explaining something simple to a child. "You have no conception of your powers, or the dangers you might face. You've done a spectacular job controlling yourself so far—" he glances at the ring on my finger, "—but in a free-for-all, where nothing can be predicted or controlled—that's too much stimulation for you. There's no telling what might happen."

"If this is an attack against The Haven, I want to help defend my home!" I proclaim.

The Queen arches one prim eyebrow. "You already consider this your home?" she asks softly.

I curse inwardly. I must have spoken in the heat of the moment. But I can't take the words back now.

"Home or not," Raul continues, ignoring both me and his

Mother, "you're safest here. There are spells protecting the castle."

"If she wants to go," Morgan says thoughtfully. "Who are we to stop her?"

Raul growls at his Mother as she sweeps by him and extends her hand. "Come with me, child," she tells me. "I thought I would need to give you three days, but it seems you've already made your choice."

She smiles, then, and I can't help the feeling it's the smile of a cat who's just caught a canary in her claws.

***

When we get to the underground caverns where the humans are held, it's absolute madness. From our vantage point high above, I see a clear divide in the mass below me. On one side stand all the villagers—yelling, screaming, shouting their lungs out—and on the other, a wall of vampire guards keeping them away from the exit.

The Queen takes one look at it and strides to the front of our group. She stops at the very end of the jutting-out rock, and hits her staff against the floor three times. On the first, nothing happens. Neither does anything on the second.

But on the third, an enormous blue flame flares from the

tip. It soars into the sky where it coalesces into a bright orb like the sun. Then, with a thunderous crash, it explodes, sending blue streamers of light down like a thousand fireworks.

That gets everyone's attention.

Her voice rings out into the sudden quiet.

"*What*," she demands of those below her, "*is the meaning of this*?"

The humans all shy back, having witnessed the power of their ruler.

"Leonardo," Morgan addresses a guard below. "You were the one charged with keeping the peace." Her voice is icy-calm, which makes it all the more dangerous. "Tell me how this all got so out of control."

"My Queen," the singled-out guard drops to his knees immediately. "The prisoners complained they were hearing voices." His inflection leaves no doubt as to how ludicrous he thinks that is. "They said a strange voice began telling them the caverns would collapse. They demanded to be let out. We refused. As per your orders."

"Voices?" the Queen asks. "What sort of voices?"

"*We* heard nothing, my Queen," Leonardo replies, motioning to the other vampires. "We considered it a ruse, an excuse for the humans to cause trouble. With your permission—" his eyes flash, "—we could select the troublemakers from their midst and remind them of their place."

"No," Morgan says immediately. "You know the rules. No human blood is to be shed except on the night of The Hunt."

"It was only a suggestion," Leonardo mutters.

"An ill-placed one," the Queen says. She turns and addresses the villagers, who are huddled together in frightened packs. "My guards claim you heard voices. Is this true?"

Only silence greets her question.

She clicks her tongue. "Maybe the voices you heard robbed you of your own?" She laughs. "Very well. You!" She singles out a villager with her staff. A beam of faint blue light shines on him from the end. "Come forward. What is your name?"

"M-Melvin," he stutters.

A ring of space clears all around him.

"You know who I am?" Morgan asks.

"Of course." The man sounds positively terrified to be speaking to the Queen.

"And if I ask you a question, you would never dream of lying to me in response. Would you, Melvin?"

"N-no."

"Good." I can hear the Queen's smile in her words. "Then tell me all you can about these voices. But know—" she adds before he starts to speak, "—that I have a *very* low tolerance for liars. You may begin."

Melvin dry washes his hands a few times. He clears his throat. "It…" he tries. "The Voice… it…"

"Get on with it, man!" Morgan exclaims.

He shies back as if physically hit. "It…"

"The Voice told us that he's going to make the caves collapse!" Somebody shouts from the midst of humans. "He said we would all die, that we'd all be crushed under the rock!"

"Who speaks now?" Morgan shines her beam into the crowd. "Step forth!"

A young boy, maybe a year or two younger than me, emerges.

"And what's your name, boy?"

The boy bristles. "It's Brayson," he says defiantly. "And I don't have a last name because it was *stolen* from me! Just like my life here in your Haven!"

"*My* Haven?" The Queen takes a gratuitous step back. "My dear child, this sanctuary belongs to all of us. Surely you understand that?"

"The *sanctuary*," he spits, "belongs to the vampires. You

keep us hostage here. We are your prey!"

"My, my," Morgan mutters. "You've got quite the spirit. Tell me, did this 'voice' also give you such dangerous thoughts?"

"The thoughts are my own," he tells her boldly. "And they're not dangerous. They're *true!*"

Morgan looks at him... and then laughs in response.

"Is that so?" she asks. "Look around you, Brayson. See how many supporters you've got."

She shines her light on the other humans, all of whom are quick to step out of the way.

"You see?" she asks. "They understand what you do not. Maybe you are still young. Maybe you are a dreamer. But understanding will come in time. I promise you."

"Oh?" he challenges her. "And what understanding is that?"

"That your place in The Haven is part of a divine equilibrium that keeps us safe. We provide you food, water, shelter. We ask for nothing in return."

"You ask for our *lives!*"

Morgan waves the accusation aside easily. "We take your blood, yes, but it is for the good of the whole. Without it, society here would collapse. Look upon your elders! They know."

Again she breaks her light through the other humans. They either keep their heads down or mumble in agreement.

"Enough of this," Morgan announces. "I came here to stem the discord running rampant amongst you. Brayson—I charge you with an attempt at high treason. The voice was a figment of your imagination and, charismatic as you are, you got the other humans around you to agree. You are the troublemaker here. And, as they say—" she gives a vicious grin, "—cut the head off the snake, and the body will follow."

Chapter Nineteen

PHILLIP

On Mother's proclamation, the entire assembly before us explodes into a riot of confusion.

"The boy is innocent!" somebody yells.

"We all heard it! We all heard the Voice!"

"It's true! It spoke to all of us!"

"Brayson's done nothing wrong!"

Mother lets the protests go on and on for a long time. She turns to me and Raul. "You see what you must do to free their tongues?" she asks with a knowing smile.

She turns back to free the villagers below her.

"Very well!" she proclaims. "Now that more of you have owned up to hearing this voice, the real questions can begin. Did Brayson speak the truth? Did the Voice tell you that these caves would collapse?"

"Yes!" a thousand voices scream in unison.

"And you *all* claim to have heard it?" Mother asks. "*Each* of you can vouch for what it said?"

More cries of agreement rain up from the crowd.

Leonardo looks up. "My Queen, if I may offer an opinion?"

Mother gestures for him to go on.

"The humans are liars," he hisses. "My guards and I have preternatural hearing, many times better than any of theirs. If there was a voice whispering in their ears, we would have heard it."

"A salient point," Mother admits. She turns to me. "Phillip? What do you think?"

I'm staggered by the sudden address. "You're asking me?"

"You are my son, aren't you? One of my two boys? Your opinion matters. So I must know."

I flinch at how obvious Mother's attempt is to disown James, and at the unnatural way she forces the 'fact' that she only has two sons.

"Leonardo might have a point," I say, thinking. "But that doesn't mean the humans are lying. Look at them! Have you ever seen them united with such conviction? Have you ever seen them with so much genuine *fear* in their eyes?"

I glance at Raul and Eleira, who have moved closer to each other.

"*Something* scared them," I finish in a low voice. "What it was, I couldn't tell you. But to ignore it now and call them all liars would have them quickly make an enemy of you. And despite everything, Mother, we *need* them on our side. The Haven would collapse if they revolt."

"They don't have the courage to revolt."

I turn around in surprise. Smithson is strolling toward us, every cocky step a measure of his arrogance.

All my instincts go on high alert. There is something terribly rotten about the man.

By the way Raul tensed at Smithson's unexpected arrival, I can tell my brother feels the same.

"If you want my advice," the Captain Commander continues, addressing the Queen, "make an example of the boy. Show them what a true ruler does when challenged by an uprising. If you do not do it with a heavy hand now..." he spreads his arms, "...they will start to think you weak. And if *that* happens—well, that's when the real danger sets in."

He finishes his walk right at the Queen's side and whispers something in her ear.

"You're right," she says finally. She leans across and kisses the older vampire on his cheek. "What I would do without your sage council, I have no idea. When I'm surrounded by fools and weaklings..."

She trails off. Then, without any warning, she thrusts her staff forward. The light singles out the human boy again.

"Brayson!" she calls loudly. "I stand by my original

147

position. You are hereby charged with high treason and attempt at rebellion. Treason against your Queen is the highest crime a human can be accused of.

"There will be no trial. I sentence you to death, at the hands of my most loyal guards, who've done an admirable job in stemming this ill-advised uprising. Leonardo—you may take him now."

The vampire guard surges forward and grabs hold of the boy's neck. The other humans are so shocked by the pronouncement that none offer their help. A few yell weak protests from the fringes, but other than that—nothing.

Leonardo drags the human boy, kicking and screaming, out of the group of humans and onto the vampire side of the divide. He puts him in a headlock and readies to sink his fangs into his neck...

Eleira steps forward. "No!"

Her order alone would normally do nothing. But with the word I feel such a strong surge of power come from her, power that all vampires respond to, thanks to the overruling hierarchy, that Leonardo goes shock-still.

He looks up, his eyes burning with bloodlust. But they're glazed over at the same time, as is what happens when a stronger vampire exerts her rule. Brayson stops struggling, too entranced by his unexpected champion.

Raul quickly runs to Eleira and takes her hand. I hope it's

to show her that she has his support, because if I know my Mother—and I do—what the Queen does next is not going to be pretty.

But Morgan surprises even me by regarding Eleira coolly. "You challenge me?" she asks.

There's a current of danger beneath her voice.

Eleira stares at the Queen totally defiant. "There has to be a trial," she says. "It's the only way the humans will ever respect you."

"And what makes you think she *needs* their respect, girl?" Smithson growls.

"Eleira's right," Raul says. "We have to have justice in The Haven. Doing something like this, acting in the spur of the moment, sets the wrong precedent. Justice has to extend to vampires *and* humans, if we're to co-exist."

"So my son mirrors his lover's ideals," Mother murmurs. "And you, Phillip? Do you side with them, too?"

I step toward the pair. "I do."

"Ah," Mother says. "It seems once again, I've been overruled." She looks down.

"Leonardo," she calls out. "Release the boy."

The guard lets go. Brayson staggers away and stumbles to a stop a good six paces clear of any vampire.

The assembly beneath us has grown ghastly quiet. Both

149

vampires and humans are waiting to see what happens next.

Mother directs the light of her staff at Brayson. "You heard what my advisors have said," she intones. "Lucky for you, you won't be made into a vampire's meal. *Unluckily*—" her voice takes on a melancholy inflection, "—neither will you leave this encounter with your life."

Before any of us can react, Morgan mutters an incantation. White hot flame bursts from the end of her staff.

Brayson is instantly engulfed by the fire.

"No!" Eleira screams. "No, no, NO!"

But it's too late. The fire winks out. Nothing remains of the boy but a pile of ash on the ground.

The Queen looks at Eleira sadly. "You see what you made me do?" she asks, in a voice barely above a whisper.

But her soft voice carries through the whole of the underground space. She must have bewitched it.

Nobody else dares breathe.

Mother turns to speak to the humans.

"Remember this day!" she tells them. "Remember it as the day you let the words of a liar, a fraud, a cheat, ruffle you into arms against your most merciful ruler. Remember that The Haven abides by the justice of the Queen, and to go against me is to spit death in the eye and expect death not to strike back. I can be fair, yes—but for that, I require your

150

trust."

"If all you wanted was to leave this enclosure…?" she spreads her hands and gives an apathetic shrug. "All you had to do was ask. Leonardo?"

The shocked guard looks up. "Yes, my Queen?"

"Escort the humans back to the village. They've been here long enough. See that the rebuild begins tonight. They have shirked that responsibility for too many days."

Leonardo bows deeply. "Of course."

Morgan addresses the human crowd one last time. "I hope this serves as a valuable lesson for you all. There was never any need for such, *ahem*, histrionics, to get my attention."

She turns and walks away. "Now," she says, only to us, "Let's go see what James has gotten himself up to."

Chapter Twenty

I wade out of the icy river, shivering as my body tries to warm itself.

Even vampires get cold. We may be more resistant to the effects, and exposure can never kill us, but that does not mean we are immune to the nasty sensation.

Especially when it comes together with tumbling around and being forced this way and that by a mighty river.

By now, I'm miles away from The Haven. I don't think even Mother knew about the river. I certainly did not.

But somebody else did.

The Voice that told me to jump was not imagined. I did not make it up. I'm sure of it now. I heard it in my head, clear as day.

As I was swimming, an uncomfortable memory bubbled up. I had heard the Voice once before, but not in my head. I heard it when its owner spoke to me outside The Crypts.

It belongs to The Ancient.

It's a measure of how badly the silver collar is affecting me that I did not pick up on the association right away. Even now, every step I take away from the river is done in a haze. The collar is not as bad as the velvet sack, but in my weakened state, it makes a close second.

I make my way to a nearby boulder and hurl myself onto it. The rushing sound of water continues beyond me. Up ahead I can see the river run out from the cave. It falls in a steep waterfall.

I can also see the sun. It's evening out there, which means I have to remain here, underground, for however long it takes for it to set.

I wish I could find another route. The more miles I put between me and The Haven, the better. Who knows how many of Mother's guards have already come after me?

I force myself to stand. I'm still woozy, but I don't want to be caught unawares by the guards bound to be coming after me.

To my relief, I find the cave is shaped exactly as I first thought. There are only two ways out, following the river back up, or through the gaping end of the waterfall.

I get antsy with nothing to do, so I decide to use the remaining hours of daylight to try getting the collar off. I know there's a mechanism, some sort of latch, behind my neck.

Yet every time I try to find it with my fingers it's not the pain from touching silver that stops me, but a chilling numbness that shoots down both arms. It must be an effect of the spell Mother put on it.

There's no way to get the collar off on my own.

I curse and fling myself down, back on the same boulder.

The sooner I get this blasted collar off me, the better.

I'm anxious waiting for night. When it finally comes, I breathe a sigh of relief and venture to the edge of the waterfall. I look down.

Whoa.

I'm standing high above the sheer cliff face of a mountain. The falling water disappears below me in a shroud of mist. I can't tell exactly how long the drop is, but I know it's sizable. Impressive. Perhaps even...

Frightening.

There is only so much force a vampire can withstand without shattering his bones. And even if the impact won't kill you, healing from such a fall could take days.

Do I have days to spend lying broken on the ground, knowing Mother's guards are coming after me? And what about the sun? I'd be unprotected down there. It would scorch my skin and eventually kill me.

"IF YOU JUMP, WE WILL FIND YOU."

154

I spin around. "Who said that?" I hiss.

"TRUST, BROTHER. TRUST IN US."

My head! It's the Voice in my head again. But this one is different from the one I heard in my cell.

"Who are you?"

"TRUST," the Voice repeats. *"TRUST AND JUMP. TRUST…"*

It fades away. In its place comes a stark emptiness.

I eye the space before me. Do I dare listen to the Voice? Am I going crazy? Maybe such a long exposure to silver is making my mind imagine things that are not there.

"Voice," I say. "If you are truly there, give me some sort of proof!"

Silence greets me.

I scoff. "Just as I thought," I mutter. I edge my way closer to the opening. Maybe I don't have to jump—maybe I could scale my way down, and—

All of a sudden the ground starts to shake. I leap back from the edge. There comes a monstrous roar, and next thing I know, the roof is caving in behind me, sealing the river off as more and more rubble comes crashing down.

The loud noise disorients me, all because of the silver collar. I lose sense of where I am, and my head starts to spin. I stumble, and, in the shaking, trip and fall.

Thankfully, I've gotten far enough from the ledge to avoid that endless drop.

After what seems an age, the shaking stops. I wipe the dust from my eyes and look out at the end result of the quake.

The way back is completely sealed. Only the tiniest trickle of water makes its way through the rocks.

"IS THAT NOT PROOF ENOUGH FOR YOU?" the Voice screams in my mind.

I bolt up. "You did this," I say.

"YES."

"And you want me to…" I look out over the edge. The fall is bottomless. "…jump?"

"IT IS YOUR ONLY WAY OUT."

"And so it is," I agree.

I mutter an oath and step out over the edge to plunge into the nothingness far below.

Chapter Twenty-One

ELEIRA

My mouth tastes of ash in the aftermath of Morgan's senseless murder of the boy.

I want to say that I cannot believe she would do something like that... but it isn't true. I know how much value the Queen places on human life.

It isn't much.

I'm part of a solemn group that follows her through The Haven. We're going back to the castle, from which point Morgan will lead us to James's cell.

"If I find out that any of you had a part to play in this," the Queen says as we delve into the darkness below her fortress, "the consequences for you will not be pretty."

Raul and Phillip shoot each other an unreadable look. Smithson glares openly at the two of them.

"Eleira, come away from there," the Queen beckons. "Walk with me."

I glance at Raul, who gives me a miniscule nod.

I walk forward and join Morgan.

"You're troubled," she tells me. "I can see it in your eyes."

I press my lips together.

It doesn't take a genius to figure that one, I think.

"You don't like the way I handled things with the villagers," she continues. "Your flaw, my dear, is that you have a weak heart. You're still hanging on to the parts of you that are human.

"That will pass, given enough time. We must both stay patient, and it will pass. Soon, you will fully embrace all your vampiric gifts. Small trifles like a single human life will mean nothing to you."

"You're wrong," I say. "If you think I'll ever be like you—"

She cuts me off with a delicate cough. "You're already more like me than you think." She glances at my free hand. "That ring on your finger. Where did you get it?"

Immediately I cradle my hand into my body, hiding it from her. "It was a gift," I say.

"You weren't wearing it when you escaped The Haven. Who did you get it from? Let me guess… James? No, that's not his style. Perhaps somebody you met as his captive? But that doesn't make sense either. Hm…" she taps her lips. Then she lifts one finger up. "Ah! Of course, I know. It came from *Raul.*"

I tense at the way she says his name. She *knew* the ring

158

was from him the entire time.

She holds her hand out. "May I see it?" she asks.

On instinct, I angle my body away to protect the piece of jewelry.

"Oh, I won't take it off your finger, don't worry," she says. "I simply want to examine it from up close."

I glance over my shoulder at Raul and Phillip. They're engaged in a deep conversation with each other and don't notice me.

"Eleira…" Morgan says. "You're not going to defy a direct order from your Queen, are you?"

I sigh and hold my arm out. "Doesn't seem like I have much of a choice," I mutter.

"Oh, but this is spectacular!" Morgan marvels once she touches the ring. "I can feel the power within. How did my son ever come across something precious like this?" She shakes her head. "That doesn't matter, since it's yours now." She gives me a most meaningful look. "You know the deadline I set of three days?"

I eye her warily. "Yes?"

"When you come to me with your final decision, you will also give me the ring."

I jerk my hand away. "What?"

"I can feel what it's doing to you, Eleira. It's preventing

you from becoming the woman you are destined to be. I will *not* have the future Queen of The Haven be suppressed the way Phillip was for so many years. I've been too lenient with him in the past. But the time for leniency ends with your coming. The Haven will be ruled with an iron fist while you are being groomed for power. The first step of that is getting you to accept your vampire nature. Without…" she casts a disgusted glance at my ring, "…without your abilities being hampered."

The worst kind of sickness settles in my stomach. It feels like all my defenses are being stripped bare.

Just when I start to look back at Raul for help, the ground starts to shake.

We're thrown against the side wall. The vampires around me quickly regain their balance.

"What was that?" Smithson yells. He casts a worried look at the stone above us. "If this place caves…!"

He doesn't get to finish his sentence. At that moment a bright blue light flows out from around Morgan. It envelops us in a protective orb.

The ground continues to shake. But none of the rubble touches us.

Raul grabs my arm and pulls me to him. He holds me to his body.

Morgan has her eyes screwed shut. She's muttering an incantation under her breath. Stones rain down from the ceiling. They rebound off the blue sphere and do not reach us.

After a few minutes, the shaking stops. The Queen holds her spell for a few more moments... and then lets go.

The light winks out. As soon as it does she stumbles back, as if a great rebounding force just crashed into her.

Smithson is at her side in a flash, holding her up and helping her stand.

"You've overexerted yourself, my Queen," he says, his voice becoming toady. "You mustn't risk so much of yourself. We could have handled it without the need to resort to magic."

"We were lucky," she rasps. I realize just how much the spell took out of her. She sounds hoarse, exhausted, and—just for a moment—I see past her regular vampire face and glimpse the tired woman underneath.

I shiver. That's one of those things only granted to those with magic in their bloodline—as the Queen had explained to me.

Does it mean that being a vampire is all an illusion? Or am I seeing something else?

It certainly doesn't *feel* like an illusion.

After a few moments Morgan pushes herself up. "That could have been much worse. The tremors came from deep underground. Had they known we were here…" she trails off. "The spell would have saved our lives."

"But that means…" Phillip begins, concern filling his words.

"It means someone is mounting an assault on The Haven," the Queen finishes for him. "Smithson—I want guards posted at every entrance. Get all the coven vampires to their homes. Don't let any wander. The humans must be kept together, too. Keep them within the boundaries of the village, but do *not* tell them what's happening."

She looks up. "The wards will inform me of any who attempt entry into The Haven from the Outside. I want you to be ready to defend at a moment's notice."

"I warned you," Raul tells his Mother. "I warned you what would happen if you sent James on his mission!"

"You think The Crypt vampires have come to get retribution?" Morgan laughs. "No, my son. Logan would not move so soon. It would take weeks for him to assemble the necessary force."

"You wouldn't say that if you'd seen what I have," Raul says softly.

Smithson stares at me.

"She's the one they want," he says. "Isn't she? But what is so special about some newly-turned vampire—"

Morgan slaps him. Full on, across the face, she slaps him. "Don't be a fool! You feel her strength. No, if they've come after Eleira, we must do everything we can to protect her. And that includes carting her out of harm's way if she's threatened." She looks at her two sons. "Can I trust you both to that task?"

The brothers nod.

"Wait!" I protest. "I don't understand. How does one small earthquake possibly mean we're under attack? It doesn't make sense."

"She's right," Smithson says grudgingly. "It could be coincidence."

"You think it's coincidence that the humans *all* heard a voice?" Morgan seethes. "No. Somebody—or something—is trying to undermine my rule. And the force is coming from the Outside."

"You believe there was a voice!" I gasp.

"Of course, I believe it," Morgan hisses. "I'd be an idiot not to."

"But you said... you *killed* the boy..."

"To stem the humans' discord and to show that I won't be swayed or influenced by them," she says. "It calmed them down, didn't it? It got them to conform?"

"That's horrible," I whisper.

"That's what being a ruler is!" The Queen glares at me. "We're vampires. You're a vampire. We're all creatures of the night! You're also a witch—the trials of humans mean nothing to you."

"You rely on them," I begin.

Morgan slices a hand through the air. "Enough of this. Smithson, what are you still doing here? I told you to run!"

"I don't think it's wise for me to leave your side," he begins.

"You think I'm under threat from my *children?*" She scoffs. "I don't like you questioning me, Captain Commander. I won't tell you again. Go. Now."

He offers a quick bow and darts back the way we came.

Morgan turns to all of us. "Now," she says. "On to James."

Chapter Twenty-Two

RAUL

I stand on the outskirts of our group, looking into James's empty cell.

The hole in the floor is enormous. Each of us have come up to the edge and looked down.

The fall into the water below would knock out the strongest vampire.

Mother tells us all to step back as she casts a probing spell underground. Just before she does it, though, she calls Eleira forward.

"You watch," she says. "See if you can pick up on anything I do."

Eleira swallows, clearly uncomfortable being around my Mother after their prior argument, but then comes close.

I turn my attention away from them and look at the crater. Who could have helped James escape like this? It's definitely not coincidence.

How many allies did he make in The Crypts?

Phillip shuffles around the edge. "It's a long way down," he says. He lowers his voice. "Do you think James could have recovered from the fall fast enough to get away?"

"I hope so," I mutter under my breath. "It's the only chance he has."

Phillip nods, deep in thought.

After a few moments, my Mother makes a horrible noise of frustration. "*Gah*," she says. The light around her dies out. Eleira shivers and steps away. "The way is blocked. A pile of rocks came crashing down to block the river. That was the earthquake we felt."

"And James?" I ask, hope rising inside me.

"Gone," Mother spits. She turns away and strides toward the exit in a fury. "Looks like we have another vampire hunt on our hands."

I don't say anything out loud, but inwards, I cheer my older brother on.

Get as far from this place as possible, James, I think. *No matter your faults, nobody deserves a fate like that sentenced to you.*

Chapter Twenty-Three

SMITHSON

Fury takes me that the Queen would so easily dismiss me from her side.

My whole purpose in coming to The Haven is to ingratiate myself to her. I must make myself invaluable. I must have her absolute trust.

Without it, none of my goals are possible.

I scowl at a rag-tag villager who stumbles into my path. The man gasps, frightened, and trips over his feet. He falls.

I pick him up by the neck and jerk him close to me. "Don't," I warn, "get in my way again." I shoot a disgusted glance at the burned-out huts and houses surrounding me. "Shouldn't you be making yourself useful with repairs?"

"Y-yes," he stammers. The other humans take a wide berth around us. None step in to help their own.

"Then get to it," I hiss, shoving him away. "If I catch you slacking again, it's right back to the underground."

He mutters a few frightened placations and turns to run the other way.

I watch him go. He doesn't know how close I came to taking his blood. It'd be against the rules governing The Haven... but not such a big transgression that it couldn't be overlooked for the Captain Commander of the Queen's Royal Guard.

I take a moment to consult with the guard from the caverns, Leonardo. He's watching over and directing the humans in their restoration work along with fifty other vampires.

"Keep an eye on that one," I say, pointing out the human who had gotten in my way. "He seems likely to make trouble."

Leonardo nods.

"The Queen wants posts around the outskirts of The Haven," I continue. "How many can you spare?"

Leonardo looks around at his team, and then at the humans milling about. "Half," he says.

"Good. I don't need more." I count out the guards who will come with me. "You've done a good job keeping order. Make sure it lasts."

Leonardo gives me a salute, and I walk away with my new retinue.

Half an hour later, all the guards are where I need them. It seems like an awful waste of resources. If the Queen would *listen* to me, she'd understand that the danger comes from that upstart young vampire-witch she keeps beside her. Eleira.

Not from an imagined, unseen foe from the Outside.

But my temper has cooled off, and I understand now that I have to do exactly as she says for me to get her complete trust. Our shared history gives me a slight leg-up, but not as much as I had assumed when I first arrived.

Once my duties are complete, I decide to turn my attention to the one vampire in here I *know* is not all she pretends to be. Victoria.

I look through the view-latch to the cell. She's sitting cross-legged in the middle of the room at the top floor of the tallest tower in the castle. Her eyes are closed. She seems to be meditating.

I snap the view latch shut and undo the main lock. I take a moment to prepare myself for the assault on my senses that all the silver on the other side will bring.

Then, taking a deep breath, I push the door open.

Victoria looks up right away. "About time," she says. "I was beginning to grow bored. I thought you'd forgotten all about me."

"Don't move," I warn. I shift one hand to the pommel of my sword. "This isn't a friendly visit. I'm here for answers."

"About what, my darling?" she wonders. She cocks her head to one side and gives a little laugh. "You don't need to be so guarded all the time. You must know that if I wanted to kill you—" she shows her teeth, "—you'd already be dead."

"Your co-conspirator, James, broke free today."

Victoria's eyebrows shoot up. "You don't say. Where is he now?"

"Far from here. Out of the Queen's reach."

She bats her eyes. "*You* wouldn't have anything to do with that, would you, Smithson?"

I spit on the ground and growl. "Don't insult me, wench. My allegiances are to the Queen alone."

"So you say," Victoria mumbles. In a smooth, flowing motion, she stands up. She stretches her bound hands over her head like a cat, not bothered at all by the silver surrounding her.

In fact, she seems perfectly at ease in this place.

"Your strength is fading," I inform her point-blank. "You're weaker than when we first met."

She shoots me a dangerous look. "It'll still take many weeks until I'm as weak as you."

"Don't test me."

"Nothing of the sort," she promises. "It's just… an impartial observation."

I scoff.

"So, you said you want answers?" She steps toward me. I shift my grip on Witchbane aggressively. She stops. "If you want answers, you need to first ask questions."

The one thing that's been bugging me the whole time I've known her comes to mind. "How can you stand the silver?" I demand. "It's not pure strength. Otherwise vampires would become less susceptible to the metal as we age. We do not. So why you?" I narrow my eyes at her in consideration. "It has to do with The Ancient's blood, doesn't it?"

"Oh no." She shakes her head and gives a perverse grin. "The Ancient has the same weakness that all vampires do."

"Then what? Is it magic?"

"Not magic." She gives a wistful sigh. "I cannot do any of the sort."

"Then what?" I ask, stepping closer.

She holds her arm out toward me. "Do you see my skin?"

"What of it?"

"Have you ever known a vampire with a tanned complexion?"

"I assumed you were like that when you were turned."

She laughs again. "How little you truly know. No. Even if I *were* like this when I was turned, my skin would pale from lack of sun. I'm tanned, Smithson, because *I go out in the sun.*"

"What?" I shake my head. "You can't. The light would

171

burn you to a crisp!"

"Oh, that's what you want to believe. The truth? Being in the sun is simply... painful. It does not kill."

"I know *that* to be a lie," I growl. "I've seen vampire's tortured by being left in the sun's rays." *I've ordered vampires tortured by being out in the sun's rays.* "The stronger ones might last longer, but in the end, they all perish. If left out there long enough."

"Then I guess I really am the strongest you've ever met." She winks at me. Then she shrugs. "What can I tell you? The pain of the sun, the discomfort of silver... I *crave* those sorts of feelings. I *embrace* them. That's why your cells, your silver, your sword—that's why none of those things frighten me."

"You're a masochist," I say under my breath.

"Maybe. Some might call me that. But you didn't come here to discuss my... personal perversions. And yet I've given them away. Could it be that I trust you, Smithson?"

"Don't," I warn. "Don't get any ideas in your head. You're still my captive."

"Yet with all you know about me, don't you think it would be *so easy* for me to break out?"

"No," I say. "You have a high opinion of yourself. I respect that. But if you are like that around the Queen, you will get yourself killed sooner or later."

She throws her head back and laughs. "Oh, I *highly* doubt that. The Queen is desperate. She needs me more than she knows. Tell me about James. He's gone?"

"Yes. We suspect your coven had something to do with it. The question is," I start to pace the cell, despite the discomfort moving around silver gives me, "why would they break him out?"

"You know it's them for a fact?" Victoria asks.

"The Queen was sure of it."

"It's easy, then." Victoria shrugs. "James knows their secrets. Logan would do anything to keep those secrets safe."

"But you know those secrets, too," I say.

"Yes." She smiles at me, and it's the smile of an opponent who knows she has the upper hand. "I know them, and many, many more."

Chapter Twenty-Four

ELEIRA

When we emerge out into the night, I feel like I can take my first full breath in ages.

I did not like the close proximity of the underground. It reminded me too much of my imprisoned arrival in The Haven.

The magic Morgan showed me... I wanted to deny seeing it.

At first I thought the streams and gossamer flowing out of her body and coalescing into the spells she cast were just my imagination. But when she called me close and used the probing spell, and I *saw* the disparate threads collect above her head and then surge forth in a rush of power... I knew that it was real. I could not deny that I could see them anymore.

I wasn't frightened by it. No, I was more concerned about the *affinity* I felt for the force. My fingers itched to try commanding something of the same sort. I *wanted* to own those powers, wanted it almost as much as I had wanted to be whisked away from my ordinary life in my early teens—

Wait a minute. I look at Raul, then at Phillip, and finally at Morgan. I'd forgotten all about that old longing, the old desire that I once had. I felt it very acutely every single night I went to sleep for a period of almost six months, after getting too caught up in a series of fantasy books I was reading.

Is that longing the reason I was so susceptible to letting these vampires take me and define my life?

My eyes go to Raul. He notices and breaks off his conversation with his brother just long enough to give me a sweet, assuring smile.

Is that why it was so easy for me to develop feelings for him?

A vampire guard I don't know runs up to us. "The Captain Commander sent me to tell you that all the arrangements have been seen to. The Haven is under the protection of the guards, all of whom are on high alert."

"Good," Morgan replies. "Take me to him. I want to inspect the posts he set."

The guard salutes her and marches off. The Queen follows.

Raul hesitates, looking at me and Phillip. "I should go with her," he says. "But Eleira, we need to talk—"

"Don't worry about me," I say. "We'll have time for that later. Go! Do your duty."

He nods. "Okay."

Just before he runs off, he pulls me in and places a chaste kiss on my lips.

I'm blushing despite myself when I turn to Phillip. He has a coy smile on his face.

"What?" I challenge.

"Oh... nothing," he says, both his eyes sparkling.

"Tell me."

"I'm just glad that someone's found love in the midst of all... *this*."

My eyes go wide and I suddenly feel short on breath. *Love? No, I wouldn't call it that...*

But my body's reaction tells a tale of the opposite.

"I want to see April," I say, shifting the conversation away from myself. "I haven't said more than two words to her since getting back. Do you know where she is?"

Phillip nods. "At the infirmary. I'll take you."

***

We arrive to find April lying in bed, a white sheet pulled up to her neck. She's sound asleep.

176

"I don't think we should wake her," I tell Phillip. He seems more anxious than me to speak to the girl.

But at the sound of my voice she stirs. Her eyes open and she sits up.

"Eleira!" she says. She smiles at me. Then she notices Phillip, and her eyes become withdrawn. "What's *he* doing here?"

Phillip flinches a fraction of an inch.

"He wanted to see you," I explain. "As did I. How do you feel?"

"Good," she says. She pushes herself up in bed. I can see the effort it takes her. With my new vampire senses, I can tell how truly weakened she is. Her heart is barely beating beneath her ribs.

Suddenly her head twists to one side. "Did you hear that?"

Phillip and I look at each other. We shake our heads. "There was nothing."

"I swear, I thought somebody spoke..."

"It wasn't either of us," I tell her.

She shivers. "Weird."

The connection flares in my mind. April's still human. Morgan *confirmed* the voice the humans heard was real.

177

Before I can speak my mind April turns to me. "You came back." She sounds almost angry. "After all we did to help you escape."

"It's not like I had a choice coming back!" I protest. I hate the judgement in her eyes.

"You were set free, and you returned to become a vampire," she accuses. The resentment is clear in her voice. "Well done."

I exchange a look with Phillip.

"Maybe we should come back later," I suggest.

"No, I'm sorry. I'm… testy. I've been having nightmares."

Phillip instantly takes a step toward her. "What sort of nightmares?"

A look of shame takes her. She draws in on herself. "They're nothing. I shouldn't have said anything."

"April, if it has to do with what I did to you—"

"No!" she snaps, going all on the offensive. "It's nothing *you* or *your kind* could ever understand."

She shoots both me and Phillip a scathing, hateful look.

"April, we're your friends," I begin. "I know you've been through a lot, but we're here for you now—"

"*You* know? *You*? You, the vampire heiress? You, the girl brought into The Haven and instantly elevated above

178

everybody? You, who's been given such great power and done *nothing* to deserve it?"

"April—" Phillip tries.

"Don't!" she snarls. "Don't defend her, Phillip. You're just as guilty of bringing her here as anybody else. You think I'd still be your friend, Eleira, after all that *they* put me through? After all I suffered for you, only to have you spit in my face by returning as you are now?" April's voice takes on a maniacal inflection. Her words get louder and louder, until she's almost screaming at us.

"But the time of Soren rule in The Haven is nearly over. You think your peace will last? You think your false equilibrium will be maintained? Oh, no. No, no. Soon, the humans will rise up. The humans will rise up and band together and they will *take what is theirs*. With The Convicted on our side and the rightful leader in His place—"

Suddenly she starts to cough. My eyes go wide when she coughs up blood.

Phillip is at her side in a flash, holding her while the fit passes. When it's done, April looks at us with stunned, dazed eyes.

"I—I'm sorry," she says in a small voice. "That... that wasn't me speaking. I don't know what took hold of me. I would never..."

She breaks off with a shudder.

179

I share a look with Phillip. He gives an almost-imperceptible nod. There's enough understanding in his eyes to let me know what he suspects.

The Voice is responsible for April's behavior.

"Phillip?" April sounds scared. "What's happening to me?"

"You'll be all right," he assures her. "You're still in recovery. You've lost a lot of blood." He smiles and brings a hand up to brush a thin strand of hair out of her eyes. "You were very brave when you offered yourself to me." His hand shifts, and he touches the underside of her jaw. "You've been through a lot." One of his fingers applies subtle pressure to a specific spot on her neck. "You should sleep."

April yawns.

"Sleep," Phillip continues, applying that little bit of pressure. I don't think I would have picked up on what he's doing were it not for my enhanced senses. "Rest. A good sleep, *without* nightmares, will help you recover."

April's eyes drift closed. A few moments later, she's sound asleep.

Phillip quickly ushers me out of the room.

"You did something to make her sleep!" I accuse. "With your fingers. I saw!"

"Keep your voice down," he hisses. He looks around to

make sure we're alone. "Yes, I did, but it was for her own good. Did you hear what she was saying? About *rising up?*" He becomes deadly serious. "If any of the other vampires heard and told Mother, she would sentence April to death in a heartbeat. But that wasn't her speaking. Somebody—something—took control of her mind."

I think of the link Victoria shares with me.

"What happened here with April, and what we saw with the other humans, it's no coincidence. When Mother sent James to challenge our Father, she drew attention to The Haven. For centuries we've remained hidden. But now there are forces on the Outside focused on us. I'm sure of it."

He starts to pace the small space between us. "If the humans could be rallied against us, The Haven would crumble from within. They outnumber vampires ten-to-one. If a *real* uprising were to begin... it would be mayhem."

"What about The Convicted?" I ask. "What did April mean by that?"

"I don't know," Phillip admits. "But have no doubt: all of this is connected."

I nod.

"Mother knows this too, I'm sure of it." He taps his lips in thought. "She's unpredictable, but not stupid. James's escape will only fuel her anger. She'll be more likely to lash out."

He takes hold of my shoulders and looks me in the eyes. "There's nobody in The Haven as powerful as you, Eleira. That puts you at great risk of becoming a target."

"If I'm not one already," I mutter.

He nods. "Dark times are coming. Keep your eyes open and your senses alert. There is a lot more to The Haven than you would believe. There's a *reason* Mother's been able to maintain the wards around this place for six centuries. I only have the most cursory understanding of magic. But I know that a single witch, no matter how strong, would not be able to keep up the wards by herself for this long."

He shifts his gaze. "I'm not sure quite how it works. Magic is not an infinite resource. It drains the user. But The Haven is special. Maybe it's the land, maybe it's something else. Make no mistake about it: whatever Mother's secret is, it *is* valued. And the more beings on the outside are alerted to it, the greater their desire to break through the wards will become. Maybe—just maybe—if you can figure it out, if you can gain Mother's *trust* and understand how she does it, it'll give us a chance to survive. Because right now?" He blinks. "It feels like we are on the verge of the first coven war in hundreds of years."

Chapter Twenty-Five

JAMES

I break through the surface of the water, coughing and sputtering.

Before I know it, two strong hands grip my shoulders and haul me out. I'm thrown on the ground a dozen paces away.

I roll over, and see a dozen pairs of hostile, red-rimmed eyes staring down at me. Heavy cloud cover blocks the night sky above.

Somebody kicks my side. I grunt, and, in my blasted weakened state, curl into myself like a small child.

Laughter comes from the circle.

The collar is still tight around my neck. The silver, combined with the enormous impact from the dive, have me in a daze.

More kicks rain down on my body. I try to shield myself.

"Enough!" a stern voice rings out.

The kicking stops. A massive vampire strolls into their midst.

I gape up at him. He must be seven foot three, seven foot four. It's not just his height that's impressive. His entire body is knotted with thick, tight muscle, the sort I've only seen on a bull.

He speaks. "You are the one known as James?"

It takes a few moments for me to regain my breath. I push myself up to my hands and knees.

"Yes," I finally say. "I am."

"James Soren?"

"The one and only." I spread my arms and give him a deep, mocking bow from my knees. "At your service."

The strike of his club blindsides me. I go back down, sputtering.

"You will show proper respect, worm," he warns. He plants a foot between my shoulder blades and pushes me to the dirt. "Or I will make your life a living misery. Understood?"

I mumble something I hope he takes for agreement. It's hard to form words with all the raw earth between my teeth.

The giant bends down. He grabs my hair and jerks my head up. "We may have been sent to retrieve you," he says. "But we weren't once asked to ensure you were in top condition!"

He spits in my face. A surge of anger rushes through me but I push it down.

184

I can be deferential when I suspect it'll save my life.

He stands, and pulls me up with him. "My name is Dagan," he tells me. "You would be smart to remember."

In the back of my mind, I add "Dagan" to the list of vampires I intend to kill.

"Where is The Ancient?" I ask when I'm upright. "He is the one who spoke to me. I need to confer with him."

Laughter, bounds of jeering laughter, meets my proclamation.

"The Ancient is safe in The Crypts," Dagan sneers. "What makes you think he would risk himself coming for you?"

"He can't be," I say. "I heard him in my mind. He could not have communicated with me through such a distance. *He* is the one who made the earth break. Isn't he?"

"My, my, but you have a lot to learn," Dagan grunts. He shoves a pendant from around his neck into my face. "You see *this?* This is called a torrial. It is a special type of object that can temporarily hold magic. It can also enhance a magical spell. The Ancient's power flows through it."

Is that what the chalice Victoria told me about is? A torrial?

My mind wanders at all the possibilities. The potential strength that something like that can give its owner...

Without conscious thought my hand moves to touch the

185

pendant. But Dagan sweeps my feet out from under me before I can make contact. I fall on my back again.

"Never," he growls, looming high above me, "try to touch the torrial again. I am the one it's entrusted to. I am the only who will hold it. Any who defy me face *death*."

A harsh silence falls from the surrounding vampires.

Struggling to keep my anger in check, I push myself up. I shoot a grudging look around the group, then say, "I respect a leader who can keep his soldiery in line."

Dagan snorts a laugh. "Your *respect* won't net you anything. Being quiet will. We came to retrieve you. Our mission is done. You are with us."

He looks back and whistles. On his cue, another dozen vampires appear from the trees. I didn't even sense them!

It's the damned silver collar.

"If I might beg a single indulgence…" I begin. I hate grovelling, but I've known vampires like Dagan before. It's the only way to get in their good graces.

Dagan looks at me. "Go on."

"This collar," I gesture at my neck, and roll my head side to side. "It's not the most comfortable of adornments. A gift from my Queen Mother, but one I'd rather do without."

Dagan grunts and nods at one of the other vampires. "See if you can get it off."

A slender male who looks like he was barely a teenager when he was made separates himself from the group and comes up to me. He has dark, hooded eyes.

"I thank you, friend," I say.

He doesn't answer. He spins his finger for me to turn around.

I do. Once my back is to him, he mutters something in a strange tongue. The words are foreign, but the cadence unmistakable.

It's the same language Mother uses when casting her spells.

The collar drops. Relief washes through me. I rub my neck and take my first full breath in ages.

I turn to face the vampire who freed me. With the collar off, I can take measure of his strength.

For a second, confusion mounts. This vampire... he's barely stronger than a human! He's weaker than even the weakest I've ever encountered—weaker than Phillip, weaker than any fledgling newly made. He's so weak, in fact, that I doubt I could sense him were he more than a foot away.

But he can do magic.

I hold out my hand to show my gratitude. The natural hierarchy between us should make him jump to take my grip.

He only turns away and rejoins the ranks.

"Satisfied?" Dagan asks from behind me.

I turn up to the monster. He's not as strong as I thought he would be, either. His strength is only a few small segments above mine. If a season passed in which I fed and he didn't, I'd match his strength.

"Yes," I say. "My thanks."

He grunts and nods. "Now we go. I'll let you roam free for now. But if you try *anything*..."

He draws his thumb along his throat in a slicing gesture.

I hold both hands up. "Say no more."

The surrounding vampires chuckle. A chill runs down my spine.

"I owe my life to you all," I say. "I will not do anything that shows ingratitude."

Dagan looks me over. "We'll see about that. Scouts!" he calls. "Ahead! The Crypts await!"

We all take off at a dead run into the woods.

Chapter Twenty-Six

JAMES

The sun starts to rise hours later. When the first tendrils of light creep into the sky, Dagan veers off and leads us into a series of underground caves.

He knows this land better than I do. I've never had much of an interest in exploring the area past The Haven's boundaries.

Now, I wish I'd taken more initiative in the past.

A hundred questions buzz through my mind. Why are we traveling on foot? What is our destination?

Logic tells me there must be a plane, or maybe a set of vehicles, waiting for us in a secret clearing ahead. How else would we return to The Crypts?

The other curiosity is the strength—or lack thereof—of these vampires. None, save for Dagan, are more powerful than I. Yet if they came on Father's orders, shouldn't they all be as strong, at least, as the vampires I'd encountered in The Crypts?

Something about this rescue rubs me the wrong way. I

feel more vulnerable in this company than I did in my cell waiting to become one of The Convicted.

Though maybe that's because I understood the motivations behind Mother's decision. Right now, I have no true idea if I'm being led to safety or slaughter.

"We rest here," Dagan announces suddenly, gesturing to a small piece of flat rock. "We wait for the sun to set before moving on. That means ten hours of each other's miserable company. I expect order—" he looks at me in a meaningful way, "—and silence. Riyu, seal us in."

The vampire who'd freed me from the collar breaks off from the group and walks back to the exit. He mutters more words of that language I do not know. A flash of blue bursts from him. For a split second I see a phantom seal wrap across the gaping entrance to the cave.

"None will see us now."

He turns around and quietly joins the others.

They all sit, start to unpack and stretch out. Dagan takes his spot on the largest rock. Then he starts to file his nails.

I look around. Nobody makes eye contact. I might as well be invisible for all the attention I get.

After an hour, I approach Dagan. He's lying back with his eyes closed. I stand by him for a few moments, waiting for him to acknowledge me.

When he doesn't, I resort to clearing my throat.

He cracks an eye open. "What do you want?" he growls. "Didn't you hear what I said?"

"About quiet?" I ask. "Yes. But now that we've stopped, there are things I have to know—"

"The only thing you *have* to know, Prince," Dagan sneers, "is that we are your rescue party. We've come to bring you back. Past that?" His eyes take on a dark gleam. "You'll find *that* out after we reach The Crypts."

"Except we're going over land," I say. I cast a glance the way we came. "I don't know if you're aware, but my Mother values me highly. If you think we can afford to stay still—"

"Look, little Prince." Dagan stabs me in the chest. I grunt and narrow my eyes. "I don't appreciate being told how to do my job. The way I see it, you got yourself caught. *We* got you out. If you cannot even take care of your own safety, why would I take your advice on this matter, or any other?"

Pompous ass, I think. I put on my most endearing smile. "I'm not doubting your abilities. I'm simply offering a perspective you might find valuable—"

He cuts me off with a stern look. "I asked for silence. Do you see any of the other vampires testing me on that? No? Do you know why?" He brings his face close to mine. "Because *they* all know what happens to dissenters in my company. So don't *test me.*"

191

That effectively ends the conversation with him.

I wander back to my spot on the ground. I cross my legs and try to think. Am I a fool for falling in blindly with this group of vampires? Then again, what choice did I have? It was either this, or remain in the cell until Mother's sentence was executed…

I look around me once more. The niggling feeling that we're doing something wrong won't go away.

But until I'm in a position to do something about it… all I can do is endure.

Chapter Twenty-Seven

ELEIRA

All the things Phillip warned me about roil through my mind as I walk alone over the hanging bridges connecting the vampire residences on top of The Haven.

The humans are hard at work beneath me. Their grim determination to rebuild their residence is both distressing and inspiring. I hate the inequality of this place. It's unfair that vampires would live in such luxury while the humans toil away in a lifestyle that ceased to exist in the 1500s.

But such is Morgan's rule. I cannot go against her now. I hardly know a tenth of what there is to know about this place. Hardly a hundredth! It'll take time for me to find my footing, discover my strengths, understand the ebb and flow of power amongst the vampires in The Haven…

I'm mired so deep in my own thoughts that I hardly notice when I bump into somebody walking the other way.

Alarm grips me when I see who it is. *Smithson.*

"Hello, Princess," he says in a deep, smooth voice. "What an unexpected pleasure to run into you this evening."

Something tells me that this meeting was no mere coincidence. I shy back. He takes my arm.

"All alone?" he asks. "That might not be the smartest idea, considering what the other vampires are whispering. Let me escort you."

I jerk my arm away. "No," I say. "Let me pass, Smithson. Morgan told me I have full freedom to go where I please."

"Yes…" he nods slowly. "*Morgan*." He looks around. "You would do best to refer to her as Queen when others are in hearing." He steps closer to me, bringing his mouth to my ear and lowering his voice. "You would not want to give them reason to hate you more. Vampires are a treacherous bunch."

Before I can respond, he steps away. "I bid you a good night."

I stare after his back until he turns the corner and disappears from my vantage.

What was that all about? I wonder.

"I wouldn't trust him if I were you."

I jump at the sound of Raul's voice. I twist around—and find him standing nearly nose-to-nose with me.

He smiles as he reaches up and touches my cheek. "Hi," he says, softly.

"Hi," I whisper back. I can't do anything against the bloom in my chest when his voice makes goosebumps run down my back like that.

He turns aside and twines his fingers together with mine. "Walk with me?" he asks.

I nod. "That would be wonderful."

Raul leads me to the forest. The humans don't pay us any attention when we emerge. They keep their heads down and remain hard at work.

"What do you make of all this?" I ask, gesturing at the remains of the village. "Why don't the vampires help? It would go so much faster if they did."

Raul shakes his head. "The Queen forbids it. They must be self-sufficient, and they need to be kept *busy*, so they don't have time to dwell on the truth of their lives."

"The truth?"

"That they are slaves. They are our food supply. And nothing more."

I shiver. "I think they know that."

"Of course they do. But idle hands make for conspiring minds. If the humans are kept busy with their chores..." he shrugs. "It's been this way for very long."

I hate the cold-hearted way he can speak of them. "Do you really believe that?" I whisper.

Raul looks at me. He brings a finger to his lips. He touches the tip of his nose, then his eyes move to the left, then to the right. "Certain things, you have to believe," he tells me. "*When others are watching.*"

I follow his gaze… and realize that he's right.

We have an audience. Off to one side is a member of the Royal Guard. He's staring at us openly. Across from him is a richly-dressed vampire, only slightly less obvious about the reason for his proximity.

"We must *both* be careful," Raul says. Under his breath, he adds, "I don't know what I would do if I were to lose you."

Is he really so enamored with me? I stare up into his beautiful green eyes, and am taken away by the sincerity I find in them.

"You won't lose me," I tell him. "I'm here, aren't I? I came back."

"But I wonder," Raul says. "Would you be here now if you were given a choice?" He shakes his head. "Never mind. We mustn't speak of such things."

I take his hand and turn him to me. "Yes," I say. "I *would* be here. After Phillip got me out of the caves, away from The Convicted… when I first found myself Outside… I ran. But it didn't feel right. I knew by then I would become a vampire. I knew my home could only be here. When I realized that, I knew I had to return.

"But James caught me first."

Raul looks at me for a long time, his expression stony and serious. "You were going to come back?"

"Yes," I say. "I didn't know what I could do to help, but I couldn't just leave you and Phillip to face The Convicted alone—"

I'm cut off when Raul suddenly wraps a hand around my lower back, tugs me into him, and seals my mouth with a passionate kiss.

I'm breathless when he lets go. "What..." I stifle a giggle. "What was that for?"

"For telling me the truth," he tells me. "For showing me how much this life means to you."

You mean how much you *mean to me,* I think to myself. I try—and fail—to supress another smile.

A spark of mischief lights up in his eyes. He grabs my hand. "Come," he says. "I don't think I ever properly showed you my rooms up in the residences." He glances up at the treetops.

Excitement runs through me as we race to our destination. We stop in front of an enormous redwood. There's an elevator carved into the trunk. Raul calls it down. I'm swept up by the pace of things and lose myself in the moment, excited to *finally* have some time alone with Raul...

Until the doors open, and the Queen steps out.

"Ah," she smiles. "Eleira. Raul. Just the two vampires I most needed to see."

Chapter Twenty-Eight

RAUL

Mother is seething. Her emotions, which are usually kept under such strict control, are on display at full force.

She'd called an impromptu meeting of the Royal Court. That's where I am now: in the anointed chambers in the castle, listening to her chastise her Court for letting James escape.

Eleira, not being yet a member of the royalty, was not allowed to join us.

The Queen slams an open hand down on the marble table. The members of the Royal Court jump.

"Is this all you are capable of?" she demands. "Is this the limit of your abilities? Is this how you repay me for all the protection I've given you? After all the prosperity you've enjoyed?"

She stops talking, and takes a moment to meet each of the vampire's eyes. Shivers run down their backs. They know the things she is capable of with her magic. To get on Mother's bad side now would be a grave, grave mistake.

The vampire seated directly across from me—Bradley—clears his throat. "Perhaps if you'd given us reason to be more vigilant," he says, "you would not have the current situation on your hands."

Mother looks at him and narrows her eyes.

Bradley has always been one of the most outspoken members of the Royal Court.

"Go on," she says dangerously.

He clears his throat and stands to full height. "It's no secret that you've neglected the Royal Court for decades," he says. "How long has it been since our last meeting? Forty years? Fifty?"

"You want to turn the table on me?" Mother asks, her voice icy. "You *dare* suggest I bear the brunt of the blame?"

"Nothing of the sort," Bradley tells her. "But I am expressing concern about the way things have been run. It's no secret you've relied on the council of your three sons almost exclusively for this whole time." His eyes sweep to me, and then fall on Phillip. "It was the third who betrayed you? Perhaps if you'd turned to the Court earlier, certain mistakes could have been avoided."

"And what mistakes, pray tell," Mother offers sweetly, "could those have been?"

"Keeping news of the succession from us!" Bradley

exclaims. Around the table, the other Court members mutter their agreement. "Did you think we would react favorably to being told of Eleira's arrival at the same time as the rest of the rabble?" The murmurs of assent pick up. "We are, as you said, your Royal Court. Our faults lie not in our negligence, but in our disuse!"

At that, almost all the other vampires start voicing their agreement.

Mother waits for the commotion to die down. She raises her hands. "All right," she says. "I see your point. Perhaps... some of the fault does lie with me."

I nearly gape. Mother *never* admits her flaws. Not to anyone.

Not ever.

"But," she continues on. "That does not excuse any of you from shirking your duties. Perhaps the prosperity I've given you, thanks to the wards, has made you complacent. Perhaps it's made you lazy. Fine. I accept that. I was too gracious. Many of you have lost the requisite discipline needed to serve me well. But not to worry—you will each have a chance to make it up to me. Starting *now.*"

A tension shifts through the air.

"How?" one of the vampires ventures.

"The first is a strengthening of our defenses. In case you

haven't heard, the humans nearly *began* a little uprising earlier." She looks around. "Good thing I arrived in time to stop it."

"An uprising?" A female voice rings out. "Please. As if mere *humans* could be a threat."

I turn my head toward the speaker. It's Deanna, the very last of vampires to be given a position in the Royal Court.

"There are nearly four hundred vampires living in The Haven," she continues. "And what? Three, four thousand humans? A little more? I say, let them rise." She looks at her nails. "A single vampire is easily the equal of ten men. It's time to remind them *why we* rule."

The Queen looks around. "Does anybody else feel that way?"

Silence greets her. There are a few soft coughs. The tension is thick.

"Just as I thought," Mother says. She sounds perturbed.

"How do you intend to strengthen our defenses?" a vampire ventures.

"Oh. That." The Queen smiles. "I will seal the wards around The Haven. Until we discover how James escaped, not a single vampire, not a single being, not a single *soul* will be allowed in or out of the sanctuary. You will inform the coven vampires of my decision." She looks around the Court. "You may go."

Chapter Twenty-Nine

PHILLIP

A chorus of voices rings out at my Mother's announcement.

"No!"

"You can't do that!"

"How will we get fresh blood?"

"The Royal Court will *not* stand for this!"

"SILENCE!" Mother screams. Her shout is accentuated by a loud clap of thunder—doubtlessly another of her spells.

It takes a few more moments for the commotion to die down. When it does, a heavy darkness hangs in the air.

"You've trapped us," Bradley murmurs. "When word spreads of what you've done... well." His voice goes an octave lower. "Humans revolting will no longer be your biggest concern."

"You wouldn't be suggesting I should trouble myself with worries about my most loyal *vampire* subjects protesting, would you?" the Queen asks sweetly.

"That is *exactly* what—"

He doesn't get to finish.

Mother's hand lashes out. A blast of blue light bursts from her fingertips. It hits Bradley square in the chest. He flies back and crashes into the wall, where he goes down hard. Smoke rises from his limp body.

Silence of the worst kind descends upon us. When the smoke clears, there is a gaping hole right where the blue light struck.

Right where his heart used to be.

"A shame," Mother sighs. "To waste someone so young. Does anybody *else* want to offer their most sage council?"

Disgust and revulsion build in my throat. But I keep my thoughts to myself.

Nobody speaks. The Queen nods. "I thought so."

I rise from my seat and immediately start out of the room. I cannot take being here in her presence.

"Phillip?" Mother calls out. "Do you have something you want to add?"

"I need some fresh air," I grumble, and leave before I can witness any more atrocities.

On the other side of the door, I find Eleira anxiously waiting.

"What's going on in there?" she asks. "I heard a crash."

"Mother just murdered one of the members of her Royal Court," I inform her flatly.

She gasps. "Raul," she begins. "Is he all right?"

"My brother's fine," I say. The doors fly open and the remaining vampires storm out. None are happy with how events played out. In fact, most look furious. But if they didn't know better than to go against my Mother before—they do now.

They cast menacing glares at Eleira as they pass. I step beside her to show them she has my support. It might not mean much, not from the strength-hierarchy perspective, but at least it lets them know she's not alone.

I wouldn't be surprised if they attempted to take out some of their anger on her, to get back at the Queen.

When all have passed, the doors to the meeting chambers remain open. Eleira and I walk inside.

Raul is in a heated argument with our Mother.

"Have you gone insane?" he explodes. "Incinerating a human slave is one thing. But attacking, and killing, a member of your Royal Court! It's unthinkable! It's maniacal. It's—"

"Necessary," she says smoothly. "I had to remind the Court who remains in control. It was a similar demonstration with the humans. The Haven is being threatened from the

Outside, my son dearest, and I cannot have discord amongst my people."

"Well, you're going to have it now," Raul snarls. He flings a finger at Bradley's body. "Word's going to reach all of the other vampires in minutes. Bradley was right. If you thought a human uprising was bad—"

"Raul." She says his name calmly. "From one murderer to another, tell me... do you really care so much for Bradley's life?"

My head swings to my brother. Suddenly, he looks a little pale.

"...What?" he murmurs.

"Come now." Mother fixes him with a sweet smile and glides to his side. "Did you think you could hide the truth of my four most loyal guards' death from me?"

Raul's eyes flash. "I have no idea what you're talking about."

"Oh really?" Mother seems amused. She glances at Eleira, who's watching all this with an unreadable expression on her face. "Did you think you could hide the fact that you murdered Andrey and his three companions from me forever?" She shakes her head. "How small your mind is if you thought you could."

Disbelief washes through me. "You're accusing Raul—" I

begin.

"Yes, I'm accusing him!" Mother snaps. "It's the only explanation that makes sense. He was always so jealous of James's friends. Why wouldn't he take the opportunity to do something about it, to *prove his strength*, in the commotion that he himself caused?"

"Raul…" Eleira says. Her voice is hoarse. "Is this true?"

Raul locks eyes with her. He looks caught, stricken, fraught with indecision. If I know one thing about my brother, it's that he's rarely undecided.

That makes his guilt plain as day.

Before he can speak, I step forward. "You placed those same deaths at Patricia and Jacob's hands!" I say. "You already carried out their sentences! Jacob's soul is locked in one of your horrid paintings for *eternity* because of what you did!"

Mother gives a casual shrug. "Better there than left running around unrestrained throughout The Haven."

"You really are mad," I whisper. "Do you understand the things you are doing?"

"Yes, I understand quite well, *Phillip*," she snaps. "I'm tired of you and Raul second-guessing me. If you could be more like Eleira… my sweet, precious Eleira…"

She walks to the girl. Raul steps in her way. "You will *not*," he growls, "approach her, Mother."

208

"I am Queen. I will do what I want."

"Your rule has gone too far," he says. "The powers have gone to your head. You are openly killing vampires sworn loyal to you! You condemned your own son to become one of The Convicted. You throw chains on your other—" he points at me, "—to force your will onto the third! No—I will not let you use Eleira. Not while I am here."

Mother steps back. She gives a coy and dangerous smile. "Given all that you've seen," she whispers, "are you sure it's wise to challenge me? Right now?"

"Somebody has to stand up to you," Raul says. "Somebody has to have the courage to tell you when you're wrong. I—"

He stops when Eleira puts a gentle hand on his shoulder. He looks at her.

"Is it true?" she asks softly

Raul looks ruffled. "Is what true?"

"Did you kill the guards?"

Before he can answer, Mother walks to both of them and puts an arm around their shoulders. "Yes, it's true," she says. "I found a witness."

Raul's eyes narrow. "Who?"

"The human slave you spared in the fight."

Chapter Thirty

JAMES

Hours pass and none of the vampires stir. None make conversation. They all sit in their spots, waiting for Dagan to give the next command.

All of this rubs me the wrong way. With every minute that goes by, my anxiety about being this close to The Haven increases. We're just sitting ducks out here. We should be moving!

At one point, Dagan stirs. I look at him, hopeful that it's time to move. But he simply rolls over to change his position on the rock.

I grit my teeth in frustration. Patience has never been my strong suit. Neither has idleness.

An hour later, Dagan actually gets up. I look at him and start to rise. He fixes me with a glare that tells me to remain absolutely still... and turns around to walk to the farther reaches of the cave.

I wait until his footsteps fade from hearing. Then I wait some more, until I can no longer pick out his presence in the underground tunnel.

Only when I'm absolutely sure he's gone, do I stand up and approach Riyu.

"You," I say. Riyu looks up. "You can do magic. How?"

He looks at me, unblinking. He doesn't reply.

I leer at him. "Look," I say. "You know who I am. If you were smart, it would do you well to get in my good graces. My Father is the leader of your coven, and if you—"

Riyu yawns, bored, and turns away.

My anger flashes. "Look, you worthless maggot," I snarl, seizing him by the neck. "If you think I'm just going to take your insults without—"

A blue halo bursts around Riyu. A sudden chill washes over my body. My limbs seize up. The cold quickly spreads, until only my tongue is left working.

"What..."

Riyu slips from my grip. He gives a little smile, a sly wink, and suddenly I'm free again.

I stagger back. Now my rage truly flares. I focus all my vampire strength onto him. He should be trembling when faced with somebody as strong as me. *All* the vampires in these caves should, other than perhaps Dagan.

"Kneel, worm," I hiss. "Kneel to me and offer your apology. I will not be made a fool of by the likes of you!"

Riyu looks at me… and starts to laugh. It's a high-pitched, almost feminine sound.

It infuriates me even more.

By now, the confrontation has attracted the attention of the other vampires. All of those so much weaker than me. Humiliation takes me that I cannot control any of them.

I try blasting my strength at him again. The vampire hierarchy is universal. *All* should abide by it. It's in our nature. It's implanted in our very souls.

But Riyu only looks at me and shrugs. The waves of power wash off him like water off a duck's back.

"Go to sleep, James," he says. His voice has a dreamy, ethereal quality to it. "Everything will go so much better if you don't fight."

Then, as if he has any right to dismiss me, he simply turns away.

I stare daggers at him, anger and hatred rising to make a vile concoction in my throat. I spin around, challenging the other vampires with my eyes. I can feel all their individual strength. *All* are weaker! Why are they not supplicating themselves to me?

That's the moment I feel Dagan returning. I cast one last menacing stare around and, almost like a sulky child, go back to my spot.

The vampires around me do not so much as whisper a single word.

Does Dagan truly have such a tight rein over them? I wonder. I remember their laughs and jeers when they were kicking me...

The monstrous vampire returns. One look at our company and his cheek twitches.

"What did you do?" he demands of me.

I try to play it cool. "Me? Nothing. I—"

The words choke off in my throat. Dagan extends his power over me, and I find myself all too eager to tell the truth.

"I wanted to speak to the others while you were gone. I attacked Riyu in my anger. He made a fool of me with his magic."

Dagan's hold on me vanishes. I gasp. How easy was it for him to bring that confession out of me? Only a vampire who is magnitudes of times stronger would ever think about attempting to do something like that!

"That's not the first time Riyu's been underestimated." Dagan snorts. Some of the others snicker.

Then they begin to laugh. Their laughter pierces my head, making my temples throb, making this feel like some sort of awful dream.

He cuts them off abruptly. The other vampires fall silent

in perfect synchrony with him. I marvel at how easy he makes it seem, at how simple their coordination comes about.

"You used the Mind Gift on me!" I accuse. But something feels wrong about saying the words. It's almost like I know they're not true.

"No," Dagan says. He swings the amulet around his neck once. "The confession came courtesy of this torrial."

"AS YOU SAID," he booms in my head, *"ONLY A VAMPIRE WHO IS MAGNITUDES OF TIMES STRONGER THAN YOU WOULD ATTEMPT TO USE THE MIND GIFT LIKE THAT."*

Shock races through me. I know the torrial gives the ability for him to speak telepathically. But can he also read my thoughts?

Before I can do anything he turns away. "Get ready!" he booms at the others. "We're leaving for The Crypts at once." He looks at me. "You'd best prepare for the journey of your life."

Chapter Thirty-One

JAMES

As the other vampires make their preparations, I sit huddled alone on the spot assigned to me, thinking furiously.

Dagan's voice was in my head. That shouldn't come as a big surprise given what I've already experienced. But the fact that he *knew what I had thought...*

It's a terrifying proposition.

Every now and then I cast a glance at him. If he notices, he does not show it. I try to simultaneously keep my mind blank while maintaining my thoughts in the background, just beyond the edge of consciousness.

If he is in my head, how much can he glean? How much can he hear? Can he see my whole mind?

How far does the power of the torrial go?

Look at me, you big, ugly brute, I think.

Dagan doesn't so much as hitch his shoulders.

LOOK AT ME! I scream inwardly. *SHOW THAT YOU CAN HEAR ME!*

Nothing.

I growl with displeasure. Dagan is not my friend. That much is clear. And he is not my enemy—yet.

The most dangerous type of foe is one you do not understand. Because those you do not understand, you might underestimate.

Just like I did with Riyu.

Finally all preparations are complete. I'm called to join the pack.

"Give me your hands," Dagan says.

I scoff. "Why?"

He takes out a pair of manacles. "Because these are to go on your wrists."

I meet his gaze. "No."

He sneers. "Do you really wish to challenge me? *Again?*" The vampires around me take a menacing step inward. "We own you, James. Either you put them on willingly, or we use force."

"Why now?" I demand, my pride making me obstinate. It was always a prickly thing, that pride. "You freed me from the collar, and now you want to bind me in chains."

"The collar was silver. It affected your head. These—" he hefts the manacles in his hands, "—are made of iron. They are meant to keep you in line."

216

"If they are iron you know how easily I'll be able to break out."

Dagan's lips twitch up in a half-smile. "Then you should not protest against putting them on."

The vampires around me are watching the interaction with hungry eyes.

Finally, I give a resigned sigh and offer him both arms. "It's a shame you don't trust me."

"It's not me," Dagan says as he clamps the cuffs over my wrists. "It's your Father. And, yes, I think it's a shame, too."

He smiles in satisfaction once they're secure. "Now, on to The Crypts. Riyu?"

The weakest of the vampires steps forward. He stops right beside me. I look at him. I don't like the secretive smirk that's on his face.

He winks.

A bright blue flash streams out from where he's standing. I shield my eyes with one arm against the light. When the spots in my vision fade, I look back—and discover a rotating sphere hovering above the ground, approximately waist-high.

None of the other vampires look the least bit impressed. But I stare at it in wonder. It's obviously magic—but magic the likes of which I did not know existed in our world.

The sphere starts to spin faster. As it does, it exerts a

suction on the air, almost like a black hole. The cavern we're in is unlit, but because of our vampire vision we can all see through the dark. Yet as the sphere spins and spins and spins, I find my vision diminishing. The corners of the room become cloaked in a black that my eyes cannot pierce.

It's more than unnerving. It's downright terrifying.

But it is fascinating all the same.

Riyu begins to chant. It's a low, slow incantation. The cadence builds until the pace of his words matches the frequency of the spinning orb. The cavern walls completely disappear from my vision. Not long after, the vampires on the other side of the orb become hidden, too.

Riyu's words grow louder. The very air shimmers. A similar resonance to that I felt right before the ground gave way in my prison beneath the earth is at hand here.

The orb expands and flattens at the same time until it's the size and shape of a round café table. Dagan gives a command.

One by one the vampires around me leap into the spinning blue light. I watch as it swallows their forms, and they wink out of existence.

Eventually it's just me, Riyu, and Dagan. "You next," the huge vampire grunts. "Quickly."

"How do I know it's safe?" I ask.

"You don't." Dagan grins.

And, just like that, he shoves me inside.

Chapter Thirty-Two

ELEIRA

Raul storms off after Morgan's declaration about the human slave. Phillip and I look at each other, unsure of what to do.

"Oh, go!" the Queen says. "Go chase after him, go bring him back, go do whatever it is you need to do." She grimaces at Bradley's body. "Somebody will need to clean this mess up."

She retreats into her own private hall, effectively dismissing us.

Phillip stops me outside the castle. "Let's give Raul some time to cool off."

I nod. The darkness of The Haven weighs on me, and it's not just from the lack of light. There's tension and turmoil in the air. Things are changing too rapidly for me to keep up.

"Where do you go when you want to just... get away?" I ask. "When you need to clear your head?"

Phillip looks at me in thought. "Usually I'd be in my suite," he says, "but I have a feeling you're asking for something else." He turns his head in the direction of the far woods. "There is...

well, I'd better just show you."

He takes me past the first row of trees. The ground beyond them slopes upward. It's rocky and uneven, but there's a feeling of cleanliness here, of purity.

We hike in silence for a long time. I appreciate the serenity. After all the commotion I've endured, this is the perfect escape.

We come upon a deer trail. I hear an owl hoot from high above. A light breeze blows through the trees.

Then the ground before us drops, and I'm presented with the view of a magnificent secret valley. At the bottom is a small lake, dark and tranquil. Smooth black pebbles line the beach.

Phillip looks at me with a twinkle in his eye. "Well?" he asks.

"Phillip, it's beautiful!" I say. "Can we go down to the water?"

"That's why I brought you here."

He offers me his arm. I take it, and we make our way down the slope. The lake reflects the many stars shining down on us from the sky.

"This used to be one of my favorite spots in the entire Haven," Phillip tells me. "Raul's, too. We would spend hours here at a time. The water has a calming effect on us, we found.

When things were getting too hectic outside, this was the perfect place to retreat to."

"I can see why," I murmur softly.

Phillip nods. "I still come here sometimes. Raul does not anymore."

I look at him. "Why?"

He exhales. "There was a girl, long ago. Her name was Liana. She..." he trails off, and runs a hand through his hair. "I don't know if I should be telling you this."

"You can't just start and leave me hanging!" I protest.

"Raul would kill me if he found out." Phillip offers a wry smile. "Figuratively speaking, of course. I think I have to clarify in light of recent events."

Is he making a *joke*?

"Can you keep a secret?" he asks.

I feel a small zap of excitement. "Yes!"

"Liana was very important to Raul. They met, I believe, when he led the coven's vampires on a hunt. This was nearly two hundred years ago. The systems we have in place today were not so developed back then. We did not have *The Hunt*, for example. Vampires made pilgrimages out of The Haven once a month to feed on humans in faraway towns and villages. We kept a few humans here as slaves, but there were always more vampires than humans in The Haven."

"What changed that?" I ask.

"The landscape of the world. As new technologies emerged, Mother realized it wasn't viable to keep sending hunting parties out. The murders would be discovered. She began the breeding program and set up the village as you know it now. That led to an expansion of the human numbers. Soon, vampires didn't have to travel anywhere to feed. The hunt Raul met Liana on was one of the last officially sanctioned by the Queen."

"So who was she?" I ask in a whisper.

"Somebody a lot like you," Phillip says. "Somebody who broke through and managed to claim Raul's heart."

I take a sharp breath. I feel like I've just been stabbed in the chest.

But then again, what can I expect? Raul's been alive for more than half a millennium. Of course he's had relationships before.

"But it was a love forbidden by the Queen," Phillip continues. "Because of what the celestial charts predicted. Mother took one look at them... and cast Liana out.

"But Raul didn't listen. He hid her here and confided the secret in only two other vampires, James and me.

"We swore we would never betray him. We saw the way Liana and Raul were when they were together. With her at his side, some of his darkness was… swept away. Much the same way it happens with you."

My shoulders tense in discomfort. "I'm not sure that's entirely true."

"Trust me," Phillip says. "It is."

He stops and looks out at the placid water. When he doesn't speak, I prompt:

"What did the celestial charts predict?"

Phillip gives an uneasy shrug. "Nothing pleasant." He turns to me. "Raul might tell you if you ask, but it's not my place to give that piece of information away."

"So what can you tell me? What happened to Liana?"

"She remained hidden for a few months. And then, one day, she just… disappeared." He grunts. "Somebody must have found out about her presence. I never told a soul. I don't think James did, either."

"Was it murder?" I ask softly.

"That's the only logical conclusion," Phillip says. "But we never found a body. We never found any hint of an escape, either." He nods into the distance. "Past that bend was where Raul built a small hut for her. It's gone now. Destroyed by him in a blind rage. I… don't know anything past that. Raul stopped talking about her when it became obvious she was gone. The next few decades were the worst I've ever seen him.

He became withdrawn and hostile. He was aggressive toward everything and everybody. The Haven's vampires started to fear him. The Royal Court even suggested to the Queen that he should be thrown out.

"She laughed at them, of course. I think that was the first seed of discord between her and the Court."

"And Raul?" I ask. "How did he recover?"

"For the longest time, I didn't think he had. Not in full. He'd just managed to suppress the anger, suppress the rage. But now, I see him with you—"

A fox darts through the bushes. We both start at the sound.

Phillip looks at the sky. "We've dawdled long enough. We should go back. And Eleira? Please don't tell Raul I said anything. Not yet."

Chapter Thirty-Three

ELEIRA

I find Raul pacing the floor in front of his desk, on top of which are piles and piles of arcane astronomical charts.

He looks up when I enter.

"Is it true?" I ask. "Did you really kill the vampires like Morgan said?"

He studies me, a curious expression fleeting across his face. Then his hands tighten into fists, and he nods. "I had no choice. They were torturing a group of humans."

Surprise takes me. "You called the humans *'slaves.'*"

"When we were in the hearing of others," Raul says wearily.

"Those guards," I ask, stepping closer. "Were they the same ones I met at the introductory ceremony? The ones who dragged Patricia and Jacob before the Queen?"

Raul nods.

"Then good riddance!" I take his hand firmly in mine. "I could tell right away they were different from the rest.

Tainted. Corrupt. *Evil.*"

"You thought we were all evil back then." His eyes pierce into me. "Did you not?"

I shake my head. "I knew you were different, too."

To my surprise he draws his hand away and turns to his desk. "I don't deserve you, Eleira," he says. "No matter what you think of me, I have no redemption. I am a monster, and I've given way to darkness, more times than I can count..."

He turns back. "I see the way you look at me sometimes. Like I'm worthy of salvation. I'm not. I've done so many monstrous things. Killing those guards is a blip on the radar compared to my other sins."

"Forget all that," I say. "That's in the past. What we have right now before us is the future. And—"

The doors fly open, and Phillip storms inside. "April is gone!" he exclaims.

"What?" Raul exclaims.

"After we parted," Phillip says, nodding to me, "I went to the infirmary to check on her. She was gone. The doctor claims not to have seen anything. I checked the village. April wasn't there. I found her adopted family. She wasn't with them."

"A human can't wander far in The Haven without drawing attention to herself," Raul says. "Somebody must have seen

227

her."

"Nobody!" Phillip exclaims. He's more agitated than I've ever seen him. "Even the guards don't know where she is!"

"Phillip, relax," Raul says. "She couldn't have gone far. The Haven is sealed inside and out."

"You think I'm worried about her *escaping* The Haven?" Phillip laughs. It's a desperate sort of sound. "No. No, it's not that, brother."

"Then what?" he asks.

Realization strikes. "You think she's been kidnapped," I gasp.

"Worse," Phillip says. He's deadly serious. "Taken hostage."

"By whom?" I ask.

"There aren't any vampires who would harm her," Raul says. "They know she's under the Queen's protection. Morgan offered April clemency at the same time she introduced Eleira to the others. Remember?"

"That was before Bradley's murder," Phillip points out.

"Which is even *more* of a deterrent not to go against the Queen," Raul says.

"You don't think Bradley had friends?"

"April wouldn't be their target. Mother considers her

unimportant." Raul's eyes sweep over me. "Only Eleira matters to her."

"But April matters to *me*," I say. "Everybody knows she's my friend. I'm strong enough to protect myself. April isn't! She's only human. What if Phillip's right, what if she's been taken hostage, what if they mean this as a warning, what if this is somebody getting back at us..."

I trail off. I'm going in circles.

"We still have to find her," I finish lamely.

"What's to say she didn't just walk out of the infirmary on her own?" Raul asks.

Phillip shakes his head. "She couldn't have. Not in the condition she was in when I saw her last."

"Fine," Raul says. "We'll look for her. But the three of us stay together. We can't risk being seen apart. With Mother acting so impetuously, we have to present a unified front. We don't yet know which of the other vampires is on our side. And if Phillip's right, and April's been taken hostage... that means we do not have much time."

Chapter Thirty-Four

SMITHSON

I drag the cuffed human girl behind me through the dank, underground tunnels of The Haven. When I came across her alone, unprotected, and unguarded in the infirmary, I couldn't believe my luck. April was *exactly* the one I needed to get an "in" with Eleira.

A few rare, precious, gold coins from a bygone era slipped to the doctor was all it took to get him to turn a blind eye.

I shove April into a chair and rip the tape off her mouth. Her eyes are red and bloodshot. She's trembling from the cold. Her entire body seems weak, fragile, and pale.

Few humans can lose as much blood as she has and still remain standing. The fact she is conscious is a testament to her internal strength. Usually, I'd respect that—find it attractive, even.

But there's nothing attractive about the murderous way she glares at me with those eyes.

"What do you want?" she demands. Her voice is stronger

than I would have thought possible. "Are you trying to frighten me? If you think I haven't seen *this* before—" she glances around the dark and enclosed dirt space, "—you're sorely mistaken. I've seen this, and experienced worse, at the hands of your guards. You don't scare me, *Smithson*. For you to scare me, I'd need to be afraid of death." She laughs. "Right now, I'd welcome it."

"Is that why you let Phillip feed?" I ask. I lower my voice. "You don't know what that cost me."

"I don't care to know. You're a nobody."

"You forget yourself, little girl." I rise up. "I am Captain Commander of the Queen's Royal Guard."

She snickers. "You've been here less than a month. You come from the Outside and strut about like you own the place. Yet you know *nothing*. You think you intimidate me? I'm under the Queen's protection. Dragging me underground, chaining me to a chair? Cheap tactics. I'm unimpressed."

"Are you, now?" I ask softly. I pull up a stool beside her and sit so our eyes are level. "What if I told you that I know who you are? Not who you pretend to be—but who you *really* are."

Her eyes narrow a fraction of an inch. "I'd call you a liar. And a fraud."

"Is that so?" I clamp a hand on her leg, pressing my claws into her thigh just short of drawing blood. "I know you're no

231

ordinary girl. I know you belong to a long line of humans, all of whom were born into an ancient cult called the *Fang Chasers*. Isn't that right?"

Her sharp intake of breath is all I need to confirm my suspicions.

"The Fang Chasers are an obsessive cult devoted to one thing," I continue. "Falling into the hands of vampires and being given the Gift of eternal life."

April's eyes widen in horror. She shies back.

The grin on my face is nothing short of maniacal. "You see, dear girl? I know more than you think. Certainly more than the vampires who've been sheltering you above ground do. But tell me—not one of them has offered you what you seek. Have they? And you know as well as I do… your time is running out."

I press my claws into her skin and sidle a tiny bit closer. "The Fang Chasers have a strict series of rules. No human can be turned after the age of twenty-four. They don't believe in, ahem…" I clear my throat maliciously, "…*wasting* the Gift on someone who's already peaked, in human years."

I touch her chin and tilt it upward. "And how old are you, sweetest?"

"Nineteen," she says defiantly.

"So you have five years left. Maybe that's enough time.

Maybe not. Who can say for sure? Do you really want to live with such uncertainty? Five years... it seems like eternity to one so young as you. Yet it is nothing to a vampire. It will pass in the blink of an eye. And you... you're so pretty. Your skin is flawless. Your hair is fair. Your body—when it's healed—is in the best shape it will ever be. Every day that passes brings you closer to old age. Closer to *imperfection*."

"Is that why you brought me here?" she asks. "To *mock* me?"

"Certainly not." I look into her eyes. "I brought you here to make an offer."

"What offer?"

"The offer of The Gift."

She sucks in a raw breath.

"My organization..." I chuckle to myself, "...has been keeping an eye on the Fang Chasers for generations. Would you like to know the greatest secret of your cult? Would you like to know why they have remained merely a fringe institution for all these years?

"It's because *not one of your members has ever been successful*."

I back off. "Think about that for a moment. Generation after generation of humans have been chasing eternal life, with none receiving it. But imagine! You could be the first." I reach out and stroke her hair. "Or, if the Queen discovered your true motivations... you could be dead within the fortnight. Do you think she would let you live, if she suspected what you want?"

April stares at me and doesn't answer. I can see her feeble human brain working feverishly behind those eyes.

"What is *your organization?*" she finally asks.

"We are called The Vorcellian Order." My lips curl up in a haunting smile. "From the blank look on your face, I take it you've not heard of us?"

April shakes her head. I notice she's trembling. From fear?

No. Adrenaline.

This one is bolder than I thought.

"You are amongst a handful of Fang Chasers to ever actually penetrate a vampire's coven," I continue.

"How do you know?" she asks.

"Because," I say. "I helped engineer your kidnapping."

"Liar!" she accuses.

"Oh no," I say. "Everything I say is true. You see, the Vorcellian Order... we manipulate things. Creatures of the night think they are the lone source of power in this world. Their arrogance is the Order's strength, the Order's opportunity. I let you be captured... because I knew you might

234

prove useful to me in the future."

I stand up and start walking around her. "It was James who abducted you, was it not? Why am I asking? We both know it was. He was also your first real lover, wasn't he? And you, fool girl that you are, thought you stole his heart."

Cracks start to show in April's façade of strength.

"You see, my order doesn't just deal with vampires. Oh, no. We watch over all supernatural beings. We separate the legends from what's real. The Loch Ness? Doesn't exist. Bigfoot? Simply a myth. But vampires, and witches? They're real. Ghouls, too, and spirits... but I don't want to scare you with stories of those yet.

"My order controls a small band of witches. Not very powerful ones—none so mighty as your Queen—but they are ours. They are on our side."

I grip the back of her chair and whisper in her ear. "I was the one who ordered a witch to give James a longing for you. You had a consistent routine in your old life, didn't you? Every day, you would go from school to the seedy diner where you scraped together just enough cash to pay the rent. Every night, you left for your crappy apartment at exactly the same time. You took the same path. You never looked up.

"Really, April. You made it too easy for us."

She breaks. Silent sobs start to rock the girl's body. Hearing of her past is undoubtedly painful for her.

235

That's why I'm so eager to do it.

"I had my witch implant an image of you into James's dreams. Just the smallest inkling of your likeness… but enough to make him obsessed.

"The hunter's instincts took over. He saw the streets you walked on, he knew the time, the place, the pathetic monotony of your life… and he whisked you away from there. He made you his lover. His pet. But never, not ever, did he intend for you to become…" I lower my voice, "…a *vampire* mistress."

I smile cruelly. "So. You now know my secrets. It's time to give me yours in return. First, who is Eleira to you?"

"What?" April's head snaps to me. "*Her?* She's nobody, some human wench—"

I slap her. "*Don't* lie to me, girl," I hiss. "You and I both know she's already a vampire. What I want to know is why she is important to *you.*"

"She isn't—" April begins.

I spin her around and take a deep breath. "You're trying my patience. We'll give this one more go, from a different angle. Tell me, please, why *you* might be important to her."

April looks at me. I see the conflict in her eyes.

Finally, she sags down and speaks.

"I was her very first friend. I was the first human she met

236

in The Haven."

"Hmm," I say. "That's interesting. Very, very interesting." I trace a claw under April's chin. It draws a thin line of blood. "So if something were to happen to you... Eleira would not take it well."

April closes her eyes and shakes her head vigorously.

I step away. "Thank you. You've been very forthcoming. I'll let you go, for now... but a word of this to anyone, and your life is forfeit."

"You... you promised me the Gift," she mutters.

I sneer. "You think I would give it to you *now*? No. Remain cooperative, don't betray my confidence, and stay alert. I'll give you orders when the time comes. Follow through on them, and eternal life can be yours."

Her eyes widen. Her breath hitches. "I'll do anything."

"Good. For now? Stay quiet and observe. I'll come to you when I need you next. Should you do anything to compromise our little arrangement, however—I will know. And trust me. You do not want to get on my bad side."

She nods quickly. "I won't say a single word."

"Good," I tell her. "That's all I ever asked."

Chapter Thirty-Five

ELEIRA

Raul, Phillip and I rush through the scattered remains of the village, searching for April amongst the humans.

She's nowhere to be found. Even worse is the reaction I receive when I try talking to the villagers. They regard me with a mix of suspicion and fear.

It's a nasty way to be looked at by people you want to do good things for.

Raul and Phillip don't seem to notice. That reaction is nothing unexpected for them.

I do catch an attractive woman somewhere in her thirties casting furtive glances at Raul. It's almost like she knows him—but then again, everybody here *should* know the Prince.

When I point her out he becomes strangely defensive. "Just a slave," he offers curtly. "Nothing more."

Could she be the one he rescued from the vampire guards?

But I don't press. April is our most pressing concern right now.

On my suggestion, after conducting a thorough search of the village grounds, we start for the castle. My thinking is that if Morgan set tracers on me to know where I am in The Haven, she might have done the same with April.

But we don't even get that far. Halfway there, we run into April walking on her own in the opposite direction.

"April!" I exclaim. "We were looking for you!"

She looks puzzled—then breaks out into a big smile. "Good. Because I was looking for you, too."

As she joins with us, Phillip gives her a quick once-over. "You're unharmed," he says. "I was worried."

"Needlessly," she tells him. "I felt better, so I went for a walk. It's amazing the things you see in The Haven when the blocks are lifted from your mind."

I wince. Every reminder of the blocks is a reminder of how the Queen keeps the humans grovelling.

"You shouldn't be out by yourself," Phillip says. "Other vampires know who you are—"

"Of course they know who I am," she says imperiously, eyes flashing. "I was introduced to all them with Eleira, remember?"

"That's not what I mean. They know who you are with regards to *us*. You don't know what the Queen has been doing. You're in more danger now than before."

"Phillip is right," I say. "You need to be careful."

She crosses her arms. "I'm *always* careful."

"You need to be *more* careful," Raul says. His voice is low and grave. He takes hold of her elbow and pulls her into our little group. "If you value your life, you'll stay with one of us at all times."

She casts a glance at all of us. "Is that why you're looking for me? To *babysit* me?" Then she sighs. "So be it. But if it's anyone I'm staying with, it's Phillip."

She crosses over and links arms with him. He looks befuddled, but then gives a short nod, all resolute again. "Fine by me."

Raul elbows his brother in the ribs. "I thought you'd be a lot happier," he teases.

"Now is *not* the time for jokes," Phillip says.

Raul holds both hands up in apology. "You're right."

"So what *has* been happening?" April asks. "The Haven seems so… quiet. Everybody is so subdued."

Raul looks at her… and then at me. "Right now?" he says. "It's the calm before the storm. And trust you me—this storm is going to be the largest one we've ever seen."

Chapter Thirty-Six

JAMES

The world spins as I throttle though the blue vortex. I cannot tell up from down or left from right. There's pressure, an enormous pressure, inside of my head, and it's pressing against my body, making me feel like I'm being flattened, like I'm being crushed, like it will never relent, like—

Without warning the torrent of sensation stops. I land on my feet and stagger forward a few steps, surprised to be upright. I hear the snickers from the vampires around me.

Somebody grabs my shoulder and yanks me out of the way just in time to avoid being crushed by Dagan. He apparates in the spot I was in, out of the other end of the portal above my head. Next comes Riyu, and then the portal winks shut.

We're in a spectacular crystal cave. That same magical blue glow is imbued in all the semi-transparent surfaces I see around me. The walls are glowing with it. Jagged shards of crystal ebb with the light.

I've never seen a place like this.

I turn my head up. The top of the cave seems to go on forever. There is a mystical beauty here. It's almost like standing in the pits of a great cathedral and looking up at all the images of the humans' false gods.

They are false, of course, because my immortality has shown me the truth of the world.

The only beings who deserve such reverence are my brothers of the night.

It's a conviction I've not forgotten, despite what these last few weeks have put me through.

"What is this place?" I wonder aloud.

"These," Dagan grips my shoulder, "are called the Paths. They are a relic of an ancient time, when magic was not forgotten, nor feared, in the world. The only way in, or out, is through the use of a portal such as Riyu summoned."

"We're… underground?" I ask, thankful Dagan is feeling talkative.

"You could say that. The Paths were created as a secure, covert way for witches and warlocks to travel. Without arousing suspicion from the outside world. They *are* beneath ground… but exist on a parallel plane. You cannot simply dig your way here. Magic must be used to enter."

"Who uses the Paths now?"

If Mother knew about such magnificence…

242

But then the glitter of the crystals catch my eye. In a flash, I realize I've seen the same sort of stone before.

Mother's crystal throne is made of the same stuff.

Dagan grins, almost like a proud father. "None but those granted permission by our King. Knowledge of the Paths has been eradicated from the world. The only ones to still know of them are members of The Crypts. The Paths are a closely guarded secret. Now that you've seen them?" he smiles a cruel smile. "You are bound to us for life."

So that's why he's so willing to divulge information. He wants to trap me.

"I already made my allegiance known to Father," I tell him. "My loyalty is only with your coven."

Dagan scoffs. "We'll see about that." He looks at Riyu. "Ready?"

The weaker vampire nods.

Dagan gestures for him to move. "So lead the way."

***

We journey slowly through the interconnected network of tunnels that make up the Paths.

After leaving the monstrous cave we arrived in, the space

becomes significantly tighter. There were parts where we had to squeeze through gaps in the crystals with our shoulders rubbing against the walls.

The deference these vampires give Riyu is strange. He's so weak. But they obviously respect his knowledge of magic.

After hours and hours of walking, we squeeze through a narrow chasm, and I find myself in…

A cavern that looks *exactly* like the one where we first arrived.

It's identical. Down to the very last fleck of crystal on the ground, it's the same.

I spin around in confusion. Have we turned around? No, we only went straight. We only went one way.

Riyu walks to the middle of the cavern. The other vampires form a tight circle around him. No words amongst us are spoken as Riyu begins to chant in that other-worldly tongue.

Another burst of light, another blue sphere. Riyu brings it close to the ground. The spinning globe does not take away the light in here. If anything, it seems to make the cavern glow brighter.

"This time," Dagan says, appearing behind me. "You go first."

He shoves me through the portal.

Pain such as I've never known takes me. It's worse than silver, worse than torture, worse than anything I've ever experienced in my existence. Coming into the Paths, the pressure was external, pressing into me. That at least made it bearable.

Coming *out*, going through the portal this way, it's all from within, like a foreign energy fighting to get out. My body feels like it's going to explode. Like my skin will rupture, and I will combust.

A burst of blistering light, then heat, then the coldest cold I've ever known takes hold of me. Then my feet hit solid ground, and I crumble down, gasping for breath, my knees unable to hold me.

"You disappoint me, son," a grim voice says above my head.

I crane my neck up, and stare at the visage of my Father.

"A member of the Inner Circle needs to be strong. He needs to be mighty." My Father starts circling me. "He cannot be seen *grovelling...*" Father plants a foot between my shoulder blades and applies pressure, "on the ground, like a pathetic worm!"

The sound of more feet landing comes. From the corners of my vision I see the vampires of my company stream out of the portal. They land right on their feet, none showing any ill-effects, and stream into formation by the far wall.

Military precision, I think.

"Good," Father says. "The rest have arrived."

Dagan comes through the portal last. He offers the King a respectful salute.

"You've brought my son back. Was the rest of the mission a success?"

"We ran into no problems," Dagan answers. He goes to one knee, takes the amulet off, and offers it to my Father.

Father's cascade of chains and rings rattle as he takes it from the larger vampire. It quickly disappears in one of his robe pockets.

I watch all that with half a mind, because, in truth, most of my attention is stolen by the vampires on the far wall.

I can feel their true strength.

The moment they came through the portal, I felt it. They're not weaker than I am—not at all.

They are, each one, many, many times stronger than I.

How...?

It makes no sense. A vampire's strength cannot simply change. And I *knew* their strength before, I *felt* their weakness, I spent time in their company!

Yet awareness of their new, collective strength crashes into me like a tidal wave. Some catch me looking. A few sneer.

246

One, so boyish in appearance that he might be confused for a woman, offers an apologetic shrug.

Dagan grabs me and hauls me to my feet. Embarrassment streams through me at being manhandled in front of my Father. I push off and steady myself.

If only I could somehow steady the turbulent thoughts in my mind.

"I know what you're thinking," Dagan says. Even *his* strength has expanded. He's bigger, more powerful, more *forceful* than before. He looks at his retinue. "You are wondering... *how*."

Father chuckles.

Dagan beckons for Riyu. Out of all the vampires, only his strength is unaltered.

Yet the stronger vampires regard him with reverence nonetheless.

"The King and I thought it prudent—" Dagan tilts his head to my Father, "—for us to take precautions before approaching The Haven. Riyu cast a spell on each of us that cloaked our strength.

"Because otherwise, how could we have gotten so close to your coven without arousing attention?"

Suddenly it all makes sense. *Cloaking*. That's *why* I couldn't exert control over any of them when Dagan left us alone in the caves.

"You've all done your duty," Father says. "Go and enjoy the reward given to those who please me. Each of you will feast on a limitless supply of blood. And, at the end... you will be given a sip from the chalice."

On that pronouncement, a raw hunger, a blistering excitement shines in the eyes of the vampires by the wall. I'm not immune. I feel it, too.

The chalice. The one Victoria told me of, the one that spreads The Ancient's power.

Father looks at me. He sees my greed. "Not you, son," he tells me.

That comes as no surprise. The fact that I so openly displayed my eagerness *does*.

The vampires file out of the chamber we're in. Riyu is the last to leave. He stops and casts one look over his shoulder at me.

Then he's gone.

But in that split-second, I catch a resemblance I never noticed before.

He looks like Father.

"It seems you have an admirer," the King says softly.

I still the features on my face and don't react to the provocation.

248

Father starts to walk away. "Come with me."

I follow him through a series of empty halls. A set of doors lead into the throne room. Shivers crawl up my spine from my last memories of the place.

He almost killed me here. This is where Victoria saved my life.

I hide my discomfort. Father continues to walk.

We go through another set of doors. The halls become tighter. Father takes a turn, and then one more, and another...

And suddenly I find myself standing in front of the doors that lead to the treasure vault.

I misplace a step. Father looks at me. "Something wrong?" he asks, too casually.

"No," I choke. I can all but feel the invisible noose being lowered around my neck.

"Good. There's something in here—" he nods ahead, "—that I want you to see."

I swallow my sudden fear and walk with him into the room.

It's exactly as it was when I was last here: the fallen chalices on the floor; all the spilled blood; the destruction from the fight between me and Eleira and Victoria and Raul...

"Nobody has been allowed in since your escape."

I almost choke. The noose is getting tighter. "It wasn't an escape. It was an ambush."

"You and Victoria tried to betray me." Father kneels down and touches the dried blood on the floor. He brings it to his lips.

"This…" he tells me slowly, after tasting it, "…is the blood of a great witch."

He surges up, and before I know it, his hand is around my throat, the other on my chest, just above my heart. His claws extend and he digs through my shirt. There is deep-set fury in his eyes.

"You brought her here!" he rages at me. "You brought the witch, you had her under my nose, and you did not give her to me! After I offered you the gift of sanctuary! After I spared your pathetic, miserable life! You are a traitor!"

His hand crushes my windpipe. I cannot speak.

"Well?" he brings his face closer. "What do you have to say? Think carefully before you speak. Your precious Victoria is not here to protect you."

I choke out a single gasp.

He turns an ear to me and hisses, "Yes?"

"I…"

Whatever remaining strength I have is being sapped from my body. I'm fading. Under Father's strength I am nothing. I hate this feeling, I hate how pathetic it is, how damn pitiful it makes me feel...

"It *was* betrayal," Father growls, tightening his grip over my heart. "And I only brought you back to me for one thing."

He lets go, and the sudden release makes me stagger and fall.

"So that I could kill you myself."

Just as he's about to attack, a female voice from the background stops him.

"I would not be so hasty about ending this one's life if I were you, my King."

Father freezes. I look past him and see a beautiful raven-haired woman flow into the room.

A gown of the deepest maroon hugs her curves, and then flows out behind her in a long train glittering with jewels. Her face is painted with smoky makeup, emphasizing her dark, dark eyes against the pale complexion. She's stunning, and, in short—just my type.

She comes up to my Father's side and places an arm around his back. He grabs her and pulls her to him, kissing her passionately.

An ugly spark of jealousy rears inside of me at the ostentatious display.

When he lets go, she turns to me. Pity shows in her eyes.

In that moment, such a violent torrent of anger surges inside me that I nearly lash out and attack Father. I know full well I would lose.

But *pity* from a beautiful woman is amongst the most humiliating feelings that I know.

"Why do you toy with him so, my King?" she asks. "The vampire who spoke at his induction was right. He has your bloodline. In it, there is strength."

"Strength to defy me," Father says.

"Look at him." She motions at me. "He is proud. You shame him and expect respect in return?"

"He is too arrogant. Such arrogance—"

"—is mirrored in you, my love." The unnamed woman smiles sweetly at him. "Could you blame James for his behavior, given the circumstances of his upbringing?" She lowers her voice. "He's been corrupted by your first wife. There was a reason you left her for me."

"Don't speak of such things in front of the boy."

I cringe at being referred to as 'boy.'

The beautiful woman offers me her hand. "Let me help you up."

I swat it away imperiously. "I don't need your help."

"But you are in need of my protection." She glances around her. "Had I not stepped in, your blood would already be on these walls."

I cast a surreptitious look at my Father. His face is blank.

"I'm sure," the woman continues, "that you had reasons for hiding the witch from the King. So tell us, while your ruler is in an indulgent mood..." she strokes his arm, "...what that was."

"I brought Eleira here, it's true," I say. "But she was still human. The transformation had not yet taken her. All this—" I gesture at the cups lying scattered on the floor, "—was meant to expedite the process. I wanted to present her to the King when she was ready. As both a powerful witch *and* a vampire, that he could do with as he pleased."

"And yet you failed," Father says in a low voice.

"She... overwhelmed us with her strength," I admit. "Neither Victoria nor I thought the ceremony would accelerate her transformation so much."

"She was alone?" Father asks. There's a dangerous current in his voice.

I eye the fourth chalice on the floor and decide to offer the absolute truth. "Raul was here, too. I captured him when he came for Eleira."

Father's eyes widen with sudden fury. "YOU BROUGHT MY SECOND SON TO ME," he screams, "AND YOU LET HIM ESCAPE?"

"Shh, shh," the woman coos. "Don't get angry."

"To hell with that!" Father flings her off. He stalks towards me. "You," he says, "do not deserve to leave here with your life." He grabs me by the throat and hauls me up, then pins me to the wall. He takes a dagger from his robes.

The woman runs up to him and throws her full weight onto his arm. "No!" she pleads. "Do not kill him! Do not waste his potential! Take him prisoner, bind him, shackle him, but *let him live!*"

"Why should I?" Father's grip tightens on the dagger held at my breastplate. The point presses into me.

"He knows things," the woman exclaims. "About The Haven. About your first wife. He can offer information that we won't get from anybody else!"

Father throws me down. He kicks me in the face. I taste blood. I try to fight him, but I'm no match. He uses the Mind Gift to keep me on the floor. The telekinetic force binds me. I cannot strike against him no matter how much I want to.

He continues his attack. Kicks rain down on me from all sides. All I manage to do is curl up in a pathetic ball and take the abuse. He's yelling and screaming obscenities as he beats me to a bloody pulp.

Finally he tires out. I look up in a daze.

"Take him to the prisoner's quarters," he commands.

254

"Bind him in chains. He'll be given a chance to redeem himself..." the King seizes my chin and forces me to look at him, "...after he's been sufficiently tortured."

Chapter Thirty-Seven

RAUL

Days pass with Mother locked in her room. After news of Bradley's death emerged, an eerie type of tension descended over The Haven.

Vampires have started seeking me out to try to understand what's happening. Mother's seal of all the exits and entrances makes them uneasy. They feel trapped, and, for the first time in our existence, uncertain about the mental stability of their Queen.

Eleira, the only one of us viewed as an "Outsider" has been more or less shunned by all the other vampires here.

"I don't understand," she tells me. "Morgan told me I have three days to decide. But when I go to her she won't open the doors."

"You're not the only one getting that reception," I mutter. "Come here, look at this."

She walks over to my desk. The charts I've been pouring over are still laid out. Constellations, astrological signs, everything that points to the succession.

"Do you really believe in this stuff?" Eleira asks. "Seeing the future in the stars? I always thought it was kind of… hocus pocus."

"When you have the assurance of living for centuries, you see patterns emerge. The stars don't decide our fates. But knowing what's going on in the heavens gives insight into what might happen on earth."

I sweep a hand over the chart that's taking up the most space on my desk. "As vampires we have a particular advantage in studying the night sky. We are only awake when the stars shine. They are a part of us, as essential to our wellbeing as the sun and vitamin D are to humans. These charts, also—" I glance at Eleira, "—told us of your birth. So you can't deny their power."

Eleira studies the intricate symbols overlaid on the canvas. "I can't make heads or tails of it," she mumbles. Then she shifts her gaze to me, eyes afire. "You can teach me! Can't you?"

For a second I'm taken aback by her interest. Then an easy smile spreads across my face. "I would love to."

I walk around the table so that I'm standing behind her. She doesn't move. I take one of her hands and draw it along a celestial line. "This one," I say softly, taking advantage of the moment to be close to her, to breathe in her delicious scent, "is called the Nocturna Animalia constellation. It's Latin for

257

'*Creature of the Night.*' Humans have never charted it. It is not important to them. But it is to us. When we watch the shifts over centuries..."

"Yes?" Eleira breathes, her voice soft and low.

I find my throat suddenly constricted. I have to clear it before trying again. "When we watch over centuries..."

Eleira turns her body and looks at me. Her pupils have widened. There's a flush in her cheeks.

She is so beautiful.

"Yes?" she presses. "What happens when you watch them?"

"I..."

My mind ceases to work. I'm lost in her amazing eyes. I start lowering my head, wanting to kiss her, *needing* to taste her lips.

Her eyes drift shut as she waits for my kiss.

We only get a half-second of contact when a loud crash from the library in the opposing room sounds. Eleira gasps and pulls away.

I curse inwardly.

"I'm all right, I'm okay!" Phillip calls, oblivious to what he'd interrupted.

I grind my teeth and share a sympathetic look with

Eleira. Then we both go to check on my brother.

He's lost somewhere beneath a huge pile of books that has just come tumbling down on top of him from a great shelf. Only his head pokes out, his glasses askew.

"Well, that explains the noise," Eleira says, trying to stifle a giggle.

I cross my arms and stare. "Aren't you supposed to be more fleet of foot," I deadpan, "given that you're a *vampire*?"

Phillip gives a cheeky grin.

"And why are you wearing glasses again?" I continue. "You've fed. Your vision should be perfect."

"They contribute to my look," Phillip says idealistically. "Besides, after wearing them so long, I feel naked without." He taps the lenses. "I replaced prescription glass with regular."

"Charming," I rib. "You're going to have to put all those books back, too." Eleira and I walk over and help him up. "How'd you manage this disaster anyway?" I look at the railed ladder on the far side of the room. "I had that installed for a reason."

"A book caught my eye on the top shelf." Phillip glances up. "I didn't have time to go for the ladder."

"And look what happened when you decided to climb on your own. Did you get what you were searching for, at least?"

"Yes," he tells me. "And Eleira—this book pertains to you."

259

"Really?" she asks. "How?"

"I'll show you."

We return to my study. Phillip lays the book on the desk. It's covered in dark, flaking leather. It looks old.

There's no title. Nothing at all is imprinted on its front, back, or spine.

For a second, I get a sense of a menacing power held inside.

"Ready?" Phillip asks.

"It's just a book," I bluff. "There's nothing to get ready for."

Phillip gives me a stringent look, then opens the book to a page at random.

The pages are entirely blank.

"Well, that was anti-climactic," I say.

"Just you wait," Phillip says. "This particular book requires blood."

"Blood?"

Phillip retrieves the goblet Eleira was drinking from. Her thirst has not abated one bit since the transformation.

"Yes," he says. "Human blood."

Carefully, he pours the tiniest trickle onto the spine.

The blood simply pools into the middle. Nothing happens

otherwise.

"That's it?" I ask. The only impressive thing—if you can call it that—is that the ancient pages don't soak the liquid up.

"Eleira, be a dear and hold out your hand, would you?"

She reaches out and gives it to Phillip. He pulls out the tiniest needle and pricks her finger.

A drop of blood leaks out. Phillip turns her hand toward the book. Gravity beckons the drop down. It falls through the air.

The moment it hits the human blood, a loud hissing sounds.

All three of us step back.

I watch, fascinated, as the pool of blood starts to trickle into the pages on either side. It flows onto them and takes shape, forming delicate lines of an unknown script. Intricate pictures full of arcane symbols flourish beside the blood-red text.

The whole book comes alive with the infusion of Eleira's blood.

"Only a witch can access the secrets hidden inside," Phillip says in a low and spooky voice.

"Good thing we have Eleira." I look at her, but her attention is fixed on the book.

Once all the blood has gone out the middle and seeped

into the pages, Eleira brings one trembling hand out. She traces some of the symbols on the page.

"I recognize these," she says in a bare whisper. "I've seen them before. These runes. Long, long ago, when I was a little girl." She shudders and withdraws her hand. "I don't like this."

"Neither do I," I tell Phillip. "What's the purpose of this book?"

"It's called..." Phillip flips it over to show the front, "*The Book of the Dead.*"

Now there are symbols on the cover, glowing in a faint, dull blue.

Eleira shakes her head. "No," she says. "No. This is wrong. No. We shouldn't be looking at this. No. This isn't ours."

"Eleira." I look at her in concern. "Don't worry. It's just me, you, and Phillip. He found it in my library. There's nothing wrong with—"

"No," she cuts me off. She backs away until her shoulders hit the wall. "No, no, no," she keeps repeating.

I glare at Phillip. "What's wrong with her?"

Eleira keeps going on. "No, no, no..."

"I don't know," Phillip admits. He spreads his hands helplessly.

"Is it the book? Is it affecting her?" I demand. "It's doing something to her, isn't it?"

The glow on the cover is getting stronger. I rush to Eleira and hold her by the shoulders. "Tell me what's wrong."

But she just keeps muttering the same word. "No, no, no, no." She shields herself against me.

I throw my arms around her body. "I'm here. I promise. Just tell me what's wrong!" Again I glare at Phillip. "Get that book out of here!"

"*NO!*" Eleira screams and suddenly a violent blue light explodes from within the pages. It knocks me back, it knocks Phillip back. It knocks everything in the room back, except for... Eleira.

She is standing upright, her eyes fixed straight ahead but unseeing. Her hair is being blown away from her by a wind that's started gusting from the pages of the book. The whole room is enveloped in that blue light.

Eleira steps forward. I try to move—and find myself unable to. None of my muscles respond.

And yet it's not like I'm locked in place. Rather, it feels like my mind has started to operate at hyper-speed, watching, seeing, processing *everything*. Yet the physical restraints of the world prevent my body from keeping up.

Or maybe time has crawled to a standstill, and the only thing operating at proper speed is my brain.

I see Phillip. He's frozen, too.

Eleira, however, approaches the ghastly book with ease.

She starts to mutter something in a horrible language. The room pulses with violent energy. Her inclination grows louder. The voice is not her own. I fight against the light pushing me down, but I'm like an insect caught beneath a panel of glass. I feel like a specimen on display in a museum— forever watching, forever unable to affect my surroundings.

Eleira reaches the table. Her voice takes on a truly terrible bass. The pages of the book flap this way and that. All the energy inside is escaping and feeding into the blue light. It pulses in time with the cadence of Eleira's speech.

A dim shape, thick as ink and dark as the deepest night, starts to rise out from the midst of the book.

No! I want to scream.

I push against the force holding me down. Panic takes over when I realize that strength is still not enough. I cannot move. I'm trapped, and all I can do is watch as Eleira draws that malevolent black shape out of the book.

The room's temperature quickly drops. Eleira keeps chanting. The shape continues to grow. It's the size of a rat, now, and I can already see its body taking form, the hideous lines, the misshaped head, the crooked torso—

Suddenly the main doors fly open. Morgan is standing there, staff in hand. She takes one look at what is happening and steps into the blue light.

Somehow she's able to penetrate the force field. Her lips move, yet I cannot hear what she says. But I feel the power of her words as they clash against Eleira's chant in the air.

Eleira snarls at my Mother. Such a viciousness contorts Eleira's face that it frightens even me. She draws her lips back and shows her fangs. Her eyes have gone almost completely black—nothing like the eyes of the girl I love. Her cheeks look hollow, gaunt, as if she is undernourished.

Eleira's incantation grows louder. She screams the words at Morgan.

But Mother's focus is all on the creature rising from the book. She deflects Eleira's words and points her staff at the black shape. The blue light draws inward, like a deflating dome. It seems to be flowing into Mother's staff, and yet...

And yet Eleira is doing everything she can to stop it.

Eleira grips the edge of the table. Her claws have come out. They carve deep marks in the wood. Her entire body is tense and sinewy. The foul words continue spewing from her lips, challenging Mother's.

A blast of white explodes from the tip of Morgan's staff. A beam of the stuff, almost like fire, scorches across the room and collides with the awful black shape.

The creature howls. The noise is worse than any I've heard in my life. Worse than the cries of The Convicted, worse than the squeals of a tortured animal, worse than...

265

Worse than damn near anything.

More and more of the white fire pulsates into the creature. Eleira is flinging spell after spell at the Queen. She deflects them all. The creature continues to scream.

There's a sudden explosion. The dark shape flies across the table, misshapen, burnt, and wounded.

But it's still alive. Alive, and gasping.

Mother's eyes line onto it. She begins the spell that will end it for good. Another beam of light shoots from her staff, aimed straight at the creature—

Eleira throws herself in the way.

The cry that is wrangled from my throat is unlike anything that's been ripped from my vocal cords before.

Mother's spell strikes Eleira straight in the chest. The girl's body is flung backwards. She hits the far wall and drops to the floor, completely limp.

The moment that happens the blue light dies. Eleira's wicked spell is gone. I can move again.

That horrible black creature jumps to its feet and dashes away.

I don't have time for it or anything other than Eleira. I fly to her fallen form. My chest constricts in agony.

I drop to my knees beside her. She's out cold. But at least—at least I can feel her pulse.

266

It's frighteningly weak.

"Get out of my way!" Mother snarls, shoving me aside. She runs her hands over Eleira's face, then rubs them together and brings them to her chest. She presses them into the spot her beam struck.

"What are you doing?" I scream. Anguish takes me.

"Saving her life," she tells me. Under her breath Morgan utters the words of a new spell. Another glow surrounds her hands, tinged red this time.

Mother pushes that energy into Eleira's body.

The girl's eyes pop open, and she gasps. She coughs— dark blood spurts out.

Then her eyelids close and she drops back to the floor.

"Delightful," Mother mutters, wiping her hands clean of the mix of blood and phlegm. She takes instant control of the situation. "Raul, you take her to the infirmary. No—take her to my rooms in the castle. They're closer to the blood banks, and she will need a near-endless supply if she is to recover."

"*If?*" I demand. "*If?*"

Phillip speaks. I was so focused on Eleira I didn't even notice him approach. "What happened to her? Why did she throw herself in the way?"

"She was possessed," Mother says calmly. She stands up, and glares at my brother. "You, my son, made a grave mistake when you brought out that book."

Phillip has the grace to look crestfallen.

"I might expect such rash behavior from James, or even Raul," she continues. "*Not*, however, out of you. I know it comes from your reawakened instincts. Learn to control them! Next time you do something like this, you will be properly punished."

I cradle Eleira in my arms. Her breathing is so shallow it's terrifying. "Forget about him!" I say. "Tell me, what's going to happen to her? What do you mean, 'possessed?'"

"And what was that thing from the book?" Phillip adds.

"I mean just what I said, Raul," Mother says stiffly. "Somebody, or something, took control of Eleira's mind and made her do what you witnessed."

"How?" I gasp.

"Being a witch makes her vulnerable. I should have taught her to shield herself. But with The Haven sealed off, I did not think she'd be under threat. At least, not so soon…"

She turns to Phillip. "That *thing,* son dearest, is called a Narwhark. I'd have thought with all of your constant meddling, all of your computer systems, all of your furtive interest in my affairs, you would have come across its mention before."

Phillip shakes his head. He looks shaken.

"Come now. You've only been looking at all things magic for twenty years!"

Again, Phillip shakes his head. He stares at his feet.

I think: *Phillip has an interest in magic?*

"A Narwhark is a type of demon," Mother explains. "It comes from the underworld—not the literal underworld, but a parallel dimension existing on a plane beneath ours. Narwharks are nasty, nasty things. They crave only death and destruction. The world is porous, you see, and at certain places there is an overlap between the planes. That overlap allows portals to be made between dimensions. Some say that is the key to discovering the true origin of vampires and witches alike."

Mother walks back to pick up her staff. "But now is not the time for a history lesson. All you need to know is that the first witches had a true purpose—they sought to eliminate all such demons from the world. The different clans banded together and succeeded in closing the portals that let such creatures into the world. When that was done, they turned their attention to other things.

"Some witches, however, were not fully committed to the cause. Some witches *rebelled,* because they saw the closing of the portals as a great opportunity lost. To have access to other worlds, to new realities, to learn their secrets… it was not a gift to be discarded so rashly."

"You were one of them," Phillip breathes. "Weren't you?"

"No. This was long before my time. I always have, however, shared their opinion. So, when I was given the Gift of Immortality, I took it upon myself to gather scraps of anything the dissenting witches left behind. I took it upon myself to collect as many artifacts as I could that were linked in any way to sorcery."

"And what did you discover?" I ask.

"The ancient witches were not able to sever the connections between worlds completely. A few, they eliminated... but most, they simply masked. They did not have the raw strength required to close the portals.

"The masking spells, however, had to be maintained. So they created objects called torrials that did exactly that. But the dissenting witches... they also created objects of power. A counter to the torrials, called contra' torrials, are used to *summon* creatures out from other worlds.

"Using a contra' torrial requires *blood magic*. The sort that you activated when you let Eleira's blood drip onto this book."

Phillip has gone an even paler shade of white. "I had no idea."

"Clearly." Mother looks to me. "Now get Eleira to my rooms. Hurry. Don't let any others see you—you don't know what they might attempt if they saw Eleira like this."

270

"Oh, I have a very good idea," I say darkly.

*I also know, that until Eleira wakes, I won't leave her side...
and the other vampires would be fools to try anything against
me.*

Chapter Thirty-Eight

SMITHSON

"There's been a complication," my Queen informs me.

I stand with my back rigid and my arms clasped behind me. I show none of the discomfort I feel at being summoned *personally* by the Queen so soon after my little talk with April. "Yes?"

"A demon has been summoned. It's loose in The Haven now."

I blink, caught completely off-guard. "A demon?"

"A Narwhark, to be precise." She peers at me. "You have experience with those, don't you? In your... previous life?"

"You mean my time with The Order."

"When you hunted down clan after clan of witches, yes," she says. Her voice is flat, emotionless. "When you burned so many of my sisters."

"I put all that behind me the day you turned me into a creature of the night," I vow. I go to one knee. "I am eternally grateful for the gifts you have given me."

272

"Hmm," she considers. "Charming. Now get up. I don't like to see the Captain Commander of my guard groveling."

I hide my scowl and rise. "I've... only heard rumours of demons, my Queen. The Order never considered them anything more than folk stories. Meant to frighten children and old folk. Not to be taken seriously."

"Then you don't know about the role witches played in cleansing the world of such demons?"

I shake my head.

"Interesting. Perhaps if you had, you wouldn't have persecuted us so."

"That was a long time ago," I say. "I know who I am now. If you brought me here to question my loyalty—"

She smiles a grim smile. "Whatever would give me reason to do something like that? You're not feeling *guilty* over something, are you?"

"I have nothing to feel guilty for," I lie.

"So you say, so you say." She sighs and sits. "Demons are real. The Narwhark is real. And it's loose in The Haven."

"What do you want me to do?"

"Keep order amongst the vampires. The Narwhark is unpredictable. It is much like us—a predator. But it kills without discretion. It's wounded now and hiding. A search would be useless. Even our vampire capacities won't help find it. Only a powerful witch has any chance of stopping it."

"So it falls onto you."

"It does. But we have to wait for it to reveal itself. In a few days it will go for the humans. They are weaker, there are more of them, and they make for vulnerable prey."

"You want me to protect them?"

"Oh, no." Her eyes shine. "All I want is for you to be vigilant. When the Narwhark strikes, I will be the first person you inform. But—" she raises a finger, "—knowledge of the demon is not to leave this room. Only you and I and my two sons know of its existence. That's how I want things to stay. There is no use causing a panic."

Yes, I think. *Especially after you've trapped all your subjects inside.*

Chapter Thirty-Nine

RAUL

I sit by Eleira's bedside, watching her sleeping form.

She looks so beautiful asleep, so very peaceful. Her chest rises and falls in smooth, soft breaths. They seem delicate rather than strained, nurturing rather than concerning. Her hair falls around her face like a darkened halo, and I'm struck by the symbolism of it.

She looks like a fallen angel.

I catch my thoughts and stop them from going down that path. There are no angels in The Haven. Only murderers and slaves. Only beings of the night and our human captives.

"How is she?" Mother's cool voice sounds from beyond me. It's completely dispassionate.

"Same as she was an hour ago," I say. "And the hour before that, and the day before that, and…"

I trail off. No matter how peaceful she looks, Eleira is fighting for her life right now.

I take her hand in mine. Once again, I've failed to protect her.

"You sound so forlorn." Mother stops beside me and draws a hand through my hair. I stiffen at the unwanted display of affection. "Don't worry. She'll wake. She's just as important to me as she is to you, you know."

"Yes, but for entirely different reasons," I say under my breath. I turn my head to Mother and glare at her. "You're going to *use* Eleira."

"I need her for her powers, yes. As do you. As do any who want The Haven to prosper."

A pillar of anger comes to life inside me. "You call *this* prosperity?" I demand. "Your subjects are frightened. The vampires are running weak. You keep our humans trapped in an age that ended centuries ago!"

"All the easier to keep them meek." Her hand stops in my hair and she makes a fist, forcing me to look up. "You know how much trouble they can cause if they are not. And they are truly only here for one purpose. To supply our banks with blood. To give sacrifice for The Hunt."

I jerk away from her. "When Eleira rules..." I begin.

Mother laughs. "That is a long time coming. I assure you of that. You think, after six-hundred years, I would relinquish control so easily? So quickly? Eleira will be groomed for the throne, and shaped into a ruler of *my* liking. The succession will not happen overnight. Transforming her before her eighteenth birthday was important. Finding her, making her a vampire, exposing her to us and ensuring she was the right one... all of those were objectives with a deadline. Now that she's here? We have years. We have decades."

"Is that why you were so reckless when you attacked the demon?" I scowl. "The blast could have killed Eleira."

"No," Mother says. "It could not have. I aimed straight for the Narwhark. How was I to know the fool girl would leap in the way?"

My lips form a thin line of displeasure. I have to concede that Mother is right.

It still doesn't make me feel better about any of this.

"So how did she come to be possessed? Was it the book, the contra' torrial that took over?"

"No. The contra' torrial is merely a device. To take possession of another's mind requires conscious will. It was done by someone who thinks herself extraordinarily clever. Someone who, in reality, is *not*."

I look at Mother. "You sound like you have a suspect."

"Yes," she says. "The woman you brought with you from The Crypts.

"Victoria."

Chapter Forty

JAMES

I come to with a horrible pounding between my ears.

Groggy, I push myself up. As soon as I do, I gasp—pain envelops my body.

I groan and roll over to stare up at the sky. The stars are mocking me in their serenity. I've never hated the night as much as I do now.

I think back to everything that brought me here... and all that went wrong.

As soon as Father said I'd be made prisoner, a dozen of his guards ran out and apprehended me. I was dragged through the many twisting hallways of The Crypts and brought through the mess hall, where Dagan and the others were taking in their victory feast.

The scent of blood was strong all around me. All the vampires had enormous goblets of the stuff. It smelled fresh, vital, and impossibly enticing. My body ached for just one drop, after all that I'd been through.

But—such a mercy was not in the cards.

I was chained to a massive spit. A fire was started beneath me. The heat it gave off was terrible. Then, I had to endure hour after agonizing hour as the vampires of my former company came up to operate the mechanism. They spun me over the flames and laughed and laughed as my skin burned and I screamed.

Again, the chains were silver. Obviously. They were silver so that I couldn't get out.

When the first round of torture was done, I was cut free and dropped straight into the fire. The agony that took me then was indescribable. My skin, already blistering, charred and burned in the flames. I leapt out as fast as my weakened muscles would let me.

I was doused by a bucket of... not water, but piss.

I still shudder at the memory.

With that ordeal over, the guards grabbed my arms again and hauled me away. I had not the energy to fight. Even though I was unchained, I was exhausted, so my feet dragged against the floor all the way up to the open-roofed tower cell.

That's where I lie now. Stinking of piss and trapped on a little island jutting out from the earth.

I have to admit, in my depravity, that this type of torture

cell is brilliant. It's a single round pillar poking out from the ground. It's surrounded by a moat—a moat filled with molten silver.

The heat that keeps the metal liquefied is immense. I feel it even now. It combines with the waves given off by the silver and coalesces into a double-whammy of agony. Above me, high above me, a long, long vertical slit is cut into the ceiling. When the sun rises in the day...

The rays will shine straight down upon me.

The anticipation of that happening? It's the worst. Worse than the molten silver, worse than the heat, worse than being doused with that foul, despicable, stinking yellow excreta.

I curl up into myself in the middle of the tiny space I have been allocated. I try not to shake.

James, I think. *How far you have fallen.*

Chapter Forty-One

RAUL

Mother and I stop outside of the room Victoria is being held in.

She looks at me. "Hold your tongue," she warns. "I know you're angry. But you have to let me take care of this."

Oh, you have no idea how angry I am, I think.

The only reason I left Eleira is because Phillip agreed to watch over her while I joined Mother in this confrontation.

The Queen opens the door. Victoria—short, tanned, blonde—raises her head and blinks at us, almost lazily.

Hatred such as I have never known it rages inside me.

"You." I snarl. "You nearly *killed*—"

"Hush." Mother cuts me off. She places a hand on my arm. "I said I would deal with this. Remember?"

I grunt and grudgingly step back.

"Trouble in the Soren family?" Victoria offers sweetly. "I wonder what ever could be the cause?"

She gives a little smile.

"All right, witch," Mother says. "Time to test your true loyalty."

"Oh, how boring," Victoria sighs. "Is that what you're here for? I would have thought after all these days of keeping me locked up you would have come with something more… interesting."

"Close the door," Mother tells me. I move to comply.

"Now," she says, seating herself across from Victoria. "I'm going to ask you a question. You'll give me an answer. If I think you're lying…" casually, Mother lets a silver whip drop from her sleeve, "…well, we'll find out just how resilient you are to the effects of the metal once your powers have been stripped away, hmm?"

That's my cue. I fly across the room and jab a syringe into Victoria's neck. I press down and deliver the serum before she screams and throws me off.

I push myself upright. Victoria hasn't moved. Her mouth works, but no words come out. She presses a hand to her neck, takes it away, looks at it, and cries out in shock. "You've poisoned me!"

"No, no, no," Morgan says. I join her across from Victoria. "The effects of the serum are temporary. They will wear off in a matter of hours. But, as I've warned you before… I know ways of making them permanent."

Victoria scowls at us with undisguised hatred. I feel her

vampire strength ebb away. Bit by bit, it drains out of her like water from a leaky hose.

Mother adjusts her skirts. "Now we wait," she informs Victoria, "for you to lose the power you've stolen from The Ancient."

"They were given to me by right!" Victoria hisses. She bares her fangs and suddenly extends her claws.

"Nuh-uh," Mother warns, all too casually. "Fight us now, and you would not like the outcome. *That,* I promise you."

Victoria glares at me, then at the Queen. I feel her sizing us up in her mind.

I also feel her growing weaker and weaker as the serum spreads.

Her body sags with resignation. "Fine," she says. "Ask me what you want to know."

"You have a connection with Eleira," Mother says. "I felt it before, so don't deny it."

Victoria shrugs. "What of it?"

"You used it to take control of her and open the *Book of the Dead,*" I snarl, unable to keep myself composed any longer. "You *possessed* her!"

Victoria looks at me... and laughs.

"The 'Book of the Dead?'" she asks. "What, like the parchment from ancient Egypt? What on earth would I have to do with—"

Mother snaps the whip forward. It catches Victoria just beneath the eye. A line of blood forms on her face.

"Lie again," Mother says, "and the next lash will take out one of those pretty blue eyes of yours."

Victoria scowls at the Queen.

I step forward, and demand, "Well?"

"Fine, so I know of the book," Victoria spits. "Anyone who's studied magic does."

"But who would give you the education for that?" Mother wonders. "The Spark you possess is miniscule. It's barely discernible. Who would waste her time teaching *you* magic?"

Victoria dabs at her bleeding face. Her strength has been suppressed so much by the poison that I doubt she would even be a threat to Phillip—*before* he broke his human blood fast.

"That's the question I asked myself the entire time," she answers sourly. "My 'education' was a farce. The one tutoring me knew I could never amount to anything. But she made me try, anyway. I can't tell you how many days I spent bashing my head against the wall, trying to understand what was wrong with me, why my spells never amounted to anything more than a pathetic fizzle, nothing more than a dull blue glow."

She raises a hand in front of her face and cups her

fingers. Her eyebrows knot together. She starts to focus. Her eyes concentrate on her fingertips. She focuses, and focuses, and focuses...

A tiny blue flame leaps from her forefinger. It disappears before I can even blink.

Victoria slumps back, clearly drained.

"There," she tells us. "That's all I can do."

"Oh, child," Mother smiles at her sadly. "How difficult it must have been for you."

"Don't mock me!" She fires backs. "It was my twin they wanted, my twin who died. My twin who would have made a great witch. But my teacher was too frightened to tell *your* husband, the King of The Crypts, that he had the wrong girl. After it all ended, I learned *that* was the true reason she persisted in my education. *That* was why I was made to suffer constant humiliation at her hand."

"And your teacher," Mother says. "Would I know her? What is her name?"

"She's dead now, so not much use to you." Victoria sighs. "She was a human caught by the vampires. Her Spark wasn't very strong, either. It was much too weak for her to be useful to the King in any capacity other than as my tutor. She belonged to one of those off-shore witch clans, the ones who cowered before the might of the original Five Families."

Mother considers this. "I know how difficult the training can be."

I stare at her. Is that actual *sympathy* in her voice?

"But I also know you are not easily broken, or dissuaded from what you want. As you've so aptly demonstrated in your time here. So the next thing I want to know..." she stands up and walks toward Victoria, "...is exactly how one so weak as you took possession of Eleira's mind. You have the connection with her. You can't hide that."

"From you, there's not much I *can* hide," she grumbles. "But if you're looking for someone to blame, you can look elsewhere. Eleira closed her mind to me the moment she discovered the link. I have not been able to communicate with her since. And that—" Victoria shoots a defiant look at Mother, then at me, "—is the absolute truth. Do with it what you will."

She draws her shoulders back and exposes her body. "Whip me, hurt me, I don't care. There's nothing more you will find."

An icy silence falls upon the room as Mother considers this. Then, in a flurry of skirts she spins around and storms out the room.

"And you?" Victoria asks, turning to face me. "What will you do now that you have me alone, and your precious *Eleira* is injured?" She fills the other girl's name with so much hate and spite and jealousy that it's a wonder she managed to keep her features so calm.

"Less than you deserve," I say. "But more than I should be capable of." I toss her a tiny vial of blood. "Drink that. It'll heal the cut on your face, lest it become permanent while your powers are subdued."

She catches the vial… and with a dismissive sneer, chucks it against the far wall.

It cracks and splatters.

"This is a battle mark," she tells me, chin raised. "And I'll wear the scar proudly forever."

"Suit yourself," I say, and follow Mother out the room.

Chapter Forty-Two

JAMES

I'm pulled out of an uneasy slumber by a force bidding me to rise.

I blink, half in a daze. I look up at the opening above me. The evening sunset filters in. It's nearly dusk.

I've survived the worst.

All my skin feels brittle. One wrong move, and I'm afraid it'll crack like the sides of an encrusted sand castle. It's dry, so horribly dry, that I half-expect it to flake off when I try to stand.

"RISE, JAMES." The Voice of The Ancient echoes in my head. In a flash I'm upright, my muscles moving before my mind can even issue the command.

The blood rushes from my head from getting up so fast. I stagger forward, woozy. I only catch myself at the last possible moment to stop from throttling down into the lake of silver below.

"Over here, son," Father calls. "Behind you."

I turn around and face the man responsible for my pitiful

state.

He smiles at me. It's the sickening, crude smile of one completely in control. He's changed into yet another one of his garish robes, replete with all the rings and jewels and bracelets that speak of his enormous wealth.

Beside him stands The Ancient.

My hands form into fists as hatred boils inside of me. Hatred, directed at both of them for subjecting me to *this*, for making me so wretched, so pathetic, so damn weak.

For torturing me, when I should be the one standing beside Father at the throne.

I force back a smile, however, that is as false as false can be. "Finally took an interest in your son's condition, have you?" I ask. "The chamber is comfortable enough. You'll have to do something about the gaping hole in the ceiling, though. Any lesser vampires might assume it's been placed there for a reason. I doubt you'll have many guests willing to return."

"Already the comedian," Father mutters. He kicks the drawbridge across. It crashes down beside me. He beckons me to come.

I cast one look at the roiling silver below me, suppress a shudder, and walk to him with as much grace as I can muster.

As soon as I'm with them The Ancient grabs my arms. I know better than to resist as he forces them behind my back.

"You've gained yourself a private audience with your King," Father informs me.

"How fortunate," I deadpan.

We walk through the myriad of twisting hallways to arrive in the throne room. Once we're through the doors The Ancient lets go and positions himself by the only exit. Father sits on the throne.

There is a small, round table with a golden pitcher on it. Beside it is an empty cup.

The moment I enter the room I smell the fresh blood inside. I salivate. It's been so very long since I've fed.

Farther motions to it. "Drink," he tells me. "I want you at full capacity before I ask my questions of you."

And what questions are those? I wonder.

I pick up the pitcher and pour myself a cup. I bring the blood to my lips and take a deep breath.

"This hasn't been poisoned, has it?" I quip.

Father regards me dryly. "Don't push it."

I look back at The Ancient. "A drop of your blood in here would make all the difference in the world, you know."

The older vampire stares at me and makes no move to respond.

"I guess not," I mutter, and down the cup in a single gulp.

As soon as the blood passes my throat I feel the strength returning to my body. My skin begins to heal. My thoughts sharpen. The awful pounding in my head goes away.

"Better?" Father asks.

"Much," I respond. I tilt the cup at him in cheers. "Thank you."

"So you can be grateful, after all," he says. "When you think it will help you."

"Honestly?" I put the cup down. I debate pouring myself another—I desperately want more—but I need to show Father that I possess *restraint.* "The way I see it, I'm entirely at your mercy. So why bother fighting? It's only you I need to convince that we're both on the same side."

"Yes," Father murmurs. "We'll see about that. Beatrice considers you a most valuable asset. She's convinced me to give you another chance."

That must be the woman. "Smart of her to recognize my merits," I say. "Does that mean no more torture?"

"For now," Father concedes. "If you cooperate. My friend has a question for you."

"I CANNOT ENTER THE HAVEN," The Ancient roars in my head. His voice is full of rage even though not a flicker of expression shows on his face. *"WHY?"*

I look at him and then back at Father. I hang on my heel

as I consider.

"Do you…" I point in a flowery gesture at the King, "… can you hear him in your head, also? Because I think this would all be much easier if we simply use our tongues."

"Don't deflect the question," Father grows. "Tell him what you know."

"What I know? Why, I think it obvious. *You*," I look at The Ancient, "cannot enter The Haven because you're all the way over here…" I make a grand, sweeping gesture with my hand, as if over an atlas, "…and my former coven is far, far away, on the other side of the world. In *North America*."

An invisible force lashes out from The Ancient and strikes me in the chest. I go flying back and crash into a pillar. The room shakes from impact.

"Not," Father warns, "a good time to make jokes."

"I'm not bloody joking," I growl. "He asked me why he can't enter The Haven. I answered. Because he's too far away!"

"That's not the type of entry he means," Father says.

"Well, unlike your precious servant, I'm not a mind reader!" I bellow. The white-hot pillar of anger raging inside me flares and burns. "If you want proper answers, ask the right damn questions!"

"He means," Father says, "that he cannot penetrate any of the minds of the vampires, or humans, inside. We want to know why."

I glare at them both. "That's what you brought me here for? What gave you any indication that *I* would have any idea?"

"Your Mother trusted you. You would know her secrets."

"Sorry to disappoint you, but last time I saw *my Mother*," I snarl the words, "she cast me into an underground cell and sentenced me to eternity without blood. Somehow, I doubt she would impart any of her secrets upon me."

"So you're telling me that I was right, and Beatrice was wrong. You are, for lack of a better term, utterly useless." He beckons The Ancient forth. "Bring my son back to where we found him."

"Whoa, whoa," I say, holding up my arms. "Let's not be hasty here."

"Give me one good reason why."

"Because even if I don't know the answer to what you're asking me, there are things I *do*. Such as..." I step toward him, "...where you'd strike first if you were to mount a successful attack."

Father's eyes suddenly glitter with greed. "Go on," he says.

Chapter Forty-Three

Visions of death, of darkness, of destruction haunt my dreams:

I see The Haven burning. Great fires engulf not just the human settlement, but also all the trees. Villagers run from the blazes screaming. Vampires shriek as they burn, caught helplessly in the licking flames.

A small shadow, the size of a skunk or racoon, darts from place to place. Wherever it goes it leaves a trail of blood. And bodies. It strikes, and bodies fall, but all I see are their darkened outlines. Humans? Vampires? There's no way to tell.

But I feel their fear acutely.

The ground shakes, the start of a great earthquake.

Disaster has struck! Disaster! *The thought is not my own, but it echoes in my head.* Disaster, disaster, disaster...!

The castle. I must *go to the castle. I exist only as a spirit here, and I fly through the air, yet when I arrive, the whole structure is shrouded in black. It's a black that's deeper than night, a black that is infinite, a black that not even my vampire vision can pierce.*

And flowing out from it, I feel such hatred, such menace and vitriol and malevolence and greed, and that echoing voice continues to wail in my head, crying out disaster, disaster, disaster!

The Haven is in upheaval, and somehow I know, *deep in my bones, that it's my fault.*

I come to with a strangled gasp. My throat is dry, parched. My body is soaked with sweat, and the moisture stains my night shift, the sheets...

Somebody is by my side in an instant. As my vision clears I see it's Raul. Relief courses through me. He hands me a glass of blood, and says, "Drink."

I grab it from him and eagerly place it to my lips. I inhale the whole thing in great, jealous swallows. When it's gone, I immediately want more. Raul already has a second glass waiting for me.

I down that, too. With the blood in me I feel a little bit stronger. I take a moment to look around the unfamiliar room.

I'm in an enormous white bed. The sheets are white, the pillows are white, my shift is white—everything is white. The room is circular and sparsely decorated, but what furniture I see is finely made.

"We're in Mother's guest quarters," Raul says, as if reading my mind. "You've been here nearly three days."

Alarm ripples through me. *Three* days? No wonder I'm ravenous. I bring a hand to my forehead. All sorts of foreign aches and pains envelop my body.

"What… happened?" I manage to ask. My thoughts are slow and murky. My memories aren't much better. "I remember you… and Phillip… and that *book*."

I break off with a shudder. The moment I thought of the book my mind nearly shut down.

Raul takes my hand. "Do you remember anything else?"

I shake my head. "No. Why do I feel so… weak?"

"Three days is a long time to be unconscious for a vampire. It's unheard of for one as recently transformed as you—for one who needs so much blood."

"What happened?" I ask again.

"You were… *possessed*."

I gasp. "What?"

"When Phillip poured human blood into the pages of the book, and added a drop of yours to it—somebody took control of your mind."

"Victoria!" I exclaim. Panic sears through me and a

confession tumbles out of me in a rush of words. "I haven't told you this, but she and I have a link, she can speak to me telepathically. She did it on the plane here. I kept it to myself, but I should have told you, I'm sorry, but it—"

"No." He cuts me off. "It wasn't Victoria. Mother and I confronted her. It was somebody—or perhaps some*thing*—else."

He picks up my hand when he sees my fright. "Do you truly remember nothing of what happened?"

I strain my brain and try to think. But all my memories are distant and blurred. It shames me, so I look away and softly whisper, "No."

"You're a witch," he says patiently. "And also a vampire. Because you have the Spark, because you can do magic, you are exposed in ways I don't understand." He hesitates. "I shouldn't be the one telling you this."

"Then who should?"

"Me."

Raul and I both look up to see Morgan enter the room.

"I heard you conversing," she continues. "It's about time you woke up." She comes to the bed and frowns down at me. "You look weak."

I feel weak, I think.

Raul scowls at his Mother. "She's been without blood for

three days! What do you expect, after you hit her with that blast of magic?"

Morgan hisses. "You say that as if it's my fault. The fool girl leapt in the way. If she hadn't, the Narwhark would have been killed. Instead, we have to worry about it ravaging The Haven." She shakes her head in disgust. "At least *that* hasn't started yet."

"Wait, what?" I manage. "I was struck by magic? Why? And what's a... *Narwhark*?"

I butcher the unfamiliar word.

Morgan brushes her son aside and settles on the side of the bed. "A Narwhark is a type of demon," she tells me calmly, "that you called forth from *The Book of the Dead*."

"No!" I protest. But then a glimmer of a memory shows itself in my mind:

Magic flowing through me, magic being channeled to open a portal and let loose one of the damned into this world...

"Ah," Morgan's eyes light up. "You remember."

I shake my head to dispel the frightening imagery. "No," I say. "Not in full."

"That's understandable," Morgan sympathizes. "When you go through a traumatic event like that, your mind can curl up into itself and blank out the painful memories. It's a method of self-preservation for your psyche. *You* do not want

298

to be responsible for what you did. So you pretend not to know."

"Mother…" Raul growls a warning. "This is not the time to scare Eleira more."

"Eleira is not some delicate flower in constant need of your protection!" Morgan snaps. "She is both a powerful witch and a powerful vampire."

"I'm not denying that," Raul says stiffly. "I just think we should give her time to come to grips with the situation."

"We don't *have* time," his Mother counters. "We need to find out who took control of her mind, and how they did it. Eleira is the only one who can help us discover that."

"Let her feed in full, at least," he says. "Give her a *few* minutes to collect herself."

My heart warms at how Raul is standing up for me. But I need to show my strength—to prove I can handle this on my own.

I place a hand on his arm and whisper, "It's okay."

He doesn't look entirely satisfied, but he relents.

I face the Queen. "Tell me what happened," I say.

"You know parts of it. Here's what I gathered. When your blood activated the book, you became like a beacon. Every witch within a hundred leagues would have sensed your presence. It's how I found you in time. It is your affinity for magic that made the possession possible."

"But I don't *feel* an affinity."

"No, but you have it nonetheless. Even if you don't know how to control it, it's there. It manifests itself in The Spark. Your body and mind are both open to the magic in ways that make you uniquely susceptible to others' malevolence.

"That's why you need me—a teacher to guide you. You need somebody who can show you how to protect yourself. You need somebody who will stop you from *killing* yourself by wielding too much magic, too soon.

"I was wrong to give you three days. I should have commanded you to begin lessons immediately. But I wanted to give you the illusion of choice. If you came of your own volition, if you yourself saw the *need* for it, our relationship would be strengthened. You would be willing instead of hesitant. Trusting instead of suspicious.

"But now the choice has been made for us." The Queen holds out her hand. "Do you remember what else I asked of you?"

Slowly, I nod. My chest constricts as I pull Raul's ring off and place it in Morgan's hand.

"What are you doing?" he exclaims.

"I'm sorry," I say in a small voice. I don't meet his eyes.

"Excellent," Morgan says. She tucks it away in a fold of her dress. "The first lesson, which you will be given now, is how to shield your mind so you cannot be made vulnerable again."

"Okay." I nod and feel a growing determination. I push myself higher in the bed. "Tell me what to do."

"*You* need do nothing... except open yourself to me."

A faint blue-ish glow appears around the Queen's fingertips. All the hairs on the back of my neck stand up.

I feel the energy she is channeling in the air.

She raises both hands and brings them to my forehead. "Lean forward," she says. "I'm going to put a guarding spell on your mind."

Raul watches us both tensely.

I start to move—then stop. "A guarding spell?" I ask. "I thought you were going to teach *me* how to protect myself."

"That type of training will take weeks. For now, this spell will protect you. It'll form a link between you and me similar to what you experienced with Victoria. That will give me warning if anybody tries to take control of you again."

I look at her, and then at Raul. I'm having second thoughts.

Suddenly, I'm not sure how smart it is to let Morgan into my mind.

Especially if I don't know how far I can trust her.

"Come, Eleira," she says. "It'll be quick." She smiles in a serpentine way. "It won't hurt, if that's what you're afraid of."

"It will… link me… to you?" I ask.

"Yes, temporarily." Morgan clicks her tongue in exasperation. "This isn't a debate. We're losing time."

She grabs my head. I gasp as a torrent of energy floods into me. I feel a force descending upon my brain, almost like it's being shrink-wrapped. My eyes roll back and all I see are alternating flashes of white and blue.

"Don't fight me," Morgan hisses. "Let your mind go. Let me in!"

"I'm not fighting!" I grind my teeth together. The pressure inside my head builds. It feels like all my powers, all my strength, are being bundled up and pressed into each other, in a space much too small to hold any of them.

My body fights back, pushing *against* the shrink-wrap, *against* the pressure…

A sudden flash of light explodes from my body. Morgan and Raul are both knocked away. The furniture near me is shoved away, slamming against the walls. A vase smashes and breaks.

And I'm left panting, even more sweat soaking my skin, as the feeling in my head slowly returns to normal.

"That," Morgan hisses, picking herself up, "was *not* very

smart."

She launches herself at me, hands outstretched—

But Raul is quick. He knocks her aside, and they both crash to the floor.

"You will *not* harm her!" he says. "Eleira." He looks at me. "Are you all right?"

I nod my head shakily. "I... think so."

"What did you do to her?" Raul demands, pinning his mother to the ground.

The Queen makes no effort to rise. In fact, she seems to take a kind of perverse pleasure from being on the floor with him like that.

Raul grunts and picks himself up. Morgan does, too. Then she laughs.

"You think we're still on opposing sides, don't you, son?" She turns to me. "We're going to try that again. But this time, you will *not* resist."

Chapter Forty-Four

JAMES

For the fifth time I go over all the defences of The Haven.

"You were smart to get Riyu to cloak the vampires' abilities," I say. "Otherwise our scouts would have sensed you. The Queen might have slackened in her vigilance, but it doesn't mean she's blind. Wards around The Haven keep humans from finding it. There are also wild, savage beasts drawn to our borders." I smile, remembering the way I killed that wolf. "They shouldn't be a problem for any of you, however."

Father has called upon Dagan and a number of other vampires to hear me speak. From what I gather, these are all of Father's most senior military commanders.

The Ancient is present, too, listening from a far corner of the room.

"The wards work differently on vampires," I explain. "You know this. Dagan's party was close. Vampires can *feel* there is something beyond the barriers. But unless we know the exact way in, it's shielded to us."

"You know these ways?" Dagan asks, sharing a look with my Father.

"Of course."

The King nods. Dagan throws a large map on the table. "You recognize this?" he asks me.

My eyebrows go up. It's a perfect depiction of The Haven—from the inside and from the outside. The human village, the vampire treetop homes, the castle, the fields—all of it is there, just as I remember it.

Father sees my surprise and chuckles. "We *know* more than you think, son."

Something grates at me that I just wasted so much time talking about things they already know.

Dagan stabs a finger at the map. "These entrances. They are here, here, and here. Yes?"

"... Yes," I grudgingly answer.

Dagan peels the top layer off the map and reveals an intricate blueprint of the underground caverns. I marvel at the detail. There are passages showing that I didn't even know exist!

"If you have all this," I say, sensing a looming trap. "What need have you of me?"

"Patience, son." Father grips my shoulder in a vice-like grip. "That will be revealed in time."

305

Dagan traces a finger in a swooning line. "This is the outline of the river that brought you to us," he says. "It was so deep beneath the earth that the wards did not extend that far. But we cannot return that way. That entrance has been compromised because of our rescue of you."

"Yes, yes, that all makes sense," I say, growing impatient. "What of it?"

"It's not *structural* knowledge we seek," Logan says. "But knowledge of your Mother. Riyu—" he gestures toward the vampire, lost somewhere in the line of others, "—just got back from a solo expedition to The Haven. He says the wards have been fortified. He says that it is now impossible for anyone to penetrate them. The entrances are sealed."

"Sealed how?" I ask.

"Sealed as to be impregnable. But while the Queen is strong, she does not have the power to maintain the reinforced wards by herself. Someone is aiding her."

"You think it's Eleira?" I ask.

"No." Father walks across the table and pours himself a goblet of blood. My mouth salivates. I've been promised more, but haven't been given any since my initial feeding. "The girl is strong, but she does not have control of her powers. She would not be able to assist in this."

"Then what?" I ask.

"We believe," a melodic female says, "that Morgan is drawing upon an external fount of strength."

I spin around. Beatrice has just entered the room.

She continues.

"A torrial of some sort, I suspect. It gives her the ability to do what would otherwise require an entire coterie of witches."

"A coterie?" I ask, not following along.

"A group of seven, linked together in a circle to join their powers. Witches are selfish creatures, you see. It is not often that a coterie is formed. Only in times of great need..."

She trails off as she reaches the table. She runs a hand over my Father's arm.

He pulls her in for a deep and hungry kiss.

Who is this woman? I wonder. *And how does she know so much of witches?*

She looks at me after Logan lets her go. "Your Mother does not have six other witches in The Haven, does she?"

I snort. "Of course not."

Beatrice shrugs. "Then it's a torrial."

The King turns to me. "This is what we need you for. You've been there. You've served there. You *must* know the object that gives her such strength!"

307

I balk. "I'm no sorcerer," I fire back. "How on earth would I know?"

The Ancient moves from the wall. He crosses the space so fast it's like he didn't even bother with the distance in between.

He grips my neck, then shoves me into the table. *"YOU KNOW,"* he booms in my mind. *"BUT YOU RESIST."*

"No, no," I growl, anger seizing me again at being manhandled in front of Father and his most trusted vampires.

"Permit me to search his mind," The Ancient rasps, out loud, for all to hear. "I can find the answers you seek, my King."

Father considers. He looks at Beatrice.

She shakes her head.

"What he is proposing is a type of rape." Beatrice speaks softly, but her voice draws everyone's attention. "We will not resort to such tactics. Not yet."

Reluctantly, The Ancient lets me go. Father stares impassively at me.

How much influence does this woman have?

"Tell me, James," Beatrice flows toward me. "Last time you saw the Queen. Did anything in particular... stand out? Did she seem different or maybe changed, somehow?"

I remember the way Mother refused to look at me until

passing her sentence. *The same she's been for hundreds of years.*

"No," I say stiffly.

"Are you sure?" Beatrice's voice is sweet as honey and clear as running water. She tangles a hand in my hair, places her lips to my ear, and purrs, "Anything? Anything at all?"

My body reacts to her sensual proximity. I do my best to hide it. "No," I say.

"Such a shame," she whispers. "We were all hoping you'd be more use."

Suddenly she places a silver needle beneath my ear.

I go absolutely still.

"There is more than one way to kill a vampire," she tells me. "And more than one way to *torture* one."

All my attention is drawn to the needle. The rest of the assembly has gone absolutely silent.

"I've been experimenting lately. A stake through the heart, exposure to fire, all of those are known to kill, yes, but such methods are not very... exciting."

Beatrice presses her breasts into me, flaunting her femininity while toying with my life. "Yet this needle, stuck in the right spot on your neck... it would lead to a slow and agonizing death. A death which is drawn out for weeks. A death where hallucinations take you. A death that exposes you to the most heinous parts of your mind."

"You lie," I growl. Still, I do not move.

"Oh? Do you wish to test me?" She applies the tiniest bit more pressure. I go on my toes so she doesn't break skin.

"Thought not," she murmurs. "Now, tell us what you know—or risk igniting my displeasure."

"I told you everything," I grunt. "Why would I hold anything back?"

"So be it." Beatrice shrugs. "I guess you're not as much use to us as we first thought."

She looks at my Father for permission. He nods.

"Wait, wait, wait," I hiss. My mind grapples for something to tell them. "There was a—a staff! When Mother greeted me, she was using a walking staff. She's never had it before."

It's the most desperate attempt at giving useful information I know. But, to my surprise, Beatrice eases the needle's pressure.

"A staff?" she asks. "Interesting. Very interesting. What did it look like?"

"Waist high, made of some dark metal, don't know... I didn't pay attention to such things when *my life was on the line.*"

"As it is now," Beatrice reminds me. "Again."

Riyu, to my surprise, retrieves a book from the side and lays it flat on the table. Without speaking, he opens it to a particular page, and points.

My eyes go wide. "That's it!" I say. "That's the Queen's staff!"

Beatrice nods. She shares a look with Riyu. "We hoped it would be." She turns to my Father. "James is now ready to prove his loyalty to you."

A dangerous grin crosses the King's face.

"If you want to live," he tells me, "you will return to The Haven—and you will bring the staff back to us." His eyes shine with greed. "With a torrial of such strength in my command..."

"...You will rule the world," Beatrice finishes, breathless.

The vampires around me start to laugh.

Chapter Forty-Five

SMITHSON

"The guards have been told to keep a keen eye for unusual activity," I report. "So far, they've witnessed none. News of the Narwhark has been contained."

I'm alone with the Queen in the room. Her massive crystal throne looms high above us both.

I'm at the bottom of the stairs leading to the gaudy thing. She's perched on its edge.

She peers at her nails and affects a disinterested expression. "No less than I expected from you."

"The village is starting to take shape. The humans are working fast. Since your display in the caves, there have been no dissenters." I allow myself a smug grin. "Of course, my guards keep watch to help ensure things stay that way."

"Of course," the Queen echoes, sounding almost bored.

It rubs me the wrong way.

"Is there something wrong, my Queen? You asked for a status report. Things are going according to plan, ahead of schedule. The humans haven't even considered rebelling. The disquietude amongst your vampire population has simmered down. And—"

"Can I trust you, Smithson?" she interrupts. "Can I *really* trust you?"

I drop to one knee. "With your life," I swear. "I am forever your loyal subject."

"As you so often say," she murmurs.

She glides down the steps and stops right beside me. "Stand," she commands.

I do. Even though I'm taller than she is, she cuts an imposing figure.

"You know..." she traces a hand along my jaw. "I always thought you were exceedingly handsome."

I clear my throat and look around. "Is this appropriate?"

"There's no one here." She runs that hand down over my chest, over my torso. "This is *my* castle. Here as in all The Haven, my word is law."

"I do not doubt that," I say. Her wandering hand reaches my waist. She tugs me to her.

"I've been so lonely, Smithson," she says. "It's a hard life at the top. Your subjects are either scared or intimidated. That's the way it was to be. But now, even my own sons have abandoned me. James is gone. Raul and Phillip are both plotting against me. Andrey is dead. There are few left for me to rely on… few left for me to expose myself to.

"And besides," she brings her lips to my ear and finishes in a whisper, "I've seen the way you leer at me when you think my attention is turned. You want me, Smithson. Coincidentally…" her sharp teeth come out, and she nips my ear. "I want you, too."

Heat rises to my chest and my breathing becomes heavy. "You are a beautiful woman," I tell her.

She throws her head back and laughs. "The most glorious woman to live for centuries, I would think."

She grabs my hand and leads me to her private rooms. As she takes me to bed, the whole time, my prevailing thought is:

You are no match for the wife I lost because of you.

***

For hours after our tumble we just lie together, unspeaking. She is curled up on my chest, content as a happy cat.

My thoughts, on the other hand, are stormy.

I gave in to my desire without thought to the consequences. If word escapes of this affair, I'll have to deal with endless problems from the guards stationed under me. Not to mention even more friction between her sons and me.

"Be a dear and raise the blinds, would you?" she asks. "I wish to look into the night."

I get out of bed, wrapping the sheet around my body, and go to the window to pull the drapes open.

A gust of cold air sweeps into the room. I take a deep, invigorating breath.

"What do you see?" the Queen asks.

I look past the window frame. The stars are shining down over The Haven. From this high up, I see the lights from the village bleeding into the night. Beyond that, the vampire treetop quarters are also visible, peeking through the dense redwoods.

"It's quiet," I tell her. "All is still."

"How I wish it were more than an illusion." The Queen rises. She does not bother to cover herself as she walks across the room to the fireplace, where her staff is secure on a spectacular mantle.

She takes hold of it and comes to me. "It's beautiful outside, isn't it?"

"Not as beautiful as you, in the glow of the moon."

"Oh, you *charmer*." She laughs. "You've already had me in bed. I don't need to be showered by your compliments."

"They are true," I tell her, "coming without subterfuge or deception."

"How refreshing." She sighs. "If only I could believe you."

I turn back to the window.

"This won't last, you know," she says after a moment.

I look at her. "What won't? Us?"

She gives a small laugh and shakes her head. "You are welcome in my bed so long as you don't bore me. No, not us, Smithson. *This.*" She sweeps a hand out to take in the tranquil landscape. "After the attack that freed James, I thought more would come. That hasn't happened, yet… but it will."

"We'll be ready," I promise her. "The guard—"

"Is no use against a full-blown army," she cuts in harshly. "The only thing keeping us safe is the new wards I put up. But they will not stand forever. And I cannot remain cut off from the outside world. I've spent over six hundred years in this place. I yearn to be free."

"I… don't know what to tell you, my Queen." I am reluctant to step over any boundaries with her. One wrong move, one wrong word, and my entire position here could be compromised.

"Then listen," she says. "You know the covens in North America. You've been inside them. You have relations with their rulers."

"I—"

"Don't deny it. You were a wanderer for too long not to

have developed friendships, and not to have been privy to information. Besides, before, you were part of that terrible order. What was the name again? It started with a 'V'."

"The Vorcellian Order," I say stiffly. "And I vow, I've had no relations with them since being turned."

"Such a pity," she muses. "Some of the information they must have archived would be of great help to us. Whatever became of them, do you know?"

"The Order's powers dwindled until they became a fringe organization," I lie. "I stopped keeping tabs when it became obvious they lost their influence upon the world."

"Careful, Smithson," The Queen purrs. "You wouldn't want me to catch you trying to deceive me."

I turn to face her and stare deep into her eyes. "That is the absolute truth."

"Hmm." She looks away. "I have a task for you. I want you to leave The Haven and approach the five covens closest to us. Let them know of the attack mounted against us. Warn that the same can happen to them. Remind them how they do not possess even a tenth of the defenses that I maintain. And then... offer them sanctuary."

I spin on her. "What?"

"Sanctuary. Free passage. We need to increase our numbers. The Haven is strong, but I fear we are not as strong as The Crypts. If war is coming, we must be ready."

"You haven't opened The Haven to new vampires for hundreds of years," I say. "Your subjects will not be happy."

"You can't please everyone," she shrugs. "Besides…" she twists my nipple. "Last I checked, I still rule. And my word is still law."

Yes, I think. *But for how long?*

Chapter Forty-Six

RAUL

"Mother is bringing more vampires in!" I exclaim as I storm into Phillip's room. "She's opening up The Haven to other covens."

He jerks up. "What?"

"Smithson went out a week ago as her delegate. No wonder we haven't seen him for so long. Word just arrived that he is returning in three days."

"That means Mother will need to lift the wards," Phillip says. "That will leave us exposed!"

"It'll be controlled," I murmur. "But yes."

"Whoever broke James out... whoever was responsible for the Voice the humans heard... if they're watching, *that's* when they will strike."

"And with the wards the way they are," I say, "we are completely blind to what's happening on the Outside."

"She could be opening us up for a major attack."

"Mother claims she's taking precautions."

"Oh? And those are?"

I grunt. "Teaching Eleira magic. She wants two full witches to be on display when the other coven arrives."

"And Eleira's going along with it?"

"It's not," I say darkly, "like she's been given much of a choice."

Chapter Forty-Seven

ELEIRA

A row of marble busts stands far in front of me.

"Focus... and... *strike!*"

The Queen's command whips through me. I channel the energy gathered in my head, concentrate the flow out to my hands, and will a violent flare of magic forward.

Light bursts from my hands. It's blinding and comes with an enormous crash. The beam hits the marble bust... and fizzles out completely.

The bust is completely unmarked.

Morgan curses. "*Concentrate,* Eleira! You're all theatrics and no substance."

My arms sag down to my sides. My whole body feels like it's been through the wringer. This type of training has been exhausting.

We started the day after Morgan deemed me sufficiently healed. She took me down, deep underground, to a cold iron chamber that reminded me of a nuclear hideout. She said the iron would prevent any excess magic from leaking out and also protect me from any spells that might be directed at me from the outside.

We haven't yet uncovered who it was that took control of my mind.

"Maybe if you *told* me what I was doing wrong," I begin.

She gives a flippant laugh. "I would if I could. But magic is highly individual. What works for one witch might not work for the next. All I can do is have you *watch*, and make you mimic what I do."

On that note, she summons three quick beams of light. They burst from her fingertips. Each hits a bust square in the middle.

The marble statues go flying. They crash into the far walls and join the rubble already there from her previous demonstrations.

"You see?" She whirls on me. "I focused my power on the *attack*. Not on being showy with flashing lights and booming sounds. Subtlety is the key to all this."

"I thought you'd be teaching me *real* spells," I say. "Not how to destroy marble carvings!" I extend my claws. "I'm more dangerous as a vampire. At least that way, instinct tells me how to kill."

Even a week ago, that admission would have frightened me. Now? Well, I've more readily come to terms with my vampiric self than I could believe.

"These are the simplest types of spells," Morgan hisses. "All they take is a concentration of energy. You're not manipulating the magical forces. You're not weaving intricate patterns with an ethereal energy you cannot see. These provide the *base*. If you cannot do even that..."

Frustration bubbles up inside. I take aim at the pile of rubble and summon the inherent magical energies lashing through the air. They flow into me like a lightning rod. I have only the barest flicker of a second to concentrate it into a destructive beam like Morgan just did.

The spell flares from my fingertips—no light, no sound— and obliterates the cracked remains of one of the statues.

"Yes!" Morgan exclaims. "Yes, perfectly done, just like that!"

I stare in amazement. I hadn't expected that to come so easily. Especially not after all the failed attempts.

Morgan starts toward me. "You see, when you just *focus*, you have all it takes—"

She stops as a violent gust of wind whips her dress up.

She looks at me. "Did you do that?"

"No—"

I don't get to finish. At that moment a tornado starts up at the opposite end of the room. It sweeps up all the pieces of rubble and blows them into a raging vortex. They spit out of it one-by-one, crashing against the walls with enormous force.

I cry out and duck as one flies straight for my head. It skims so close, I feel my hair blow out by the tailwind.

Morgan grabs my arm. "We have to get out!" she screams. The tornado is flinging bits of rubble everywhere. Projectiles fly at us with deadly speed. "We—"

A huge piece of debris comes straight for us. Morgan casts a defensive spell. A glowing blue orb surrounds us. The jagged rock hits the edge and disintegrates, like a meteor striking earth's atmosphere.

"Come on!" Morgan shoves me to the door. Behind us the tornado rages on, darting across the floor like an angry caged animal.

The Queen pulls the door open and we stumble out. Just before she closes it, something catches my attention within.

In the middle of the floor, right beneath the point of the tornado, a black hole is opening.

"Morgan!" I scream. "Look at that!"

She sees what I'm pointing at and curses. The darkness spreads, like a blot of spilled ink across a page.

A jagged, crooked arm extends from the darkness. It's thin as a gnarled branch, and covered entirely in a sickly black slime. Its fingers grip the edge, and it pulls itself up.

One of the most horrendously misshapen creatures I've ever seen comes out. It has no eyes, only a wide, open mouth showing rows upon rows of sharp, gleaming white teeth. The teeth are completely at odds with the smooth, inky black of its wide and bulbous head.

A beam of light, a beam of power, shoots out from Morgan's hands. It hits the creature in the face.

It gives a vicious scream, high and loud, like a hissing, boiling pot of water. And then it—it pushes Morgan's attack back.

For a moment I'm stupefied. The creature not only repels the spell, it actually forces the beam back toward Morgan.

"Don't just stand there. Help me!" the Queen commands.

I try to focus and cast another spell but my attention is shot. I can't look away from the awful creature. I feel almost a... a kinship toward it. Like it's a part of me, like it's mine, like I'm responsible for it.

"*No*," I snarl, and throw myself at Morgan to stop her attack.

The move takes her by surprise. I crash into her and we both go to the floor. The protective spell she cast winks out. The wind from the tornado howls around us. A menacing force radiates out from that creature, and I feel its triumph as keenly as if it were my own.

"Stupid girl!" Morgan screams. "You've doomed us, you've—"

She doesn't get to finish. Because at that moment, a blurred shape moves from beyond us and slams the door to the iron bunker closed.

The magic storming inside the room immediately cuts off. I come to myself, realize what I am doing—I gasp and scramble off the Queen.

She dives for her staff, which I've inadvertently knocked away. With it in her hands, she mutters a powerful spell. It surrounds the iron shell of the bunker. Morgan's incantation grows louder as she draws on as much of the latent magic around us as possible.

There's a loud crash like a thunderbolt. It's accompanied by a massive explosion of blinding light. The whole underground caverns trembles.

When I open my eyes the bunker is gone. Only the faintest bit of ash remains on the ground where it once was.

Morgan is leaning against her staff, gasping for breath. I'm struck dumb in momentary shock. I look at the third member of our company, and realize that it's Smithson.

He was the one who had slammed the door.

Morgan catches her breath and turns on me. She looks more vindictive than I've ever seen her.

I take a trembling step away.

"So it's true," she says finally. "I only had a suspicion before. But this confirms it."

Her voice is laced with deadly potency. "What's true?" I whisper.

"It is as I feared." She takes one more step toward me, holding out her staff. "Your Spark has been tainted in your youth. You are a dark witch."

And then she strikes the staff against the ground, and a blistering pain explodes in my head. I cry out and fall to the floor. But before I even hit it, silver chains lash out from Morgan and bind me tight.

Chapter Forty-Eight

JAMES

"We have a way in." Beatrice's voice brings me from my uneasy slumber. "It's time to prove your loyalty to your King."

I look at her through the bars of my holding cell. "Father sends you," I say. My voice is full of disdain.

"Do you have trouble taking orders from a woman?"

"When I don't know who that woman is, or where her loyalties lie? Yes, I'd say it's a daunting prospect."

She laughs. "Look around you, James. Look at where you are. Consider your position. You have no friends in The Crypts. You are only alive because of the mercy of your Father... and the trust he shows in me."

"So I owe my life to you, is that what you're saying?"

Beatrice comes closer to the bars. Her face looks hollow, but at the same time hauntingly beautiful, as the shadows dance across it.

"That, my darling, is exactly what I'm saying."

I pick myself up. "What will you have me do?"

"A delegation from a neighbouring coven is being led into The Haven in three days. They are your ticket in."

"Impossible," I sneer. "The Haven has not opened its doors to any of its neighbors in hundreds of years. Whatever information you have is wrong. Mother would never risk it."

"Desperate times…" Beatrice says. She finishes with a shrug. "You know how it is. Things change, James. The world will pass you by if you are not watchful."

"Fine," I grunt. "I believe you. Tell me what I have to do."

Chapter Forty-Nine

RAUL

"You did *WHAT*?" I demand, my anger flaring.

No—the emotions I feel are worse than anger. Much, much worse. They're a poisonous mix of hatred and disbelief and rage and above all... Horror. Utter terror.

Tinged with helplessness.

"Eleira displayed characteristics that make her a danger to The Haven. To the vampires, to the humans, to our entire way of life. Until we can be sure of her..." Mother pauses, "... stability? She will remain in the silver cell."

I can't believe it. My whole world feels like it's come crashing down on itself.

"I will *not* let you keep her there," I growl, stalking up to her. "This is your fault! You were supposed to be teaching! Not abandoning her when things became rough."

"Rough? You dare call what I witnessed *rough?*" Mother's voice goes up. "My son, you were not there. She is a *dark* witch. Her Spark has been corrupted. She opened a portal to the underworld. Something much worse than a Narwhark tried to climb out. Only through Smithson's quick thinking were Eleira and I able to escape with our lives. Only because of him I was able to act fast enough to banish the horrendous creature before it could devastate our lands."

"If her Spark has been corrupted," I say softly, "*un*corrupt it." I take a menacing step to the Queen. "If—"

"That's far enough," Smithson tells me, coolly placing a hand on my shoulder.

I glare at him. Full of spite, full of venom, full of hatred, I glare. If it were just Mother and me here, perhaps I could make her see reason. But no, she had to have the Captain Commander of her guard with her.

"That's all right," Mother coos. "He's just upset his precious girl is not who she pretends to be."

"You say that as if it's her fault!" I explode.

"Of course it's her fault," the Queen contests. "She's had exposure to magic at some point before she got to us. It tainted her mind—the part of her being responsible for controlling the elemental forces that give right to magical ability. If I had known… if she had *told* me—"

"You should have asked her!" I exclaim. "You should have been more careful with her! And now she—she's suffering upstairs in that godforsaken holding cell because of you!"

"Not because of me, my son. Because of herself. Because

she cannot be trusted. Because all of it is outside of her control."

She turns away and walks to the bookshelf. She runs her hand along the rows of books before settling on one with a blood red cover.

She pulls it out. The title is engraved in thick, gold letters—but it's all in runes, and thus in a language I cannot read.

"This is the last surviving copy of the Witch's Covenant," she informs me. "It lays out the rules of how a new witch is to be trained. It is—it was—a sacred text to the five great families. We devoted our lives to the teachings of this book. The rules governing witchcraft are clear." She flips it open and points to a page. "*One who is found tainted,*" she quotes, "*shall be deprived of all magical knowledge, shall not be taught, and shall be put in isolation until such time that all her abilities are leeched out of her.*"

Morgan looks at me. "You see? It's quite clear what needs to be done."

The blood drains from my face. "What does that mean? 'Leeches?'"

"It's simple," Mother says. "Much as we drink the blood of humans, there are beings who feed on a witch's magic. Eleira will be bound until one such being is found. Then, she will be given a choice. Give up her magical abilities forever, or…"

332

Mother's eyes shine, "...die."

Chapter Fifty

ELEIRA

The silver surrounding me makes every breath I take a misery. The foul energy from the accursed metal pounds into me from all sides. It not only disorients me, but it makes me feel vulnerable, weak, sickly, confused…

I remember little of the aftermath of my training with the Queen. All I know is she thought the tornado was my fault—and that the horrid creature attempting to crawl through the floor was my doing.

The door to the cell rattles. I look up. A muffled curse comes from the outside.

My heart leaps in my chest. I recognize that voice.

"Raul?" I say, standing up—

Instantly I wish I hadn't. A savage bout of vertigo takes me, induced by the silver. I sit back down, hard, and *oomph*.

A moment later the view latch comes open. I see Raul's beautiful green eyes shine through.

"Eleira?" he calls. "Eleira, are you in there?"

Morgan cast a spell that deflects the light in this room. For anybody looking in, I'm invisible.

But that doesn't mean I cannot use my voice.

"Yes!" I say. I yearn to run to him, to press against the door and feel his presence on the other side... but I cannot.

This spot in the center of the room is the only place I can stay in without suffering crippling nausea.

"Where? Dammit, why can't I see you?"

"Your mother cast a spell," I say. "It bends the light."

He curses again. "I'll get you out of there, Eleira. I promise. I *won't* have you ripped away from me again."

That's such a sweet sentiment... but I've been through enough at the hands of these vampires to know it's misplaced.

"I don't know if you can help me." Melancholy fills my words.

"*Don't* say that!" Raul shouts. "Eleira—don't. Don't give up!"

I blink through eyes that are suddenly moist. How many times must I be made prisoner? How many times must I find myself in a position of utter helplessness—even if I seemingly did not do anything wrong?

I wipe at the tears angrily. "I'm not giving up," I say. "I'm just realistic. What can you do? What can anyone do, when the Queen holds all the power?"

"I *will* get you out," Raul promises. "I hold it on my own life, on Phillip's, on anybody's who's ever been important to me. I swear it. I'll find a way."

A noise sounds from beyond him. "Someone's here," he says. "I'll be back when I can."

And, without waiting for a goodbye, he slides the little panel shut. I'm left all alone in the room of icy silver once more.

Chapter Fifty-One

PHILLIP

I stand next to my brother, half a step behind the Queen, as a marching procession of Wyvern Coven vampires flows down the main pathway of The Haven.

They are a raggedly bunch—without order, without discipline. Their adopted coven name is a mockery of the great creature a wyvern represents.

They march in a straight enough line, but so many of them look bedraggled, weak, and perhaps even... frightened?

And why not? There isn't a single one amongst them who matches us in power. These are the castaways, the unwanted, the ones who'd been kicked out of their original homes and banded together as nomads.

They are the gypsy wanderers of our time. And for some inane reason, Mother decided to open the doors of The Haven to them.

I look behind me. All the vampires of our coven are here. The humans have been ushered back underground. They'll remain there until the newcomers can familiarize themselves with the rules governing The Haven.

There is undisguised hostility on the faces of all of The Haven's vampires. From those of the Royal Court, to those of the regular rabble—none are pleased that the Queen opened up our home to them.

Especially after sealing the wards and locking us in for weeks.

The front of the line stops before the Queen. It takes a few moments for the disorganized vampires in the back to come to a standstill.

"They are intimidated," Raul whispers to me. "They don't know if this is a trap or not."

"I agree. They've come out of desperation."

I look at the guards Smithson posted in the trees. All have their shining armor for display. It's an ostentatious display of wealth compared to the primitive clothing of the Wyvern guards.

"They brought coffins." Somebody sneers from behind me. "How quaint."

I go on my toes and realize he's right. At the very back of the line are row upon row of coffins, being carried by hand.

"They must not know we're graced by eternal night," the speaker's companion says.

"How many do you think there are?" I ask Raul. "Two,

three-hundred?"

"More," he answers. "Easily enough to match us. Where is Mother planning on housing them?"

"I doubt they'll be particular. Coming into The Haven should be enough of an honor for this bunch."

"It would be an honor for any vampire who know of us," Raul grunts. "Too bad this is who we're stuck with."

"Welcome!" Morgan steps forward and greets the three leaders of the delegation. "We are so grateful that you took us up on our offer of sanctuary. My Captain Commander has told me much about you in anticipation of your arrival. It's a pleasure to make your acquaintance."

A grizzled vampire with a long, disarrayed beard steps out of the trio and extends his arm. "The pleasure of meeting the mighty Queen of The Haven is all mine," he says. "I am Collin. My two companions are Mark and Nestar."

Mark and Nestar give their greetings.

"At first, we were not sure what to expect," Collin admits. "But when Captain Commander Smithson assured us of your intentions... well, we could hardly refuse joining the most feared coven in existence."

"He's lying," I say. "Look at the way his eyes are shifting. He's nervous. Something is wrong."

"He speaks like a snake," Raul agrees. He turns his head

slightly to me. "Is April safe?"

"I snuck her out of the group of humans as they were led underground. She's locked in my rooms."

"Good," Raul says. "Because I have a feeling that if something goes wrong, the humans will be the first to—"

A sudden gut-wrenching shriek comes from deep in the woods. My head spins toward it. It rings out for only a second before being cut off.

Collin, Mark, and the rest of the new vampires instantly turn in its direction. Mother steps smoothly in front of them to block their view.

"A misbehaving human," she explains. "Nothing to concern yourselves with." She looks at Smithson. "Have one of your guards check it out."

"That didn't sound like a human scream," I whisper to Raul.

He nods in thought.

Before Smithson can pick someone to investigate, Raul steps forward. "I'll go," he volunteers.

A look of angry surprise flashes across Mother's face. It's quickly replaced by a fake smile. "My eldest son, ever the protector of The Haven," she says to the newcomers.

"I'll join him," I say.

This time there's no denying the look of displeasure that

crosses the Queen's face. "My *second* son," she says curtly. "Forgive them, they have no tact for politics."

"We are not here to interfere," Collin says. "Let them do as they wish. This welcome is more than enough."

Mother shoots me a scathing look, but then nods. "Very well."

In a second Raul and I take off into the trees.

We run in the direction the scream came from.

There, we stumble upon a ghastly sight.

Patricia is bound to the trunk of a tree. Her clothes are in tatters. There is blood on the front of her shirt, pooling from a horrendous gash in her neck.

Her head hangs limp, and her eyes are open... but unseeing.

She's dead.

"No!" I gasp. "No, it can't be!"

Raul approaches the area carefully.

"She was left here as bait," he says. "But the trap was set improperly."

He picks up a rock, takes aim, and flings it at the spot just below the dead vampire's feet.

A silver net, just large enough to catch an animal the size of a bear, shoots down from the tops of the trees. It hits the ground and folds lamely in on itself.

My brother and I share a concerned look. "The Narwhark," I breathe.

"I suspect so."

Raul creeps closer to the hanging vampire. He touches his fingers to her blood, then brings them to his lips.

He spits it out immediately.

"Tainted," he says. He points at the cut across her neck. It's savage and uneven and lethal, almost like somebody took a wood-axe to her throat. "No vampire would kill like this. You're right. It was the demon."

"A failed attempt to capture it. Would Mother be desperate enough to try?"

Raul shakes his head. "No. Not yet. Not if she knows what the demon is capable of."

"Then who? Smithson?"

"He's the only other one who knows about it. Maybe he thought this would help curry favor with the Queen."

I grunt. "He was keenly aware of her hatred for Patricia." I look away. I can't take the sight of her lifeless body.

Raul places a hand on my shoulder. "Are you okay?"

"I saved her," I say softly. "I gave up my ideals to grant her life. And she ends up being... slaughtered... like this."

I spit in disgust. "Let's get her down. No vampire deserves to be seen like this."

Chapter Fifty-Two

RAUL

An enormous feast is hosted for the visiting vampires later that night. It takes place in the middle of the village, where most of the homes have already been rebuilt. All of The Haven vampires attend. It's an unusual opportunity for members of the Incolam to mingle with both the elite and the Royal Court.

Mother had kegs and kegs of blood brought out from her personal stores—the ones separate from the blood banks. They are mixed with wine, so that as we drink, tongues become looser, inhibitions are abandoned, and friends more easily made.

There is music playing and dancing. I get asked to dance by more than my fair share of pretty female vampires. It is a rare chance for them to attach themselves to the Prince.

I turn each offer down. My thoughts are solely on Eleira, suffering in that horrible holding cell.

I've been weighing my options all day. If I break her out, I'd be going directly against Mother—again. And I've already exhausted her reservoir of goodwill for me.

But if I use my wits... if I somehow convince the vampire Queen that Eleira should be given another chance... then maybe, *just maybe*, Mother will see reason and let Eleira go.

I look up at the table at the head of the room. Mother is sitting in the tallest chair with a jewelled crown atop her head. I haven't seen that gaudy thing in centuries.

On her left-hand side sit Collin, Mark, and Nestar, drinking from their goblets and sharing stories with each other. Mother glances at them occasionally while granting them a small bit of her attention.

Most of her focus, however, is on the man on her right.

Smithson.

When did she and he become so... *comfortable* together?

I see the way she clings onto his every word. As the night progresses, she touches him more and more, on the arm, on the wrist, on the chest...

It quickly becomes obvious that if I want to influence Mother, Smithson is the man I have to go through.

At a certain point he excuses himself from the table. I take it as my chance. I follow him into the night.

The door behind me barely has a chance to swing shut as he steps out from beside the building and lunges for me. I'd been expecting that, however. I parry the attack, spinning us both so his back collides against the outside of the building.

One hand wraps around his neck. I protract my claws and press them none too gently into his skin.

"Well done," he growls, with a particular sneering inflection. "I never thought you much of a warrior."

"Then you've been blind," I say. I let him go. He straightens and dusts himself off.

"I felt someone following me," he explains. "I did not know it was you. I would never have attacked the Queen's son."

"Somehow, I find that hard to believe," I say. I look around. It's quiet out here compared to the raucous party inside. "Why did you leave the festivities? You looked so comfortable with Mother."

"Is that what this is about? Your jealousy?" He stands taller. "Are you worried someone will take your place? You're not *threatened*, are you?"

"I know my place, Smithson. I'm concerned about yours."

"Morgan would have me believe otherwise."

I narrow my eyes at him. "Since when are you and she on first-name basis?"

"Come now. It's just us men." He smiles. "There's no need for pretense. You came after me for a reason. Tell me what you want."

"I want to know what your intentions are with the

346

Queen."

"Intentions? No, no." He shakes his head, and I *know* the next words coming from his lips are falsehoods. "I have no intentions. I am her humble servant. I do everything as she commands."

"*Bull,*" I accuse. "You wouldn't be here if you didn't have some ulterior motive. What are you trying to gain, Smithson? Why did you come to The Haven in the first place?"

"Are you always so suspicious? That should be my role as Captain Commander of the guard. Perhaps we should trade positions."

"Cut the crap."

"Fine. Why did you follow me?"

"I had to speak to you in private."

His eyes shine. "It wouldn't happen to be about that... thing... you found in the woods earlier today, would it?"

My gut clenches in both anger and distaste. "That was a horrible thing you did. Patricia—"

"Is no longer a thorn in the Queen's side. I think I'd have the Queen's gratitude."

"You know the laws against killing a vampire," I hiss. An awful cognitive dissonance stirs up inside me.

I've killed four.

"But I did not kill her," Smithson smiles. "The Narwhark did."

"And you thought your pathetic silver net would capture it?" I snort a laugh. "The mechanism didn't even go off."

"No." Smithson walks around me. I turn my head to follow his movement. "The net was for a vampire who might stray too close. I did not mean to capture the Narwhark. I simply wanted to see what it was capable of."

"You put her there as bait."

"Better her than one of us, hmm?" Smithson asks. "Better a *nobody,* a weakling vampire, than one of the vampire elite."

My rage takes me. I cannot help it. I grab his shoulders and slam him into the wall. "She was my *friend,*" I hiss.

Smithson's eyes are ablaze. "Do you know how many friends *I've* lost over the years? Do you know how many people I've had to watch perish, how many vampires I've seen die on the Outside?" He shakes his head. "But of course you don't. You've been protected here for centuries. You know nothing of the cruelties of the world. You're soft and pompous. You—"

"I am *not,*" I growl, pressing him harder against the surface, "—soft."

"And yet where is your beloved? Where is Eleira? Oh, that's right. She's left suffering in the silver cell because you're

348

too cowardly to do anything about it."

More of my anger boils. "*Don't,*" I warn him, "accuse me of cowardice."

"What, then?" he asks. "You consider *doing nothing* a declamation of love? Please." He looks down at my hands. "You might as well let me go, since we both know you're not going to dare harm me tonight."

With a grunt I shove off. How is it that I let this vampire get so deep under my skin?

"That's better," Smithson says. "As it so happens, you and I are not enemies. We both want the same thing."

I eye him skeptically. "And that is?"

"Peace," he tells me. "Your Mother fears a war, but she does not realize that her actions are inciting one. She opened The Haven up to all the covens of North America. Do you know why only the weakest came?"

"Enlighten me," I grunt.

"Because," Smithson says, "the others fear a massacre. They considered the invitation a Trojan horse. Get them here, get them comfortable—and slaughter them in their sleep."

"We would never—"

"*You* might not," he interrupts. "But the Queen? Have you noticed her behavior recently?"

Smithson steps away. "You aren't aware of the mystique

surrounding The Haven in the outside world. This coven is spoken of in hushed, reverent tones. It is the only one on this continent that has survived for *centuries*. It is the only one governed by a witch. The other covens are nowhere near as organized. Mostly it's a clan here and there, wandering through the world, mixing with the world of humans. Some live in cities—New York, for example, has fifteen blocks around Central Park secretly owned and lived in by vampires. They feed using the Little Drink and mingle with humans as if nothing separates our species. They go to plays, they explore the nightlife, but they are always—always—vulnerable and exposed to the currents of the outside world.

"Compare that with what you have here. A perfect piece of paradise. Nothing can touch you. You are free to feed. Yes, yes, I know all about The Hunt, but that is mostly for ceremony and sport, isn't it? You keep the blood banks full. No Haven vampire has to worry about a crusader against evil murdering him in his sleep."

I narrow my eyes. "Crusader?"

Smithson laughs. "You don't even know?"

"Tell me."

"Crusaders are humans devoted to hunting down and killing every last vampire in existence. They make their purpose known openly. Most regular humans think them insane. After all, how many regular humans believe in the preternatural? In a world of science and discovery, it is precious few.

"But the crusaders have weapons. They have funding. They are almost fanatics in their zeal to seek out and kill." Smithson lowers his voice. "Do you know the best thing about killing a vampire?"

I wait for him to tell me.

"They leave no bodies. A week, two weeks, after the death, the force that gives us eternal life dissipates. All the shells we inhabit, our stolen bodies, waste away with breathtaking speed. They disintegrate, first into dust, then into nothingness.

"So the crusaders can kill, if they're smart, without being caught. Not caught by vampires, no. Caught by other *humans*. By the police, by the authorities." Smithson spreads his hands. "Without bodies to give evidence, there is no crime."

"Why are you telling me this?"

"Because I want to open you to the world around you! To the vampire existence you are utterly blind to, shielded here in these magnificent redwoods. I'm trying to show you that not all live a life as privileged as what the Queen provides. And as such, in the vampires of the Outside, there is jealousy, jealousy and suspicion. The best thing the Queen can do is to remain hidden, to let the rest of the world forget The Haven exists. Instead, she is at the top of the mountains, screaming with all the brashness God gave her: '*WE ARE HERE, WE ARE HERE, COME WITNESS US*!' And if you think that can end in anything but disaster... I pity you."

Smithson stops talking. I look at him for a long moment, taking it all in.

Could he be right? Could the world outside The Haven really be so dark?

"You've gone quiet," he observes. "I trust you'll leave the matter of Patricia's death on the down low. In return, I'll speak to your Mother about Eleira. That is what you really want out of me, isn't it?"

Before I can answer, he turns away to rejoin the party. "Have a good night," he tells me. "Please try not to do anything stupid. The Queen is going to be very much occupied until the false morning. The guards I've posted around the castle are bound to let their attention waver. It would be such a *shame* if something unexpected happened to Eleira the night we welcome another coven to our midst, don't you think?"

With that, he closes the door, stranding me outside. I turn immediately for the castle.

A more blatant hint of what he's given me permission to do I could not imagine.

Chapter Fifty-Three

JAMES

Supressing the almost insatiable urge to cough, I push the top of the sarcophagus off just a sliver, and test the air.

I hear nothing. No movement. No sound. No indication that my hiding spot has been compromised.

Then again, this is exactly what Beatrice promised.

With a grunted effort, I push the massive stone slab the rest of the way off. I sit up. My eyes pierce the dark.

I can't help but smile.

I'm in the very familiar lower keep of Mother's castle. This was the place originally reserved for outside guests. It is just one level below the main floor. It was designed before she cast the spell that maintained eternal night over The Haven— back when she actually entertained delegates from other covens.

Being underground, these dungeons were the safest place for visiting vampires to sleep without fear of being burned by the sun.

And now, after all these years, she seems to have found

use for them again.

I look around at the coffins lying on the floor. They are all filled with gold and jewelry and precious gemstones. As payment from the Wyvern coven for letting them in.

When Beatrice first told me of the plan to smuggle me in, I was incredulous. I would never believe that Mother would be so careless as to openly *welcome* vampires from another coven in, especially not after what I heard about her reinforcing the wards and blocking access in or out.

But the delegation's entry was the one moment the wards would be relinquished. It was my only chance.

Of course, any Haven guard worth his salt would sense a vampire as powerful as me hiding in one of the coffins. That's why Riyu cast a concealment spell that camouflaged my powers.

I stretch my neck from side to side and roll my shoulders. Four days of being confined inside that coffin have made every muscle in my body extraordinarily stiff. The effects of Riyu's spell make it worse. It feel like I have a wet suit three sizes too small wrapped around my body. There's not a part of me that doesn't feel the tightness.

But if this grants me freedom, and proves my loyalty to Father... who am I to complain?

After all, Father is the only vampire I've ever recognized to share my ideals about the world. He wants our kind to rise to power. He wants vampires to have dominion over humans because we are greater than men.

The trick, of course, is getting him to see I share the same sentiment.

I do another cursory scan of my surroundings. Nobody is even remotely nearby. Beatrice promised she would have somebody help me once I arrived—a mole on the inside—but I doubted that possibility very much.

Seems like I was wrong.

It makes me all the more curious about the woman. She is ruthless, yet tactful. She is everything Mother wishes to be, but is not.

It only makes sense that Father would align himself with one such as her.

With one last, final push, I shove the slab all the way off, and rise to my full height.

"My, but how good it feels to be back," I say to no one in particular. A crude smile forms on my face. "Mother, you have no idea what you have coming."

I creep toward the door and crack it open. I'm pleased to find it unlocked. Whoever was charged with arranging my arrival did a superb job.

I creep up the hallway toward the hidden entrance to the castle. Riyu's spell is uncomfortable, but it gives me a rare advantage. I can sense other vampires—they cannot sense me.

For all intents and purposes, I am like a ghost stalking the halls.

I touch the amulet on my chest. The torrial is my one existing link to The Ancient and to Father. Even with the wards up, I was assured it would allow telepathic communication, just as before.

My new goal is simple. Find Mother's staff and retrieve it. Present it to Father. Fall into his good graces, and, if all goes according to plan, be gifted a drop of The Ancient's blood.

My mouth salivates at the prospect. If I had my own strength augmented by what The Ancient could give... why, I'd rival Eleira in might. I might even rival Father.

Prove yourself, first, I think.

The whole castle is abandoned. I remember snatches of conversation I heard while in the coffin. There was to be a great welcoming feast tonight. I guess that's where everyone is.

I suspect it'll take days of stalking The Haven before I find the staff. I don't know if Mother carries it on her at all times. That would make my job more difficult, but not impossible.

If only I had a *visible* ally here...

Then it strikes me. *Victoria*! She is still in The Haven,

likely still a prisoner. The little blonde spitfire would be someone I can definitely count on to have my back.

Especially if I rescue her.

I change paths and start for the holding cell reserved for the usual prisoners and dissenters. Halfway there, I stop.

Mother wouldn't put Victoria below ground. She'd want her close at hand, somewhere she could extract information from her.

She'd keep her in the *silver cells*.

I run up through the castle, taking the stairs three at a time to the uppermost level. The haunting portraits on the walls seem to follow me with their eyes. I ignore the uncanny chill that they send down my spine.

Finally I reach my destination. I pull open the doors leading to the five silver cells. Their entrances are spread in a circular pattern around a small lobby.

To my surprise, *two* of the doors are closed. That means Mother has *two* prisoners.

I frown. In all the time I've lived here, there's only been one instance that warranted a prisoner being held here. And currently Mother is holding *two?*

I go up to the first one. The silver within makes it impossible to sense a presence on the other side. That's why the view-latches exist. I slide it open and take a look.

357

The cell is empty.

I step back, confused. What little I know about Mother's magic has always given me the impression that actuating one of these cells required her constant concentration. It's not just the silver artifacts inside that exert their unpleasant effects. No, it's the way her magic warps them to make the interior absolute hell for a vampire.

And the cells are only locked *when* they're activated. To keep one closed and empty... it makes no sense.

I look into the second cell. Sure enough, Victoria is inside.

Triumph shoots through me.

I pry open the door. She's faced away from me and doesn't bother turning around.

"I've already told you all I know about the girl," she begins scornfully.

"Victoria!" I hiss. "It's me." From the corner of my eye I think I see a small shadow dart inside. I blink and look.

No, it was nothing.

Victoria gasps and spins around. "*James?*"

"The one and only," I grin. "Come to get you out." I beckon her to me. "Come on."

"But I... I don't understand," she begins. "Last I heard you were to become a Convicted. How are you here? What happened?"

"Plans change," I grunt. "Now hurry. I'll explain later."

She picks herself up. "I never thought *you'd* be the one to help me escape."

Suddenly, the stupidity of what I'm doing strikes me. *I can stalk around The Haven unseen. But when Mother realized Victoria is missing, she'll put on a full-scale manhunt—*

Before Victoria can reach me I step back and slam the door in her face.

An enraged scream comes from the other side. "You bastard!" she accuses. "Why come back only to taunt me! What are you doing? Let me out, let me out!"

She pounds on the other side of the door. But her ferocity is quickly lessening, as her strength is being sapped by the silver.

"I'm sorry," I whisper. "I'll come back for you if I can, once this is done."

I start to walk away. That's when a blood-curdling shriek comes from Victoria's cell.

I spin around. Suddenly the sounds of a battle flit to my ears. I fly to the view latch and yank it open.

Victoria has her claws extended and her fangs bared, fighting against a pitch-black... shadow?

What the hell?

Blood is pouring from multiple gashes on her body. The black thing attacks her without mercy. It rips at her throat, at her neck, all with blistering speed. It moves too fast for me to keep up with all its frenzy.

I hurl the door open, forgetting all pretense, and charge into the room. The shadow looks up. It stays still just long enough for me to see its true shape. It's a horribly grotesque creature, maybe the size of a large rat. Its whole body is swathed in wisps of black that fall from it like pluming smoke.

A snarl comes from its throat. The moment it sees me it flees into the far corner of the room.

I run to Victoria. She collapses before I get to her. She's still breathing—but barley.

Her eyes are halfway lidded, and the stench of corruption washes over me from her wounds.

"Kill... it," she whispers.

I rise. I can't do anything for her, not now, not with that creature in the room.

But what is it? I wonder.

With an ear-splitting screech it launches itself at me, all teeth and claws and hate-filled fury. I can't move out of the way fast enough, but I manage to twist my body just enough for the thing to glance off.

My claws come up and I cut it on the underside, in that

precious moment when we're together. A thick, viscous liquid coats my hand and immediately starts to burn the skin.

This isn't blood. It's much worse than blood.

As fast as I can, I wipe it off on my cloak. The creature lands on its back and scrambles upright, hissing and snarling.

But it doesn't attack again.

I position myself between it and Victoria. It snaps its jaws at me, but does nothing more.

Suddenly, all the silver in the room makes its effect known. I don't know how I endured it before. Maybe I was running on adrenaline. But now, all my senses start to wobble, and vertigo and nausea and disorientation hit as a horrible trifecta of afflictions.

I stagger back, refusing to take my eyes off the creature, knowing that if I fail it will kill Victoria. I'm no hero. I don't know what it is about Victoria that would have me risk my life.

But I'm doing it now. So be it. I've committed. I can't turn back.

"Come on, you bastard. Let's see what you got." My lips curl back and I show my fangs.

The creature stops its hissing. It looks at me...

Then turns around and flees out the door.

I stare after it, stupefied.

That was all it took?

Then I hear Victoria groan below me. Immediately I twist back. Blood is oozing from her wounds. It's not healing as it should.

I fall to my knees beside her. I pick her up and cradle her head in my arms.

"Victoria... Victoria, no," I say. A torrent of unwanted and unexpected feelings gush through me. Fear. Failure. *Guilt.*

"I'll get you out," I say. I lift her up and stagger to my feet. She feels so frail beneath me. I can feel the life force draining from her body. Her eyes flicker back and forth from seeing to unseeing. The wounds smell ripe with corruption.

Stumbling and disoriented because of the silver, I manage to find my way out of the room. I fall against the wall in the hall, a strange fatigue setting in.

I hear footsteps racing up the stairs.

I curse. If I stay, my whole purpose here would be compromised. If I'm caught now, I might as well forsake my own life.

As gently as I can, I put Victoria down. She groans as her body touches the floor. I look through the open door of the cell and see her blood staining the stone.

My hand still feels like it's on fire, despite having wiped all of the creature's internal fluids off.

The footsteps get louder. I can feel two—no, *three* vampires running up toward us. I look around.

The stairs are the only way down.

I'm trapped.

From below me I hear the creature's hissing shriek again. A blast shakes the chamber, like a stick of dynamite going off. The castle rumbles. From around the corner comes the briefest flash of blue light.

Those snarling, hissing, guttural sounds of the creature continue on below. It's engaged with the three vampires, one of whom is Mother, I'm sure.

My eyes search the walls for a cavity, for some sort of hiding place. I find one, far in the corner, right by the second closed door.

"Don't move," I tell Victoria. A part of me wants to run down and aid the others in the fight. Not from any great sense of altruism, but because I want the opportunity to finish the thing that maimed Victoria and embarrassed me so.

Whoever heard of a vampire being bested by a *rat*?

She groans something incomprehensible in response. I debate just pulling her with me, but her strength would give us away. The only reason I stand a chance hiding is Riyu's magnificent cloaking spell.

So, feeling both a coward and a fool, I jump into that tiny

pocket of darkness, hoping against hope that whoever comes up and discovers Victoria won't notice me right away.

Three against one aren't the best of odds... but with the element of surprise on my side, I reckon I'll be able to do a little bit of damage if it comes down to a fight.

Chapter Fifty-Four

ELEIRA

Something jerks my attention to the door. The view latch slides open... and James peers inside.

Shock ripples through me. What's *James* doing here? Could I be seeing things? Could my senses be so addled by the silver?

But no, it's him. I'd recognize those cruel, vindictive eyes anywhere. Although, now, they look somehow... subdued. Somehow... haunted.

A million questions rifle through my mind. Where did he come from? Why did he come? Is he searching for... me?

I stand up and raise one arm. James makes no response. His eyes glide over the entirety of the room, completely unseeing.

Morgan's spell is still active.

Then abruptly he slams the latch shut. I start to sneak for the door. If he swings it open...

But he's gone. The faint hint I had of his presence disappears like the scent of a wilting flower on a cold wind.

I return to the middle of the room. Barely any time passes before I hear a blood-curling scream.

I blink in confusion. *Victoria?*

Suddenly a torrent of images pours into my head:

A dark, silver cell nearby, identical to this one. James is standing at the door, having flung it open. Movement, dark movement, movement that's getting nearer, nearer...

I grunt and blink through the barrage of images, bringing a hand to my head. They're so *real*, it feels like I'm seeing them before me now, like I'm in some sort of vivid dream.

They continue to assault my mind:

A streaking black object leaping into the room. Panic flaring. James throwing the door shut in my face...

I hear it slam shut and realize that what I'm seeing—it's happening in real time, in another cell nearby.

I'm looking through Victoria's eyes.

But how can that be? I thought I'd blocked her off. The connection—

The connection suddenly flares into life once more, and there is no hesitance, no doubt this time: I am completely in her mind.

And it's not just images I see. I *feel* what she feels. I *know* all she knows.

I feel her rage at being abandoned by James. I feel her hatred toward me, and all that unguarded jealousy. Her mind is a storming cauldron of emotions.

But she doesn't know I'm there.

Victoria only gets the briefest chance to react as something heavy and fast slams into her and knocks her to the ground. She cries out as she lands on her back.

And there, through her eyes, I see *it*. The evil, menacing, raging Narwhark I'd unleashed. It attacks her like a savage dog.

Her hands come up in self-defence and her claws and fangs come out. But the Narwhark is too fast, too hungry, too angry. It rips right through her defenses and sinks its curling pointed teeth into her shoulder, her arms, her abdomen.

Victoria screams. I hear it both in the air and in my mind. The pain she feels is doubled in my body.

I crash to my knees and grab my head, willing the images out, out, out. But as the Narwhark continues to attack, and all I can see is its blurred black form, my connection with Victoria only strengthens, until I'm fully inhabiting her body, until I'm trapped inside like in some sort of horrible dream.

The cell door opens. James is there. He rushes back in.

The Narwhark leaps off. Victoria's eyes droop shut. Her vital energy is draining out of her. The wounds she sustained are corrupted with the demon's spit, and her body cannot heal them, cannot close them up in time.

Her head rolls one way. She looks toward the creature.

And I see, for the very first time, just what the Narwhark is.

The little black shadow is but a tiny piece of its horrifying body. I see the demon as a faint outline traced in blue light. Its head is massive, its arms and legs thick as a bear's. Long, terrible claws extend from paws that are gnarled with finger-like digits. Its skin is cracked and leathery with nauseating splotches of color here and there, like a diseased reptile. Its neck curls right before it protrudes into the head, giving it the look of a spindly thing, almost like the curved ark of a reaper's deadly blade.

Then the vision fades, and the Narwhark is that little black blur again, streaking toward James.

Victoria's eyes fully close.

I don't get to see what happens next. I'm plunged into sudden darkness. I feel a sudden crack at the back of my head.

Pain. Horrible, blistering pain as the connection between Victoria and me severs.

I fall to the floor. The pain continues unabated, lashing through my head in sharp jabs of agony. My jaw clenches as I clutch my head.

Pain, pain, and more pain washes through me, unrelenting, unstopping, and there's nothing I can do to lessen it. I cannot even cry out. It feels like my mind is breaking,

As the reverberations of the cut connection with Victoria continue to pulse through my body, my last thought is of Raul and how I never told him how I feel.

The world pitches into a thick and inky black.

Chapter Fifty-Five

SMITHSON

I race up the stairs ahead of the Queen, Witchbane unsheathed and at the ready in my hand.

When she alerted me to a potential breakout from the silver cells... I was sure that I'd been compromised. I never thought James would be stupid enough to rescue his woman from the tower.

For a few minutes, I'd dared to hope it had been Raul, gone to save Eleira as I'd none too subtly suggested...

But when I ran into him while racing to the castle, all hope went out. Now, the only thing I can do is pledge ignorance about James. But that's a horrible demonstration of my worth as Captain Commander.

We run up a flight of stairs. From the top a snarling black blur flies out. "Watch out!" I scream and jump in the way of the Queen.

The Narwhark strikes my blade with a sickening hiss. The force of impact nearly knocks the weapon from my hand. The demonic creature falls back, then picks itself up again.

Black liquid oozes down the blade. I watch, aghast, as the metal starts to warp and droop like a melting icicle.

Such rage takes me then. In all my centuries of life this blade has been my sole companion, the one constant, the only thing in which I could trust. And now, a single parry against the Narwhark, and it's... ruined.

Before I can do anything the Queen strikes out. Blue light explodes from her staff. A solid beam of it sears the spot where the Narwhark had been.

But the demon is deceptively fast. It leaps out the way so the Queen's attack hits nothing but stone. The force of impact makes the whole chamber shake.

Morgan swears. Meanwhile, I drop my sword, knowing it will do me little good. I extend my claws and ready myself to attack—

Raul is there before me. He jumps for the demon, trying to get it with his claws. Again the damnable creature darts away, quick as silver.

"Go!" Morgan grabs my shoulder and shoves me up the stairs. "Go, check on Eleira and Victoria! You cannot fight the Narwhark. Only I can!"

"I won't leave you," I start.

At that moment the demon mounts its own attack.

It leaps up and hits me in the side. Both of us go hard into the wall. I only just manage to get my hands up in time to prevent it from digging its teeth into my body. Then there's another beam of light, more compact and thinner this time, like a laser beam. The Narwhark cannot get disentangled from me in time.

It screeches as the ray of magic hits. In a fury, it spins around and jumps off. Then, seeing the way down blocked, it bounds up the stairs, back the way it had come.

For half a second I'm too dazed to move. The Queen's attack was precise, and perfectly aimed, but if the Narwhark had moved even a fraction of an inch… if that beam had hit me…

In that brief moment, I fully realize what sort of woman she is. And the guilt that has started to creep up about my true intentions after she had taken me to bed instantly vaporizes. I'd let myself grow soft, let myself be taken in by her.

Well, no more.

I jump to my feet. I share a look with Raul. He realizes, at the same time, exactly what I did: *The Queen would have killed me if she missed.*

There is no sympathy in his eyes.

"Come on," he grunts, and chases after the Narwhark.

I follow him, Morgan quick on my heels.

We get to the top. I skid to a halt and curse. The door to

Victoria's room is wide open. But the tanned vampire lies on the floor in front of us. There are nasty, infected wounds all over her body.

I scan the surroundings for the demon. I don't see it.

"It must have gone in the silver cell," I exclaim. I run forward to close the door. "If we seal it inside—"

Just then, a tall, man-shaped streak blurs toward the Queen. I'm too startled, too thrown off, too distracted by the loss of my sword, to do anything.

I hadn't noticed the vampire hidden in the shadows.

He collides with the Queen and knocks the staff from her hand. It skitters across the floor.

I catch a glimpse of his face, and realize that it's James.

Chapter Fifty-Six

JAMES

The creature comes leaping up the stairs. I watch from my hiding place as it pauses for a flicker of a second, looking at Victoria.

My body tenses. If it tries to attack her, I won't just turn the other cheek. I'll need to help.

But the decision is taken out of my hands when the sound of pursuit scares the thing into the silver cell.

I go absolutely still as three vampires spill out into view. First is Raul. Next is Smithson. And finally...

My own Mother, the Queen. She is carrying her staff.

I can hardly believe my luck.

If I'm only given one chance, this is it. As Smithson rushes to slam the door shut, I spring from my hiding place and go straight for Mother. The only reason I stand a chance is because she is momentarily distracted by the sight of Victoria on the ground.

I body-slam into her. The staff flies out of her hand. Such a look of surprise flashes on her face—she hadn't been expecting to be taken unaware. But then she sees that it's me. Her mouth twitches up in a crude smile.

"Come to claim your place as one of The Convicted?" she mocks.

I have no time for fun here. I push off and dive for her torrial.

But somewhere in all the confusion I had forgotten about my brother. Raul reaches it at exactly the same time as I do. His hand wraps around the staff simultaneously with mine.

"Don't get in the way, *little* brother," I snarl. "This doesn't involve you!"

He flashes accusatory eyes at Victoria. "You did that," he condemns.

I laugh, even though I don't feel it on the inside. "Don't tell me you care about her. I thought Eleira was the one true love for you. Bored of her already?"

"Never," Raul snarls. He tries to jerk the staff out of my hands. I hold on tight.

In the back of my mind I wonder how it is neither Mother nor Smithson have tried to interfere.

I cast a quick glance back. Mother is kneeling over Victoria's body, eyes closed, muttering some sort of incantation while running her hands over the other woman's wounds. Smithson has his shoulder jammed against the door of the silver cell. It shakes and trembles as the thing inside tries to break out.

"What are you doing here?" Raul demands. "You got out, you were free. Why did you come back?"

We grapple some more over the staff. "I came for precisely this," I hiss. "If you know what's good for you, you'll give it to me *now*!"

"Why should I?" Raul challenges. "What do *you* want with it, James?"

"That doesn't concern you."

"On the contrary. Anything of interest to you does."

I swear and try to fight him off, but his grip is impossible to break.

"Raul!" Mother gasps his name. "Eleira—you must get Eleira to me! If Victoria dies, and the connection still exists between their minds, there's nothing I'll be able to do. Hurry! Forget about him!"

Raul casts one last look at me... and shoves off. He runs for the door of the second silver cell. The empty one, with nobody inside.

I don't have time to contemplate his irrational behavior. Glorious triumph seizes me as I hold the staff in both hands. With *this* I will be vindicated, with *this* I will be redeemed in my Father's eyes.

A maddened sort of laughter takes hold. With this staff in hand—

I don't get to finish my thought. The amulet around my neck quivers with sudden energy. A surge of power explodes out from it and runs through my body.

"YES, BOY!" The Ancient roars in my mind. *"YES, YOU HAVE GIVEN IT TO ME. YES, YES, YES!"*

The power concentrates in my fingertips and flows into the staff. I lose all sense of self as The Ancient takes control of my body. I feel him in my head, in my limbs, I hear his snarling, zealous, depraved euphoria spoken in a language I do not know.

Suddenly, all the power from the amulet surges into the staff. A light brighter than anything I've seen explodes outward from it. Mother, in shock, cries out, "No!"

The light swells and then constricts. It concentrates into a point at the staff's top.

Still unable to control my body, I thrust the tip down, straight into the floor.

A sound like thunder crashing comes from the spot I struck. And all the light, all the energy, all the magic, all of The Ancient's *hate* surges down into the stone, into the very marrow of the castle. My body starts to convulse, but still I cannot do anything. I cannot let go. It feels like I'm being burned alive, burned from the inside, the power raging through me is so foreign and great.

In a wink it cuts out. For a second all is still. I recover from my daze and hurl both amulet and staff away.

But then the ground starts to shake.

Chapter Fifty-Seven

ELEIRA

A deep-set, heavy male voice pitches through the darkness.

"WAKE, ELEIRA. WAKE, YOU ARE NEEDED. WAKE!"

The final scream jerks me to my senses. I open my eyes, feeling the phantom after-effects of the lashing pain that raced through my head after the connection with Victoria broke.

I roll over with a groan. I steady both hands against the floor, start to push myself up—

A terrible shaking takes the room.

I'm on my feet quickly. *Not another earthquake,* I think. But then I sense a great effluence of power coming from the other side of the door. Enormous power, terrible power, enough magical energy to make me instantly afraid.

There comes a sound like glass breaking. A giant, splintering fissure races across the floor. I jump away, and wobble when I inadvertently land in a place where the silver's power is amplified.

For a moment, all is still. And then the fissure breaks—
and the whole floor gives way from under me.

I scream as I fly down with the rubble. All the silver
artifacts rain down with me. I hit the story below. Great rocks
come crashing down from the ceiling as it caves in from
above. I shield my head with my hands, knowing if one of
those slabs lands on me I'll be done for, vampire or not.

Then the breaking stops. Everything goes still, still and
eerily silent. I open my eyes hesitantly, amazed that I wasn't
hit.

And there, in front of me, picking themselves up from the
dust, are Raul, Smithson, James, Victoria, and the Queen.

They all look as dazed as I feel. Except for Victoria, who is
unconscious. I gasp when I see the awful wounds on her body.

The reunion lasts no longer than the second it takes to
make eye contact. Another deep groan takes the castle. The
floor we're standing on pitches in on itself and collapses
down.

I scream again as I'm sent throttling through the air.

We crash from one level to the next. The entire castle
starts to collapse inward, as if a great gaping hole has been
opened in the earth beneath its core.

My body strikes one hard surface after the next. I'm
bounced around like a ragdoll. Down, down, down I continue

to fall, as the Queen's castle crumbles around me.

We hit the ground floor and stop. The reprieve lasts barely a second. Another massive roar comes from beneath the earth. A gaping hole opens in the middle of the castle floor.

All of us go screaming down.

It all happens so fast. I'm tossed this way and that in the landslide, rebounding off rocks and objects I cannot even see. The fall into the earth takes eternity. *If this ever ends, I swear—*

The final impact knocks all the air from my lungs. I only have the vaguest sense of my body. All I know is that the motion has stopped. We're no longer falling.

Beyond me, the sound of settling debris continues. I close my eyes and mutter a prayer of gratitude. Somehow, through all that, I'm still alive. Somehow.

I look up. We're far beneath the earth. There's a gaping hole above me, and the night sky is so distant I can barely see the stars. All the broken pieces of the fallen castle surround me.

I know the only reason I survived was my vampire strength. But it seems incredible that any sort of creature could live through a fall like that.

Alarm grips me when I realize my leg is pinned beneath a boulder. I cry out. I can't even feel the pain!

I try to yank my leg free. But even if my body is whole, it's still in a very weakened state. The adrenaline is ebbing away, and a weary exhaustion starts to take over. Dust catches in my throat. I start to cough violently.

"Eleira?" Raul's voice, distant and fragile, calls for me. "Eleira, where are you?"

"Here," I croak. "I'm over here."

I hear him curse, and then, a few moments later, see him stumble down a pile of rocks.

He looks like absolute hell. His clothes are torn, there are long cuts all over his face and body. He staggers to a stop, searching the ruins for me. The moment he sees me he picks up the pace, then drops to the ground at my side.

"You're hurt," he says. Concern paints his voice.

"I'm fine," I lie.

He looks me up and down. "Your leg," he says. "Hold on."

He stands and shoves his shoulder into the boulder. It takes him considerable effort, but he manages to lift it just enough for me to pull my leg free.

"It's not broken," he observes, a trace of wonder in his voice.

"No," I echo. In fact, considering the distance I fell—we all fell—I would have thought we'd suffer more injuries. "How is it we're still alive?"

"Vampires are a resilient bunch," he mutters.

"No kidding."

The sound of scraping stone makes us both spin around. James is picking himself up from the dirt.

Before I know it Raul is on him. He pins his brother to the ground.

"You have ten words to explain what you did up there," Raul growls.

James coughs, and I think it might be an attempt at a laugh. "Only ten?" he starts. "Surely that isn't enough—"

"Four left," Raul warns. "Make them count."

James leers up at his brother. He must see something frightening in Raul's gaze, because he sighs and rumbles out exactly four words, "Father wanted the staff."

"The staff!" Raul curses. "Where is it? What did you do with it?"

"It wasn't me." James shakes his head. "I was possessed. The Ancient—"

"—used you as a surrogate to mount an attack on The Haven."

All three of us turn to see Morgan emerge from darkness. Smithson trails her, carrying an unconscious Victoria in his arms.

"He succeeded," the Queen concludes.

I'm surprised by how little anger I hear in her voice. She simply sounds... weary.

"If you're wondering how we survived the fall," she continues. "I cast a protective spell over each of us the moment I realized what was happening. Good thing, too." She looks around. "We would have been crushed were it not for that."

I stand up and face her, the hairs on the back of my neck prickling.

"What she giveth, she taketh away," Morgan mutters. She makes an intricate, circular motion with her fingers. A faint blue orb, about the size of a fist, retracts from each of our chests and flies back to her.

As soon as it happens all the pains and aches of my body crash into me. I stagger down. I'm barely able to hold myself upright. I grit my teeth against the pain.

Slowly, it starts to ebb away as my body begins healing itself. The process is not pleasant. Being shielded by Morgan's spell and then having it ripped away is like being wakened from a pleasant dream by being dunked into a tub of ice.

I look around me. All the other vampires are suffering similar afflictions. I presume, because of my strength, I'm the first to recover.

All the others, that is, except Morgan. Her eyes land on me, and she sends me such a look of revulsion, such a look of disgust, that I feel no better than a maggot she might have found in a stale piece of bread.

Raul is the next one to stand. He lumbers to me. I meet him halfway. We fall into each other's arms. He holds me against his hard body and strokes my hair.

"You're safe," he whispers. I'm not sure if the words are meant to assure him or me. "You're here, you're with me, you are safe."

I gulp down the welling emotions that try to rise in me from the sincerity in his voice.

He really does care for me, I think.

"AS IF THAT WAS IN ANY DOUBT."

I jerk away. "What was that?"

Raul looks at me in concern. "I didn't say anything."

It takes my frazzled brain an extra second to process that the Voice came from *inside* my head. When the realization hits…

"YOUR LOVE IS YOUR WEAKNESS," the menacing Voice booms. *"IT WILL BE THE END OF YOU. IT IS WRITTEN IN THE STARS. ONLY I CAN BE YOUR SALVATION. FOR THAT TO HAPPEN, YOU MUST COME TO ME."*

"I… no!" I grip the sides of my head and stagger away

385

from Raul. My foot catches a stray rock. I trip and fall.

"YOU WILL COME TO ME. IT IS NOT A CHOICE."

"Get out of my head!" I scream. I try to block the Voice's presence, just as I did Victoria's. But I cannot pinpoint its source. It's all-pervasive, sounding from every corner of my mind at once. It's not a single link but an envelopment of my mind.

"YOU WILL COME," the Voice threatens, *"WHETHER YOU WILL IT OR NOT."* Then it laughs. *"YOU MUST BE PERSUADED FIRST. I SEE THAT. WITNESS MY STRENGTH!"*

The ground starts to shake once more. A piercing blue light comes from a crevice in the stone beside me. With a start I realize I didn't trip over a rock.

I tripped over the Queen's staff. My ankle is still touching it.

"Eleira!" Morgan screams. "The torrial, get away from it! Get away from it now!"

I try to move but my body is paralyzed. An external force takes control of my limbs. It's the Voice, taking over my body. Without willing it, I reach down and pick up the staff...

A glorious flash of light bursts from the end. James, Smithson, and Victoria are knocked backwards. Raul is, too.

Only the Queen is spared.

She looks at me. "Eleira..." she begins.

386

"NO!" I scream, and the words that come from my throat are not my own, but that of the Voice. They echo through the cavernous enclosure and boom around with the stark intensity of the deranged.

"YOU WANT TO SEE POWER, YOU WANT TO SEE MIGHT? WITNESS ME AS I STAND BEFORE YOU! WITNESS ME AS I MAKE YOUR KINGDOM CRUMBLE TO DUST!"

With a savage, uncontrollable roar, I slam the staff into the ground. Magical energy pours through me and into its end. It concentrates there, many times greater than what a single witch could conceivably hold.

Then it all lashes out, as a thunderbolt, in the direction opposite where all the vampires are standing. It flashes and shoots straight as an arrow into the farthest reaches of the cave.

With that, the foreign force vacates my body. The power in the staff dies. The top of it is singed and black and ruined.

I barely have time to recover when a piercing shriek comes from the depths of the cavern. It's taken up immediately by hundreds more.

I know that sound. But Morgan gives voice to exactly what I fear.

"The Convicted," she gasps. "They've been released."

Chapter Fifty-Eight

RAUL

I fly to Eleira's side as the horde of Convicted races toward us. There are hundreds of them, but through some trick of the light their numbers seem greater. "Stay behind me," I tell Eleira in a tight voice. "You're in no condition to fight."

"Neither are you!" she protests, taking in my torn clothes and many cuts.

"None of us are," Morgan says wearily. She steps to our side. "Luckily, this isn't our fight. Look."

As if on cue, the first of the running Convicted make a sharp turn and start scampering up the wall toward the open night sky.

"They're escaping," I breathe.

"The barriers holding them down are gone," Mother says. "Obliterated by the power of the one who manipulated you and James. There's nothing keeping them here anymore."

I twist on her. "You have to get the barriers back!" I exclaim. The mass of Convicted is already halfway up to freedom. "You cannot let them run loose!"

Mother picks up the staff, and just as quickly tosses it aside. "Without this," she says. "There is nothing I can do."

"Where's James?" I spin around and look for my older brother. *He* is the cause of all this. How he got back, how he betrayed us yet *again*...

About three-quarters of the way up, the mass of Convicted find a ledge and pool onto it. I watch as they regroup for a moment and then start to move once again.

But they're not going for the opening above us anymore. No, they've turned to go deeper in the caves.

But why...

"The humans!" Eleira gasps at exactly the same time the thought hits me. "The Convicted are going for the villagers!"

I curse. But how would Eleira know the humans had been taken underground in advance of the other coven's arrival? She was locked away when it happened.

I ask her as much.

"I can sense the humans in the distance," she replies. "*All* of them."

"That's because of your strength," Mother interrupts. She's pacing the small spot in front of us, her skirt swishing at her legs. "The Convicted do not have senses as attuned to that as you. No, it is the Voice that is directing The Convicted. The

389

Voice that is telling them where to go."

"How can you know that?" Eleira asks.

"Because," Mother says. "I hear it too."

"What are we going to do? We can't just stay here!" Eleira protests. "We have to help!"

"I agree," I say. "Smithson, get the guards. I'll collect the rest of The Haven vampires to help. We won't stand pat and let The Convicted slaughter our villagers! Smithson? Smithson!"

But as I look around, the Captain Commander is nowhere to be seen.

"He's gone," Mother says softly.

She sounds... completely resigned.

"What's wrong with you?" I scream at her. "Your kingdom is under attack! The humans are about to be slaughtered! The Convicted have just escaped!"

She shakes her head. Self-pity as I've never seen it haunts her eyes.

"I've failed," she says under her breath. "I've failed The Haven. I've failed my people. I failed, I failed, I failed..."

"Snap out of it!" I yell. "You're the Queen, you're the Monarch!" The sounds of The Convicted are becoming dimmer and dimmer. The longer we wait, the farther they get from us...

And the closer they get to the humans.

Mother looks back at the remains of her castle. "Six centuries..." her voice cracks. "Six centuries it stood, only to be lost like this." A despairing sob comes from her throat. "It's gone. It's really gone, it's all gone..."

Eleira steps up to her and swings her arm. Her angry slap connects with Mother's left cheek.

Morgan looks at her, eyes wide, almost trembling.

"You are a powerful witch," Eleira says in a steely voice. "You are the ruler of The Haven. You *owe* it to your subjects to show your strength. The castle fell—so what? It can be rebuilt, just as the village was rebuilt. The barriers are down—but you can erect them again! And I'm *not*," she stresses, "a dark witch. Whatever you think that means, it is not me. Not who I am. Not here."

She touches her chest, right at the heart. "Maybe something happened when I was a child, but I can fight it. I *will* fight it, if you guide me, and together, we will defeat it."

She takes hold of Morgan's shoulders. "But right now, that's not the threat. If you stay here and bemoan what has happened, *then* your kingdom will be ruined. *Then* you'll lose all you have built. But if you show courage, and if you fight— The Haven vampires will fight alongside you. That I know."

Whoa. Chills run through me at that rising speech. I see Eleira in a new light.

Suddenly, she seems to realize what she's doing, who she's talking to. She gives a small gasp and shrinks back.

But I'm right there. I grab her waist, spin her around, and kiss her passionately.

When I let go, she looks at me with wonder-filled eyes. "What was that for?" she breathes.

"For kicking ass," I say. "And for being amazing."

I turn to Mother, who seems to have been roused from her mini pity party.

"Will you stand with us?" I ask. "Or will you cower and hide?"

Mother looks at me, then pushes herself up to full height. "A Queen," she says loftily, "never hides."

She's back, I think.

For now, the thought comes with no small measure of relief.

Chapter Fifty-Nine

JAMES

I stumble in a half-crazed daze after Smithson. He runs fast, urging me along, through caverns that I should know as well as the back of my own hand.

When he grabbed my arm and pushed me to go, in the aftermath of our fall into the earth, at first I resisted. But then he said the words that made me know *he* was the one who'd arranged my passage in:

"Beatrice would want you safe."

So I went with him. I ran from my Mother and brother and Victoria and Eleira, while being consumed with shame at what I'd done. I let my Father play me like a second-hand fiddle. I thought he'd wanted the staff, the torrial, for himself.

I did not ever imagine that he wanted it for The Ancient to destroy The Haven.

But the first domino has fallen. And I am wholly responsible.

Somewhere from beyond us come the shrieks of The Convicted. They've been let out, thanks to me. And now, after being deprived of blood, for so long, they will wreak havoc on the world above.

Smithson darts into a crevice in the rock. I follow him—and am blindsided when his fist catches me square in the jaw.

I stumble back. A white-hot pillar of rage erupts in me. My vampire instincts are instantly unleashed. I snarl and launch myself at him, claws out, going for the heart.

He knocks me off as easily as if I were a babe. I crash into a wall. Smithson laughs.

"Do you think you're the only one under protection of a cloaking spell?" he growls. He draws a dagger from his belt. It's tipped with silver. "Come on," he says, "show me what you've got."

I launch myself at him. We collide and grapple for position. He tries to dip the dagger under my ribs. I swat the attack away, managing to get my claws up in time to swipe him across the face.

Four red marks form on his cheek. He laughs and spits out blood.

"Is that all you have?" he asks me. "Is that all the strength contained inside the son of the greatest vampire king this world has ever known?" He looks at me in disgust. "That's pitiful."

My anger strikes up another notch. Raging, I throw

myself at him. He was right, he *is* cloaked, and that's why I'd always considered him weaker. But he isn't like the vampires from The Crypts. He doesn't have the gift of The Ancient's blood.

In fact, he and I are closely matched.

He tries to stab me with the dagger but I parry each of his attacks. I can tell from the way he holds it that he isn't the most proficient with the weapon.

"What's wrong, Smithson?" I ask cruelly. "Missing your precious sword?"

That riles him up. He roars and throws himself at me. I go entirely on the defensive, only just managing to deflect his attacks.

Maybe taunting the man wasn't the best idea.

He flashes his dagger. Every single jab gets closer and closer to hitting the mark. I grit my teeth, grimly aware that I am weakening—

With a sudden stab he breaks through my defenses. The dagger sinks into my side. I cry out. The silver tip, *inside* my body, is more than I can handle.

I go down.

Smithson looks at me and laughs. A sudden flurry of stabs descend upon me. It's all I can do to shield my heart. The dagger dips into my chest, my shoulders, my arms, my back. Pain and agony take me. The wounds do not close because of that horrific metal.

Finally, when I lie broken and bleeding on the ground, he stops.

He sneers as he wipes the dagger clean on his pants. I groan. "Killing you was never part of the plan. But you *had* to go and visit Victoria. You *had* to make yourself seen. Beatrice asked me to get you in. She said nothing about keeping you alive."

He tosses the blade on the ground. It skitters to a halt before my face.

"Do yourself a favor. End your misery. Take the honest way out." He kneels before me. "Take the dagger," he whispers. "Plunge it in your heart. You know death comes for you no matter what. You can extend your misery, and slowly bleed to death. Or you can accept my final mercy, and go out as a *man*. Because," he stands again, "in all the behavior I've seen you display, you're nothing but a frightened child."

With that he walks away.

"Wait," I croak, dragging myself forward. Blood continues to pour out of the wounds and pool around me. "*Why do this?* Who is Beatrice to you?"

He considers the question for a moment. Then he decides to indulge me.

"Beatrice," he says. "Is the wife who was stolen from me. And for *that* little nugget of information..." he plucks the dagger away, "... you lost your last chance at a swift and easy death. Goodbye, James. I *won't* be seeing you again."

He walks out of the fissure, leaving me to bleed dry on the ground.

Chapter Sixty

VICTORIA

Somewhere in the commotion I come to. I crack an eye open. Sounds filter to my ears.

Eleira—she's alive! Eleira is screaming at the Queen, something about her being a dark witch and fighting for The Haven and other such nonsense that I cannot make heads or tails of. Beyond her, I see Raul. Handsome, stunning Raul, with his flame-red hair and blazing green eyes. If only *he* had been the one to first come to The Crypts, and not his arrogant brother James...

A sudden spasm in my neck makes me whimper in pain. I bite down the sound. I have to avoid drawing attention to myself.

My eyes go up. Far above me is an opening to the sky. I'm surrounded by rubble and debris from the castle.

Glimpses of what happened come back to me. The fight against that awful black... *thing.* Succumbing to its ghastly claws. Willing my body to heal, but finding it incapable of closing the wounds...

With enormous effort and through tremendous pain I force my arms to drag me to a hiding spot. I crawl behind a jagged rock and huddle there. I try not to shake.

I don't know how much time I have left. But I know my death looms on the horizon. I don't feel the link with Eleira anymore. It's been severed completely.

Death always comes to the weaker vampire when the link breaks.

At first, I thought it would have been her. But my body has been ruined by the fight. And Eleira is obviously still standing. Which means...

Well, I try not to dwell on what it means.

From far above me come shrill, eerie cries. No, they've always been there—they've been constant since I woke up—my mind is only just starting recognizing them.

What type of wretched creatures can make sounds like that?

Suddenly Raul, Eleira, and the Queen rush off. I curl into myself as they pass, praying they don't notice me.

Somehow, they do not. Or maybe they wouldn't pay attention to someone as ruined as me.

Long minutes pass. I look down at my body and wince at what I see. The deep wounds in my skin are marred with oozing corruption.

No wonder the other vampires did not cast a glance at me. I'm clearly as good as dead.

My hand slips from under me. I go down and fall on my side. I don't even bother picking myself up. All I can do is wait for the reaper to arrive.

The spark of a distant object catches my eye.

My eyes widen.

No. It couldn't be!

Determination replaces all despair. I force my muscles to move. Inch by agonizing inch I pull myself forward, leaving a trail of thick, stinking blood on the ground.

My fingers fall upon the spot where I saw the sparkle. I start to dig, throwing dirt and rock this way and that...

And then I see it. The only hope I have of salvation.

The Ancient's amulet.

I grab it and clutch it to my chest. I can't believe it's real. I can't believe it's here, I can't believe it's been forgotten.

I throw it over my neck. Summoning what little magic I possess, I slide the link between me and the most revered vampire into being.

His voice greets me. *"YOU. WHAT DO YOU WANT?"*

In a flash of images and memories I show him the state of my body. I pray it'll be enough.

"Please," I whisper. "Please help me."

"WHAT CAN I DO FOR YOU?" The Ancient wonders. *"THE MAGIC SOURCE HAS BEEN DEPLETED. I CANNOT MEND YOUR WOUNDS."* A pause, and then, *"BESIDES. YOU ARE A TRAITOR."*

"No!" I exclaim. I clutch the amulet to my chest. "No, I am not, I swear it, I—"

"GOODBYE, VICTORIA."

And then the precious stone in the amulet cracks, splinters in two, and falls apart.

"No!" I gasp. "No, no, no, no!"

But I know that without the stone, the torrial is useless.

I collapse on all fours. I roll over, cough, and stare at the night sky. Those screams continue from above me. I barely pay attention. They're so far away, and so very far from affecting me.

I close my eyes and wait for my life to wink out.

Suddenly there are hands on my shoulders. Someone is pushing me up. Something is thrust to my mouth.

A second later, blood, hot, precious, warm, viscous blood breaks past my lips.

I grasp onto the forearms in front of my face and suck as much as I can.

"Easy, there," Smithson's gruff voice makes me snap back

401

to myself. "Easy. There you go. That's enough."

He pulls his arm away. I stare at him in wonder. *That he would feed me his own blood...*

And then the strength inside me is unleashed. My wounds begin to close. My body starts to heal. I feel myself rising up from the abyss of death where I nearly met my end.

"You saved me," I gasp. "*You!* Why?"

"You are not the only one here for your own gain," he tells me. He looks up. "When The Haven falls, it's time for true loyalties to come out. I think we can help each other, you and I. We are more alike than you know."

What game is he playing at? I wonder.

He stands and offers me his hand. "Will you join me, and help bring everlasting power to our race?"

Power. My mind clings to the word.

I look around and see the desolated ruins of the castle.

Is this all that is left of the mighty vampire sanctuary?

If Smithson is my way out... then I have no choice but to take it.

I grasp his hand and let him pull me up. "Yes," I swear. "I will join you."

Something dark and malicious glitters in his eyes. It's only there for a second—so quick in fact, that it's gone before

I can blink.

But the memory of it is clear in my mind.

He has the same floating specks in the whites of his eyes that Logan does.

Chapter Sixty-One

RAUL

I stand on the edge of battle as hordes of Haven vampires rain down on The Convicted, who are tearing through the humans below.

I want to be there. I want to be leading my people.

But Mother forbids it. She says that a general, a leader, is only good to his people alive.

I hate the truth in those words, as much as I hate how much of a coward they make me feel.

Screams a thousand times worse than anything heard during The Hunt echo across the massive caverns. The humans are running scared, fighting as much as they can against the deranged, bloodthirsty Convicted let loose on them. My vampires, the vampires of The Haven, have been given free rein to kill any Convicted on sight. And to save the lives of as many humans as they can.

It's an absolute bloodbath down there. The humans have no organization, no leaders. They are being picked off one by one by The Convicted. The Haven vampires fight, too, but they are distracted, and rightfully so, by the powerful lure of human blood.

They are also badly outnumbered by The Convicted. That shocks me. I never knew so many of the zombie vampires existed.

It means Mother's been making them not *just* from Haven criminals. But who else, and how many, and *why*?

Suddenly the Queen casts a fireball spell. It flares and crashes into the midst of the fight. Humans and vampires alike jump to get out of the way. Some make it. Some do not.

I turn on her. "What are you doing?" I demand. "You're killing our own!"

Grim determination is all I see in her eyes. "In a war, there are casualties," she answers, readying another spell.

"No!" I yell, and charge into her to knock her off her feet before she can cast a second one.

"Get off me!" she snarls. "Can't you see we're *losing?*"

I look down—and to my horror, realize she's right. Half, or more than half, of the humans are dead or dying. The Convicted, having fed on fresh blood, are only getting stronger. Stronger and more enraged.

The Haven vampires, on the other hand, don't have the benefit of fresh blood in their veins. And they've taken casualties, too.

Where are the Wyvern vampires? I think. *Why are none of them helping?*

But the answer is obvious to me. This is not their fight. It never has been.

This is not even their home.

I cannot take sitting on the sidelines any more. In a blinding rage I tear down the steep cliff and jump into the heart of the battle. Convicted after Convicted leap at me, but I fling them off. One jabs a clawed hand at my heart. I spin, avoiding the attack, and pierce my own hand through his chest.

I rip out his heart.

The killing blow gives me only a sliver of satisfaction before more of The Convicted fling themselves at me.

I dance with them all, operating on instinct alone. I am the strongest one down here by far—that gives me a considerable advantage.

My one thought is on keeping as many of the humans alive for as long as possible, while giving The Haven vampires a chance to finish off The Convicted.

"HAVEN VAMPRIES!" I scream out. "WITH ME! STAND WITH ME!" I rip off the head of a Convicted who gets too close. "HUMANS! GET BEHIND US! NOW!"

With someone taking up the lead, the chaos becomes a

bit less... chaotic. The Haven vampires rush to form a wall around me. The humans run to get behind the line.

It's not clean, of course, nor pretty. As the arrangement is being formed, more humans are picked off by The Convicted. Screams ring out as hungry fangs sink into vulnerable necks.

"WITH ME!" I scream. "HAVEN VAMPIRES, STAND WITH ME!"

Some of the sharper vampires, seeing what's happening, pick up the humans and carry them to safety faster. It seems like it takes ages, but eventually, the humans are all behind us, separated from the rabid Convicted on the other side by a wall of vampires.

Vampires fighting for humans in The Haven - who would have ever thought?

"We protect *all* the humans," I inform my comrades. "And we *destroy* all The Convicted." A cheer raises around me. Some of The Convicted still run at us. They are flung away like waves against a rocky beach.

The others, seemingly more aware of what's going on, stop and stand back.

Slowly a great divide forms between us. The Convicted ebb away and take shape like an assembled army. Snarling, hissing, snapping, they challenge us.

But none attack.

One steps forth from their midst. His face is half ruined, one eye missing and an entire cheek ripped off. He opens his mouth, but instead of the blood-curdling scream that I expect, The Ancient's voice comes out.

"YOU DARE CHALLENGE US, BOY?" He raises an arm. All The Convicted beyond him fall silent. "YOU DO SO AT YOUR OWN PERIL. STAND ASIDE. LET US FEAST!"

I look back at the cowering humans. They don't stand a chance on their own.

"*Never*," I snarl.

The Convicted leader throws his head back and laughs. Then, with The Ancient's voice, he says, "Then prepare to be destroyed."

There's a moment of silence, and then The Convicted charge.

I know one thing: This will be the longest and bloodiest fight of my life.

Epilogue

RIYU

A long time after all the commotion outside dies down, I release the protective spell cushioning me in the coffin and slowly lift the lid.

A smile spreads across my face as I survey the destruction before me. Everything has gone exactly according to plan. The Haven's castle lies in ruins around me. The shrieks of the battle between The Convicted and the Haven's vampires are like music to my ears.

Father would be so proud.

I catch that unbidden thought and glower. I am not allowed to think of *him* as my Father. I am not allowed to consider my own lineage. One such as me... is better off forgotten.

Quickly I hop out of my hiding place. Time is of the essence if I am to get away unseen. So far, none know that I am here. I'd prefer to keep it that way. Direct combat has never been my forte. But striking from the shadows, striking from where none can pin the blame on me... *that* is what I live for.

I think of that pompous fool James, and I snicker in laughter. He undoubtedly thought The Ancient channeled magic through him, and used the staff torrial in order to destroy.

But The Ancient cannot do magic. The Ancient does not have The Spark.

No, it was never The Ancient... it was me.

I touch Dagan's amulet hung around my neck. The one given to James was a poor replica, a red herring. *This* is the real one, and there was a reason it was entrusted to me, and me alone.

The Ancient is powerful, and this torrial links me to him. The Ancient has command of the Mind Gift, which makes weaker vampires, and obviously humans, vulnerable to his telekinetic force. He pierced James's mind, but the link went through *me* first... and it was I who channeled the spells that rained destruction onto The Haven.

My body shudders in ecstasy as memories of controlling so much power take me. It was only through The Ancient's protection that I could control that much. Actually, it was a three-way buffer: the torrial, James, and The Ancient. But then Eleira picked up the staff, and I was given access to her mind...

Why, nothing in life could ever compare to the absolute euphoria that gifted me.

She's far away now. Tendrils of our connection still linger

in the air. She's immensely powerful as a witch, but her mind's been locked. She is blind to her own potential.

The better the world is for it. If she knew the things she is capable of...

My coven will expose her to them when the time is right. When she is safely in our hands, we won't hesitate to exploit every last ounce of her abilities. But good things come to those who wait, and for now, patience is key.

I climb out of the crater my coffin ended up in. I cast a very small probing spell to check for any other vampires—

A warning jolt runs through me. I mutter a curse and throw myself down. One other is here, left abandoned. The spell does not tell me who it is, only the approximate direction of the living body.

Close. The vampire's close. But he—or she—is not moving. In fact the life essence I picked up on is so faint I think it might wink out at a moment's notice.

So. There is an injured vampire, then, a would-be casualty from the castle's collapse?

Stealthily, I sneak toward the source. I'm three-quarters of the way there when my probing spell picks up another vampire approaching.

I stop and flatten myself against a stone. I focus all my vampire senses on the newcomer. But I am pitifully weak, and those senses only give the barest advantage compared to when I was human.

I sense the two vampires come together. I hear voices.

I recognize one of them. It belongs to Victoria, that upstart pretend witch who tried to usurp my place by Father's side...

The 'witch' with The Spark no greater than an ant's, the one who my own mother taught—or tried to teach—when she should have been teaching me.

I hate her. I've always hated her, because of her failure, because she caused my mother's death. Father refused to give mother eternal life when it came out that Victoria could barely do magic.

Rage pulses through me. I have not been given permission to kill. Killing would give me away.

But I want Victoria dead with every bone in my body. I want her dead; I need her dead. I—

I stifle a gasp. The probing spell alerts me to what is happening. Victoria is gaining strength. No more is she clinging onto life by the barest string. The second vampire, damn him, must be feeding her his blood.

I remain in my hiding spot, seething. If I had come across Victoria alone... maybe, just maybe, I would have risked ending her life. She's been a thorn in my side ever since she was made some forty years ago. It was only after she left The Crypts with James that Father recognized my utility to him again...

I wait for them to leave. Then, when I'm sure that I'm alone, I get up and start deeper into the caves.

The spell alerts me to somebody else underground. None should be here, especially with The Ancient taking control of The Convicted and directing them against the humans.

As I get closer and the spell gives me more information, I realize this other vampire is barely clinging on to life, too. I smirk. What are the odds of coming across two stragglers like that?

The smirk fades when I reach the small entrance hidden in the cavern wall and see that it is James bleeding on the floor.

Immediately, I mutter a spell that forces his eyes closed. I cannot risk him seeing me. He groans as the magic sets in, straining his already-spent body.

I go to my knees at his side. His wounds are numerous. They're not healing, either.

That means they've been made with a silver weapon.

Conflict wanes through me. If James managed to get himself killed, there'd be nothing for me to do. But he's not dead yet. If I turn a blind eye, however, he'd only last minutes more.

What to do, what to do?

Eventually, loyalty to my family wins out. James might be a bastard, he might be an asshole, but he is still my half-brother. Despite the secrets of our connection, and the tenuousness of it, *I* know.

And if I let him die, guilt will haunt me for ages.

Shaking my head, I bring my wrist to my mouth. My fangs protrude. I pierce two small holes on the underside of my arm.

I let a drop of blood fall on each of James' wounds, watching as it fizzes and mixes with his and begins to heal him.

I bring my arm away when the worst of his injuries are sealed. Doing it this way, instead of feeding him my blood, makes the process less efficient. But I've been forbidden to feed any vampire my blood, because of The Spark I possess. Because of the unintended consequences sharing such blood with others could bring.

James groans and rolls over. It'll take a while for him to get up. But with the worst of his injuries gone, I've pulled him away from the precipice of death. That, in and of itself, is a more precious gift than he has any right to expect.

I rise and focus my energies on ripping that hole in

reality that'll allow me to escape. The familiar blue light greets me. A portal opens to the Paths.

Without looking back I leap through. Only when I'm on the other side do I realize I neglected to lift the spell binding James's eyes shut.

A perverse sort of glee takes me. The spell might last a day, maybe two. James will think he's gone blind. Wouldn't that be frightening?

But I think, if he knew, he'd agree: a bit of discomfort is well worth keeping his life.

The End

THANK YOU FOR READING!

Want More of The Vampire Gift?

The Vampire Gift 3 comes out Summer 2016!

Don't want to miss it? Sign up for my mailing list (http://eepurl.com/bYCp41) to get an email the day it comes out!

Loved the book? Let me know by leaving a review on Amazon! Or come say hi to me on Facebook – I love meeting and interacting with my fans :)

www.Facebook.com/AuthorEMKnight

Free Book Offer!

Want to get the next book in The Vampire Gift series for free? Here's how you do it...

1. Leave a review on Amazon.com for *The Vampire Gift 2: Kingdom of Ash.*

2. Once the review is posted, email me a link to it with the subject "Free Book Offer". My email: em@emknight.com

3. As soon as the next book comes out, I'll send you a special link to download the book for free! You can request any book in the series as your free "thank you" book.

71043559R00234

Made in the USA
Middletown, DE
19 April 2018